·ALISON CHERRY·LINDSAY RIBAR·
·MICHELLE SCHUSTERMAN·

Point

All rights reserved. Published by Point, an imprint of Scholastic Inc., *Publishers since 1920.* SCHOLASTIC, POINT, and associated logos are trademarks and/or registered trademarks of Scholastic Inc.

The publisher does not have any control over and does not assume any responsibility for author or third-party websites or their content.

No part of this publication may be reproduced, stored in a retrieval system, or transmitted in any form or by any means, electronic, mechanical, photocopying, recording, or otherwise, without written permission of the publisher. For information regarding permission, write to Scholastic Inc., Attention: Permissions Department, 557 Broadway, New York, NY 10012.

This book is a work of fiction. Names, characters, places, and incidents are either the product of the author's imagination or are used fictitiously, and any resemblance to actual persons, living or dead, business establishments, events, or locales is entirely coincidental.

Library of Congress Cataloging-in-Publication Data available

ISBN 978-1-338-15172-5

10 9 8 7 6 5 4 3 2 1   18 19 20 21 22

Printed in the U.S.A.   23
First edition, April 2018

Book design by Maeve Norton

IF YOU LOVE SOMETHING
WITH YOUR WHOLE HEART,
BE IT MAINSTREAM OR UNUSUAL,
THIS BOOK IS FOR YOU

CHAPTER ONE

CALLIE

There were two ostriches, a water buffalo, and a flock of wild turkeys between me and the registration desk.

"Dad, can you scoot the turkeys over a little?" I asked. "We're blocking the door." I was careful to keep my voice upbeat and positive, even though I was tired and stiff from the twelve-hour drive to Orlando. I wasn't exactly thrilled with how that drive had gone, either; instead of talking to me, Dad had spent most of the time making calls about his latest restoration project while I listened to podcasts.

Then again, I hadn't expected him to invite me to the World Taxidermy Championships at all, and the fact that he'd brought me to this place he loved felt like a step in the right direction. Maybe after we settled in a little, the good memories would kick in and soften him up, and then we could do some real bonding for the first time in forever. We still had five whole days together, and if he was ready and willing to act like a family again, I was on board.

The turkeys stared up at me with their reproachful glass eyes, as if to say *Good luck with that.* "Shut up," I murmured to them, then glanced around to make sure nobody had heard. I was *not* going to become one of those people who talked to dead animals.

My dad pushed the luggage dolly holding the turkeys a little farther into the convention center, but it rolled forward faster than expected, and a guy crossing in front of us had to dodge out of the way. He had a scraggly ponytail and deer tracks tattooed up his forearms, and he was carrying a bundle of blankets with a scaly tail poking out one end and a pair of toothy jaws protruding from the other. "Watch it, buddy!" he snapped.

"Excuse me, I'm so sorry," my dad said. He peered at the bundle. "Black caiman? That's a beautiful specimen."

The guy smiled, and he suddenly looked a lot less menacing. "Yup," he said. "Good eye. And those are some fine-looking turkeys, man."

"Thank you," my dad said, all puffed up with pride. He'd brought an ibex and a pair of cerulean warblers for the competition as well, but the turkeys were his babies.

Caiman Dude reached out a beefy arm and clapped my dad hard on the shoulder. "Good luck," he said, and he took off.

Two doors down, there was a flurry of excitement—my dad's archrival, Harley Stuyvesant, had just pushed an enormous musk ox in from the parking lot on a rolling cart. As his fans and colleagues crowded around to admire his new mount, he pulled a comb out of his pocket and started grooming the musk ox's flanks in this showy way, even though judging didn't start until tomorrow evening.

I nudged my dad with my elbow. "There's your favorite person," I muttered. If there was one thing we could definitely bond over, it was that Harley was a complete douchenozzle. "Remember two years ago when he ran over that woman's foot with his rhino, and Mom had to drive her to the hospital because—"

"Yes, I remember," Dad said, but his voice was sharp and final, like that topic was off-limits. I should've known better; bringing up Mom was probably the worst thing I could do if I wanted to get on his good side.

"I'll go get our badges from registration," I said. "Will you watch my stuff?" I put my purple duffel bag down next to the traveling crates and leather tool bags that held the supplies for my dad's "Mounting a Strutting Turkey" demonstration.

"Sure," he said, a little gentler this time. "Thanks, Callie."

I navigated around an articulated snake skeleton and a flock of penguins and got in line under the welcome banner. The lobby was a sea of camo, denim, fur, and testosterone as far as the eye could see. It was impossible not to *think* about Mom, even if I wasn't allowed to talk about her; I'd never been to this convention without her, and she had always made me feel less out of place. While Dad was in his sessions, she and I used to dig through the bins of glass eyes on the trade show floor and people-watch in the lobby, guessing what animal each attendee had brought for judging. Dad would join us when he was done for the day, and we'd all squish together on one of the big hotel beds, watch a dumb comedy, and order burgers from room service.

Of course, that was before Dad started getting really

high-profile museum work and he and Mom started screaming at each other every night about how he spent way more time with his dead animals than he did with us.

I heard a high-pitched giggle and turned to see a group of girls my own age. For half a second, I felt a little flare of hope, but it immediately became clear that these girls weren't here for the taxidermy. Even though it was May, they looked like they were on the way to a Halloween party—one wore a jumpsuit and carried a Chinese parasol, one was in full body armor, and the third wore wings and a gold spandex bodysuit. Another girl in normal clothes followed several paces behind. When she turned to stare at someone's leopard, I saw that her shirt said *I <3 Harry Potter* in yellow puffy paint, and I realized the gold girl was probably supposed to be a Snitch. There must've been a different convention going on in another wing.

"Next?" called the woman behind the conference registration table.

I stepped forward and handed her my confirmation email. "Hi. I'm picking up two badges for Hamish Buchannan."

The woman's eyes widened. "The turkey man? Oh my god, do you work with him?"

"Yes." It was true, but it made me a little sad to hear her say it. Even at home, I usually felt more like his assistant than his daughter.

"Tell him how much I love his work, okay? I'm signed up for his seminar on Saturday. Do you think he'd autograph his book for me?"

"I'm sure he'd be glad to."

"Amazing. I'm *so* looking forward to it." The woman beamed as she handed me two badges and registration folders. "Judging begins tomorrow evening at seven o'clock sharp, so be sure to turn in your forms and deliver your competition mounts to the ballroom by six. There's a map and a schedule for all five days in your folder, as well as your drink tickets for the awards banquet on Sunday. I hope you and Hamish have a wonderful time!"

"Thanks," I said. "I hope so, too."

I turned to head back to my dad, but I almost tripped over a largemouth bass when I saw who was with him. I hadn't seen Jeremy Warren in years—he'd been living in London for a while now—but he'd spent countless hours at our house when he'd done his college internship with my dad. Even though I was only a little kid back then, he'd always treated me like a friend. He had even learned all the Pokémon characters so he could discuss their relative merits with me as I helped scoop brains out of deer skulls. My whole family had always loved Jeremy, and the fact that he'd be around for the next five days would definitely put my dad in a better mood.

"Hey!" I called to him. "I didn't know you were coming to this!"

"Cal! It's so good to see you!" Jeremy's smile was blindingly white against the brown of his skin, and he held out his arms for a hug. When I stepped into them, he squeezed me so tightly my feet almost left the ground. "Man, it's been forever. How have you been?"

That answer to that question was way too complicated to

handle, so I just said, "It's great to see you, too. Are you back in the States for good?"

"No, just for a job. I wasn't planning on being here, but one of the judges had a family emergency, so they asked me to fill in. I'm doing Waterfowl and Turkeys." Jeremy lightly punched my dad's shoulder. "I hear I'll be judging this old man."

My dad smiled, and it looked totally genuine, unlike the tight half smiles he'd been giving me all day. "I hope you'll go easy on your favorite mentor."

"I'm sure I won't need to. Your mounts are always flawless, Hamish, and these are no exception." He gave the turkeys a fond look, like they were long-lost friends.

"Oh god, they're a mess right now," my dad said. "No peeking until they've been groomed."

I raised an eyebrow at Jeremy. "He's been grooming them all day. Every time we hit a rest stop, we had to unwrap these guys and make sure every feather was in place. I bet you can imagine the kinds of looks we got in the McDonald's parking lot."

"They probably thought you'd brought your own meat for McNuggets," Jeremy said, and I snorted, but my dad frowned at me.

"I wasn't *grooming* them," he said. "I was checking for damage."

"Yeah, checking with a comb," I said, hoping he'd finally give in and laugh like he used to when I teased him about being a perfectionist. I knew not to try to banter with him while he was working these days—since the divorce, he'd been quiet and focused in the studio, instead of playing music or asking about my day. But I figured things might be different here in the place he liked best. Two Taxidermy Championships ago, he and Mom had made a bet about whether he could go the entire drive without unwrapping his competition animals. He'd lost when she'd caught him peeking at his turkeys at a rest stop in South Carolina, and as her prize she'd made him buy her an ice cream sundae every day of the convention.

But apparently being here now hadn't lightened his mood at all, because all I got was a look that said *Shut up, Callie.*

Jeremy must've sensed the tension in the air, because he immediately changed the subject. "So, you must be . . . what, a sophomore now?"

"A junior," I said.

"God, that makes me feel so old. I remember when you used to sit in the corner of the studio in your My Little Pony pajamas and make the stuffed squirrels talk to each other."

"Yeah, and I remember when you used to bring your laundry to our house because you didn't know how to use a washing machine," I said.

He laughed. "Oh man, that's embarrassing. I'm pretty great at laundry now, I'll have you know. I use dryer sheets and everything."

I rolled my eyes. "Congratulations. Your medal's in the mail."

"What are you up to these days? You starting to think about colleges?"

I was about to tell him how I wanted to go to Northwestern for communications, but my dad jumped in before I could open my mouth. "She's been my assistant for a year and a half now," he said. "You should see the raccoon she mounted a couple of months ago. Very impressive."

"Good for you, Cal. That's great. And how's Regina? Is she here?"

"Regina's . . . fine." I braced myself for the part that I knew would come next; seeing that predictable look of pity cross Jeremy's face would be the absolute worst. But instead my dad said, "She's out of town right now. For work."

Well, that was bizarre. Did he always pretend they were still married when he talked to his colleagues?

"Is that Jeremy Warren?" called a voice behind us.

Jeremy turned to wave at a middle-aged guy with a Moses beard. "Hey, I've got to go. It's so awesome to see both of you. We'll catch up later, okay?"

"Absolutely," my dad said. "We should have dinner. I heard you've been experimenting with erosion molding. I want to hear all about it."

I made a face. "Or I could order room service while you two talk about guts and pelts, and then Jeremy and I can have dessert and a normal conversation once you're done."

Jeremy laughed again. "You were always so funny, Cal. I'm glad to see you haven't changed." He gave my dad a little salute as he walked away.

"Come on," Dad said. "We need to get all this stuff upstairs. I don't want to leave the ibex and the warblers in the van too long."

"Okay, sure." I crouched down and stuffed our registration

folders and judging forms into my backpack. "The walkway to the hotel is over—"

There was a deafening crash, and one of the supply boxes on my dolly lurched sideways and hit me in the ribs. I threw my arm up and managed to catch the box with my elbow before it fell, and pain shot up my arm. That would definitely leave a bruise, but it was better than the alternative. My dad would murder me if anything happened to the turkey armature inside.

"God, Brian, watch where you're going!" a guy shouted.

"I can't see anything behind all this stuff! You were supposed to be steering!"

"What's wrong with you? You ran someone over!" A girl's freckled face peered at me over the supply boxes. "Are you okay?"

"Yeah." I scrambled to my feet to see what had happened—if anyone's animals were damaged, I was really in trouble—but instead, I saw drums and cymbals lying all over the carpet. A rack of chimes had fallen on top of a gong, and one of those giant xylophone things had slid halfway off a hotel luggage rack. As I watched, a drum rolled lazily toward the registration table, narrowly missing a rack of deer heads.

"I'm really sorry," the girl said.

"It's okay." I retrieved the leather bag that held my dad's sculpting tools from where it had landed near the gong. I glanced over at him, wondering if he was going to help me clean up, but he was completely focused on his turkeys, making sure the nearby crash hadn't ruffled any feathers.

"I told you it was going to fall," snapped one of the guys.

"Just get everything back on the cart! We're already late!"

As the girl righted the chimes, a guy with a red buzz cut moved one of my dad's boxes so he could retrieve a bunch of fuzzy mallets. "Man, this is heavy. What's in here?"

"A turkey carcass."

He stared at me. "Like, to eat?"

"No, to study. This is a taxidermy convention."

"That's a thing?" I pointed at the giant banner that said *Welcome to the World Taxidermy & Fish Carving Championships!*, and the guy said, "Huh. What's fish carving?"

"Brian, come *on*!"

The drummers heaped their stuff precariously back onto the luggage rack and started wheeling it toward the next wing of the convention center. "Sorry again!" the girl called to me. It was only after they were out of sight that I wondered what they were here for. Maybe they were some sort of Harry Potter band?

I opened the box that had fallen to check on the turkey armature and was relieved to see that nothing was broken. "Everything looks fine," I told my dad, angling for a little gratitude—I *had* made a pretty excellent catch, after all. But he just sighed and started wheeling the turkeys toward the elevators in silence, so I gathered the rest of our stuff and followed.

Neither of us said anything else until the elevator doors closed behind us, but the second we were alone, my dad turned on me. "Callie, if you're going to be here, I really need you to act professional."

If I was going to *be here*? The words made my stomach hurt.

We'd been in Orlando all of fifteen minutes; had he already changed his mind about bringing me?

"It's not my fault those drummers knocked me over," I said. "And I caught the box. I told you nothing's damaged. I even—"

"I'm not talking about that. I'm talking about the way you mocked me in front of a judge."

I blinked at him. "A judge? I didn't . . . Wait, you mean *Jeremy*? He's our friend! We were just messing around. You two used to make fun of each other all the time."

"It doesn't matter which judge it was. That was still out of line."

"I didn't mean to embarrass you," I said. "I was just kidding."

My dad sighed. "Cal, you're here in a professional capacity. You're not a child anymore—you're my assistant, and everything you do for the next five days reflects on me and my business. You can say whatever you want when we get home, but for now I need you to think before you talk and try to control yourself. All right?"

This was not how this trip was supposed to go. I came here to reconnect with him, to remind him that he could actually have a good time hanging out with his only daughter. We were supposed to *bond*. And right now, all he saw when he looked at me was an assistant who wasn't living up to his rigorous standards.

Then again, maybe I should try to cut him some slack until we settled in. Travel days were always stressful. He and I hadn't taken a trip together since Mom left, and maybe falling back into our old patterns would take some time.

"All *right*, Callie?" Dad said again.

I swallowed hard. "Yes. All right."

The elevator stopped, and the doors dinged open. "Good. Now, help me get the turkeys into your room."

We unloaded the birds near the mini-fridge, then headed back downstairs to retrieve the ibex and the warblers from the van. (Thank god we weren't sharing a room this year—there's no way Dad and I would've fit in one with all those animals, boxes, and suitcases.) As we passed through the hotel lobby, I scoped out the scene and considered possible plans for the rest of the evening. The Mexican restaurant looked pretty good, and there was a sports bar—maybe there would be a decent baseball game on. Maybe Jeremy would be free for dinner tonight; I'd have to be super careful about how I talked to him, but it would still be nice to hang out. Or Dad and I could just people-watch in the lobby and play the guess-which-guy-brought-which-animal game, then resurrect our room-service-and-movie tradition.

We always used to have fun together at these conventions. Maybe if I tried hard enough, we still could, even without Mom.

CHAPTER TWO

PHOEBE

Every spring, the Ridgewood High School percussion ensemble packed up our junky equipment and drove almost twenty hours east to prove to Orlando, Florida, that we still sucked.

It wasn't our fault most of the other schools owned timpani that probably cost more than our entire band hall. Like Bishop, our rival high school from back in Austin, who pretty much always placed in the top three at the Indoor Percussion Association Convention. They had two sets of everything: one for marching season, one for concert season. They even had a vibraphone with gold bars. Not actual gold, but still. Our poor old vibes were held together with duct tape and happy thoughts. One of the wheels had fallen off when we'd unloaded the truck an hour ago, and we'd wasted five minutes searching before finding it wedged under the ramp. And at competitions like IPAC, where the schedule was so tight that getting from truck to stage was like running a marathon, every minute was precious.

"Look at that, Phoebe." My best friend, Brian Krantz, pointed up ahead as Bishop's legion of band booster parents began wheeling their gleaming, perfect equipment into Hall 1B for their performance. "Look at those timpani. Real copper. I bet those are calfskin heads, too."

"I see them," I said distractedly, trying to untangle our wind chimes. "Hey, you might want to check the pedal on two—it looks jacked again."

Groaning, Brian pushed his glasses up his nose and crouched next to the second-smallest of our dented fiberglass timps. That drum had become the stuff of legend during football playoffs sophomore year, when one of our linebackers dove straight into it helmet-first a few seconds before halftime. His game-changing interception had made him the hero of the night, and the pedal hadn't been able to get higher than B-flat ever since.

"Figures we have to follow Bishop," Scott Lloyd muttered as he retied the knot on one of the crash cymbal handles. "How are we supposed to sound halfway decent when—"

"It's about the musician, not the instrument," Mr. Mackey interrupted, handing me a lug nut that had fallen off the wind chime stand. "And don't even start all this *why can't we have nice things* stuff with me right now. Especially after you two just sent our instruments rolling all over the C-wing lobby."

"That was Brian's fault," Scott said immediately. "He was steering the cart." I could tell Brian wanted to argue, but he just rolled his eyes. He was too much of a suck-up to gripe in front of Mr. Mackey.

"There." I finished untangling the last two wind chimes and examined them. Six—no, seven chimes were missing, up from only three. "Crap, I think we lost a few more in the lobby," I told Mr. Mackey. He opened his mouth to respond, but a sudden, muffled *BOOM* and a familiar ringing chord sounded from Hall 1B. Brian straightened up slowly, a look of horror on his face.

"Is that . . . ?"

"Yeah." Mr. Mackey closed his eyes briefly. "'Big Top Circus.'"

"Oh, *sharks*." I opened my music folder and stared at my sheet music. *Big Top Circus: Percussion 3 (Xylophone, bass drum, wind chimes, suspended cymbal, 4 toms)*. My eyes followed measure for measure, like I was trying to prove to myself this wasn't the same music. Being played by our rivals on concert-hall-worthy instruments.

"We're screwed," said Scott. "We're so screwed."

Mr. Mackey rubbed his eyes and sighed. "We'll be fine." He joined Christina Gonzalez and Nuri Hwang, who were inspecting the marimba keys to make sure everything was in order after the crash in the lobby. Scott wandered over to where the other boys were sitting against the wall, drumming on the floor. I sat on the edge of the cart next to Brian.

"Nervous?" he asked, running his hand over his head. It was a new tic he'd developed after randomly deciding to buzz his curly red hair over spring break.

"Meh. Not really. Maybe a little about this part." I pointed to the wall as Bishop reached the xylophone feature: twenty-four measures of nonstop rapid sixteenth notes played with extra-hard plastic mallets that exposed even the tiniest flaw. Every wrong note, every rushed rhythm would be as noticeable in the giant, echoey hall as a crystal chandelier crashing to the floor. Of course, the Bishop kid was nailing it. And he was probably playing on a xylophone that didn't have a huge crack in the low C-sharp key.

"When's your solo?" I asked Brian. "Mine's tomorrow afternoon."

"All the timpani solos are Saturday," he replied. "Marimba's Friday."

Ridgewood might have had a bad rep as far as ensembles went, but we made up for it in solo competition. Christina and Brian were amazing, and Scott, Nuri, Amy Robinson, Jorge Ramirez, and I always placed pretty high. A lot of that had to do with the fact that all soloists used the shiny, new instruments of whatever company was sponsoring the competition that year. Which kind of blew a hole in Mr. Mackey's theory about the judges not judging our shoddy equipment. But I guess that's the kind of crap you have to tell students when their school doesn't have a budget for extracurriculars unless they involve helmets and balls.

"I think they scheduled me and Christina last, since we won our categories last year," Brian added. His eyes flickered over to Christina as he spoke, and she glanced up and shot him a grin. A flush crept up Brian's neck as he smiled back, and I rolled my eyes. The two of them had started dating last month and they were still in that kind-of-cute, kind-of-annoying early couple stage. I'd been trying hard to hide my irritation, because they were clearly crazy about each other. But my current best friend dating my former best friend made for a pretty uncomfortable third-wheel situation.

Brian spread his "Big Top Circus" music out in front of him and started air-drumming along with Bishop's timpanist, his brow knit with concentration. The sight made me smile. We could roll into a competition with paint cans and a busted tambourine, and Brian would still take it as seriously as a performance at the Grammys.

When Bishop finished, the muffled sound of cheers and applause sent a fresh wave of nerves through me. I wondered how much of their crowd would stick around to hear the other school from the suburbs of Austin play the same arrangement as their better, richer rivals. Anyone who wanted a good laugh, I figured.

The double doors flew open, and Bishop's students poured out, flushed and talking loudly as they rolled their flawless instruments down the corridor. A few noticed us and waved or called, "Good luck!" I waved back and tried to smile. Brian looked so smitten, he might as well have been running toward their timpani through a field of flowers while an orchestral arrangement of "At Last" swelled up in the background.

"Here we go!" called Mr. Mackey, pushing the vibes at the front of our line into the room. Brian grabbed the handle of the timpani cart, and I followed him, pushing the xylophone with one hand and carrying the wind chimes with the other. Twice, the leather bag with all of our harder mallets and triangle beaters slipped off the xylophone, and each time I stopped to catch it, Scott bumped me with the bass drum. (I was pretty sure the second time was on purpose.) By the time we were in front of the judges on the floor, irritation had almost completely replaced my nerves.

The hall was maybe two-thirds full, mostly with students from schools who'd played earlier in the day and wanted to check out the competition. Three tables, one for each judge, sat spread out in front of the sea of chairs. As Mr. Mackey shook hands with the announcer, the rest of us went into setup mode, moving quickly without speaking. IPAC had a one-minute setup, one-minute breakdown rule that could supposedly get a group disqualified if they went over. No one knew how closely they timed it, but we didn't want to take any chances.

I had my station ready to go—bass on the left, xylo in front, toms and auxiliary on the right—in half a minute, and unzipped the leather bag on the trap table Scott and I shared. I stared at the contents for a solid five seconds before clearing my throat.

"Um, Scott?"

"Yeah?" He looked down, and his eyes widened. "Uh . . . what the hell is that?"

Like our mallet bag, this bag had three rows of deep pockets. Unlike our mallet bag, this bag did not contain mallets. Instead, each pocket held a tool, silver and highly polished. There were curvy scissors, tweezers, knives, scalpels, and a bunch of other weird tools, all with clear plastic safety caps. Every pocket was labeled: *Caliper. Tail Splitter. Fleshing Knife.*

My hands shook as I flipped the bag and saw *BUCHANNAN TAXIDERMY* neatly stenciled in bright white letters on the back.

"That girl you plowed over in the lobby," I whispered. "With all the dead turkeys—this is her bag!"

"That was Brian's fault!" Scott hissed back. Gritting my teeth, I looked over at Mr. Mackey just as the announcer stepped up to the microphone.

"Next up, from Austin, Texas, the Ridgewood High School percussion ensemble! Ridgewood will also be performing 'Big Top Circus,' arranged by . . ."

I waved frantically at Mr. Mackey, but he was already stepping up on the podium. Leaning over the toms, I tugged Brian's sleeve.

"We lost the mallet bag, give me any extra mallets you've got!"

Brian's eyes widened. "Um . . ." He reached into the bag hanging from the third timpani and handed me a pair of super-puffy mallets. I grabbed them and spun around as Christina handed Scott an extra pair of yarn mallets for his vibraphone part. I did a frantic, three-second assessment of my situation: I could use the puffy ends of the mallets on the suspended cymbal and the bass, then flip them over and use the harder back ends for the toms and—I winced at the thought—the xylophone. Mr. Mackey would kill me if I dented the keys, but hey, better that than no xylophone solo at all, right?

I barely had time to feel a surge of panic about getting through the next four minutes when Mr. Mackey lifted his hands. Taking a deep breath, I adjusted the bass drum slightly, lifted the timpani mallet, and nodded to let him know I was ready.

BOOM! The piece started loud and fast, and for the next

minute and a half I almost forgot about our predicament. Christina's yarn mallets worked fine for Scott's vibraphone part, and I was doing okay with Brian's timpani mallets—Mr. Mackey hadn't even noticed that anything was different yet. As we slowed into the chorale section, I set the mallets on the trap table between me and Scott. The next thirty-six measures were pretty much a big solo featuring Christina, our marimba rock star. All I had to do was add a little wind chime accompaniment. Christina was on her game today, too—I saw the judges nodding and jotting down notes on their comment sheets, probably praising her *flawless technique* and *expressive musicality*, as usual.

With four measures left of the chorale, I reached for the timpani mallets. They weren't there.

My stomach plummeted as I looked around the trap table and under the weird taxidermy bag. Then I spotted them. In Scott's. Freaking. Hands. He was using the back ends on the bells like I'd been planning to do.

"*Scott!*" I hissed. His eyes stayed glued to his music, but he lifted a shoulder and an eyebrow as if to say, *Sorry, bro.*

Two measures left. The yarn mallets sat on the vibes: the yarn was way too soft for the xylophone, and the handles were lightweight plastic. Even if I used those backward, I might as well not be playing at all. And clearly Scott was too much of a douche to realize my part was a little more important than his. Now I had nothing to use. I'd just be standing here dumbly behind the xylophone while everyone, including Scott, accompanied a solo that wasn't happening. I stared down at the trap table, unable to look at Mr. Mackey, and my gaze fell on a pair of scalpels.

Heavy duty, said the label.

Screw it, said my brain.

I grabbed both scalpels and whirled around right as Mr. Mackey cued the tempo change for my solo. The label hadn't been kidding; I was holding both scalpels by the plastic caps, and the handles were made of some seriously heavy silver. The resulting sound as I hammered the keys was probably similar to what you'd get if you dumped a sack of marbles on a toy glockenspiel. Really *accurate* marbles, though. Terrible implements aside, I was kind of nailing this feature.

Twelve measures in, the caps started to slip off. For a split second, I thought for sure the scalpels were going to fly out of my hands, and I adjusted my grip, loosening my back fingers and letting go of the caps. The scalpel blades dug uncomfortably into my palms, but I ignored them.

I chanced a glance up at Mr. Mackey. He looked horrified.

Laughter bubbled up inside me, and I stared at my hands. *Yup, I'm at a massive percussion competition in front of hundreds of people, destroying a xylophone with scalpels probably used to gut fish. Aaaand I think my hands are bleeding. Eight measures to go . . . four . . . two . . .*

And then it was over. Nothing left but half a page of suspended cymbal rolls. I tossed the scalpels down, and Scott handed me the timpani mallets. Our eyes met, and his mixed expression of horror and admiration was so ridiculous that I had to bite the insides of my cheeks to keep from smiling. If Mr. Mackey saw me giggling about this, he'd kill me.

When we finished, the applause was mixed with a good deal of murmuring as we schlepped back out of the hall. I kept my gaze fixed on Scott's back, waiting until we were out of the judges' sight before ramming the xylophone into his butt.

"Hey!" he yelped.

"You aardvark!" I yelled, but that only made him giggle. "You knew I needed those mallets! What the hell is wrong with you?"

"I don't know, I guess I didn't really think about it." Scott glanced down at the taxidermy bag. "Nice save with those knives, though. That was epic."

"They were *scalpels*. Look at my hands!" I held up my scratched-up palms, and his eyes widened.

"Whoa, you're bleeding!" he exclaimed gleefully. A few seconds later, the entire percussion section had surrounded me, inspecting my hands and asking what had happened. I explained, starting with the bag mix-up in the lobby and making sure to lay as much blame on Scott as possible. But with every sentence, his smile grew broader and broader. Nuri elbowed him in the side.

"What are you so happy about, jerkface?"

"She's *bleeding*, for chrissake," Amy added.

Scott grinned at me. "I know; it's so hardcore."

"But it's *your fault*," Christina said pointedly. Amy and Nuri looked at me, probably waiting for me to chew him out.

But they were just scratches, really. And this would definitely become a classic band tale, retold year after year: that time Phoebe

Byrd rocked a xylophone solo with taxidermy scalpels until her hands bled. I found myself grinning back at Scott, pretending not to notice when Nuri and Amy exchanged disgusted looks.

"Mackey's coming," Brian said, and everyone hurried back to the instruments they'd abandoned. Mr. Mackey was talking to Christina's dad and a few other parent chaperones. I hung back once we reached the service elevator, letting the others pack our stuff inside to take down to the loading dock. My palms were still stinging, and I wanted to explain everything to Mr. Mackey.

"You say you met the people this belongs to?" he asked when I finished, pointing to the leather bag.

"Sort of. It was this red-haired girl in the lobby of C-wing," I said as Brian walked up. "You talked to her, right?"

I held up the bag, and Brian nodded. "There's a taxidermy competition or something going on here," he said. "She had a dead turkey in a box."

I raised an eyebrow. "So this could've been worse. We could've mixed that up with the snare drum case." Brian snickered, then stopped when Mr. Mackey shot him a look.

"I'll bring the bag to the front desk at the hotel tomorrow and see if I can find her and get our mallets back," I said. "My solo's in the morning, so I can do it in the afternoon."

"Thanks, Phoebe. Mrs. Hwang is getting the first aid kit— she'll be back in a few minutes to check out your hands, okay?"

"Sure." I paused. "Mr. Mackey? How bad was it, honestly?" I nodded in the direction of the hall. Mackey sighed.

"All things considered, it was . . . not the worst thing ever. I'll explain to the judges about the bag, although I don't expect them to cut us any slack for it." He smiled, patting my shoulder. "Nice improvising, I guess. Although if I find a crack in one of those bars, I'm coming after you."

"Don't forget the bottom C-sharp was already cracked!" I called after him as he headed over to the elevator to supervise. When I turned back around, Christina had appeared next to Brian.

"I brought a ton of Band-Aids," she said, rummaging through her purse. "Are your hands still bleeding?"

"Um . . . just a little." I scowled at my palms. "Scott is such an aardvark."

Brian snickered. "Your parents aren't here, you know. You don't have to worry about the swear jar."

"I know, I just don't want to risk slipping up when I get home." I accepted two bandages from Christina and smiled briefly at her. "Thanks."

"Sure." She flashed a quick smile back, then slipped her hand into Brian's.

An awkward silence descended. It was broken when a guy with longish, greasy black hair sprinted around the corner and tore down the hall past us, wearing nothing but gray briefs and swinging black robes over his head like a lasso. The three of us gaped at him. Brian spoke first.

"Is it just me, or does that guy look kind of like . . ."

Christina and I said it at the same time. "Snape."

A split second later, a massive, glowing, puffy thing flew around the corner in hot pursuit. It was a second before my brain registered what I was seeing: a person in a costume that appeared to be entirely made out of cotton balls and green Christmas twinkly lights.

"Todd!" the glowing, puffy thing hollered as it raced after Undies-Snape. "Todd, you drunk idiot! Get back here!"

"Imma cast the Dark Mark over Florida!" came the slurred reply.

By the elevator, Scott and Jorge were doubled over laughing. We all watched as Undies-Snape almost made it to the exit before getting tackled by his friend. A small crowd—some in costumes, some not—had gathered at the end of the hall to watch. They cheered as the puffy thing led Undies-Snape toward them. The laughter faded as they all disappeared around the corner again.

"Well," Brian said, pushing his glasses up his nose. "That just happened."

I grinned. "I remember seeing someone in a Harry Potter shirt in the lobby. I guess there's a fan convention going on, too."

"Awesome," said Christina, and this time we shared a real smile. Back in middle school, when we were best friends, we would have completely freaked out over being at a Harry Potter convention together. But by the end of our freshman year, she'd decided she had more in common with girls like Nuri and Amy, and suddenly everything was about shopping and selfies. So we'd stopped hanging out. No fight, no drama. Just a slow fade-out.

It was fine, though. I had Brian and the guys, she had Nuri and Amy. Apparently the three of them were even starting a band together. Christina was almost as good at piano as she was at marimba, and I had to admit Amy had a decent voice. Frankly, I was way better at drum set than Nuri, but whatever, it wasn't like I'd expected Christina to ask me. It wasn't awkward or anything.

But her dating my best friend? *That* was awkward.

The whole bus ride to Orlando, I'd pretended to enjoy sprawling out over two seats while they sat together across the aisle. But I missed sitting next to Brian, playing games on our phones and arguing over our wildly different theories about the next *Star Wars* movie. And when my mind eventually wandered back to middle school band trips, when Christina and I would pretend we were on the Knight Bus and annoy everyone with our periodic shrieking as we squeezed through traffic, I felt infinitely crappier.

The two of them got back to loading the elevator while I ripped open one of the Band-Aids. Christina still used the kind with smiley faces. Looking at them made me feel more sad than happy.

CHAPTER THREE

VANESSA

Just outside the door of room 1502, I paused and took a deep breath and forced myself not to run away and hide, no matter how much I wanted to. Except I didn't *really* want to because . . . well, because this was it. After eight months of writing together and six months of being best friends and four months of dating, this was the moment I was finally going to meet my very first girlfriend face-to-face.

Soleil had arrived at the convention center's hotel about half an hour ago, while I was still on the road, which I knew because she'd sent me a text saying Guess where I am??? accompanied by a selfie that she'd just taken with a *Fun Things to Do in Orlando* brochure—the kind of brochure you only ever saw in hotels.

Taking out my phone, I turned around and positioned myself so the room number was right over my head and I angled the camera just so. I snapped a pic and sent it to Soleil, accompanied by the same text she'd sent me earlier: Guess where I am???

Within seconds, the door flew open—and there she was. Exactly as beautiful in person as she was online.

Soleil was about my height, but that was where the similarities ended. While my skin was medium-brown, hers was super pale. While my hair was aggressively curly and, again, brown, hers was straight and shiny and corn-silk blond. She wore eyeliner and lip gloss, and even her clothes—just a plain black T-shirt, jeans, and boots—looked like they'd been picked out by a Hollywood costume designer.

But my embarrassment about my lack of makeup skills and my hand-me-down jeans only lasted half a second, because that was when Soleil flung her arms around me and squeezed me like her life depended on it, and I kind of *hoped* her life depended on it, because right then mine definitely did.

"Nessie! Oh my god, I can't believe you're a real live person!"

I laughed into her shoulder because, oh god, I couldn't believe she was real, either. Especially since, you know, most real people were boring and annoying and watched TV shows with*out* immediately logging on to FicForAll to look for fanfiction of their favorite characters. They didn't speak Internet, and they didn't speak Fandom.

And none of them, absolutely none of them, ever called me Nessie.

She probably knew it, too, because probably none of her real-life people called her by her screen name, either. Probably they just called her Sarah.

"Soleil," I said, and we squeezed and squeezed, and I breathed deeply. She smelled like something floral. Well, fake-floral. But pretty.

For a minute after we finally broke apart, we looked at each other. Just looked. And I wondered if this was when we were supposed to kiss.

"You look nothing like your avatar," she said, and stepped back a little and, okay, maybe it wasn't time for kissing yet. "Thank god."

I laughed. My avatar on the FicForAll boards was the Loch Ness Monster, which came from my screen name, Ness, which was short for my real name: Vanessa.

"Neither do you," I said, because obviously a person looking like a smiley-faced sun was totally an option.

"Har har." She stepped back a little and took me in from head to toe, which was kind of awkward but also a little bit great. "God, look at you! You're so cute!"

"Cute?" I said, feeling my cheeks go hot. Maybe it *was* time for kissing.

"Yeah," she said. "Your shirt. It's adorbs. Where'd you get it?"

Adorbs. That was an internet word that I'd never heard anyone use in real life and, oh god, this was finally happening. After almost eighteen years of being stuck in classrooms with people who basically didn't speak my language at all, I was finally meeting my *own* people.

"My cousin made it for me," I said. "She's seven."

Soleil nodded. "Hence the puffy paint."

"Yeah, hence the puffy paint." With my index finger, I traced the bright yellow words: *I <3 Harry Potter.* It had been a birthday gift last year.

"Super cute," she said again. Then her eyes flicked over to the mirror, which was hanging over the tiny desk. "Ugh, I'm so gross. You wouldn't believe the flight I had. I had to sit next to this horrible sweaty woman, and baggage claim took decades, and the line for cabs was like eighteen miles long. You know."

"That sounds like the worst," I said.

Seriously, I was so lucky that I hadn't had to fly here. My family lived right outside Orlando, so it had only taken my parents about forty-five minutes to drive me to the convention center and, sure, it was forty-five minutes of them lecturing me about internet creepers, reminding me to call them at least once a day, and threatening to ground me if I drank anything alcoholic—but that was still way better than an eighteen-mile-long cab line.

Although it probably would've been way worse if I'd told them that Soleil was my actual girlfriend instead of just my online best friend. If I'd said all that, they probably wouldn't have let me come at all. Not because Soleil was a girl—they were totally cool with me being gay—but because they had a strict rule about only dating people who were still in high school, and Soleil was in college and, sure, she was only a freshman, but still.

"Hey," said Soleil. "Wanna help me pick out an outfit?"

"An outfit? You're not wearing that?"

She laughed. "God, no. These are travel clothes. You don't change into the good stuff till the con actually starts. I mean, it's not like you're wearing that to the welcome dinner, right?" She meant my shirt. The same shirt she'd called *super cute* twenty seconds ago.

"Um. Should I not?"

"A Harry Potter shirt? Sweetie. Come on."

Okay, clearly I was missing something. "Wait, do you mean you have a costume instead? Because I didn't plan on—"

"No, no, no!" She laughed, waving her hands expansively. "God, I'm sorry. I was so excited about meeting you, I totally forgot this is your first convention. You don't know the rules."

"Rules . . . ?"

"Well, okay, not like literal *rules* rules. More like . . . things that you're just supposed to know. Like how you don't wear shirts for mainstream fandoms—except if they're old enough to be vintage. Otherwise, the smaller the fandom, the better the shirt."

"So, like, a *Wonderlandia* shirt would've been okay," I said. That was the web series that Soleil and I wrote our fanfic about: a low-budget *Alice in Wonderland*–inspired thing that she and I both loved beyond all reason.

"Exactly," she said. "But let's be honest: advertising your fandom at all is kind of cheap. The really classy thing to do is just walk around looking fabulous. You get me?"

My limbs suddenly felt heavy. How could I possibly have known all that? It was the same thing that happened on a daily basis at school, where you walked in one morning and ninety percent of your classmates had suddenly decided that side ponytails were fashionable again, or that wearing purple was no longer cool. Nobody ever said these things out loud, but somehow everyone knew—or at least, ninety percent of everyone knew, and the other ten percent, which always included me, were left to fend for themselves. It was social Darwinism at work, and it was pretty high on the list of reasons I liked the internet better than real life. Online, no matter what rules you followed and what you looked like and what you wore, there was a place for you.

I'd found my place on the message boards of FicForAll, my favorite fanfiction website, where fanfic authors from all around the world posted their stories, critiqued and praised each other's work, and talked about their fandoms. The result: friendships that were thousands of times stronger than anything born of being shoved into a high school classroom with a bunch of people who had nothing in common except an age and a zip code.

FicForAll was where I'd met Soleil. She was the most popular ficcer in the *Wonderlandia* fandom—so popular that whenever she posted new fic, other people then wrote fanfic of *her* fanfic. Including me. I'd written a little sequel to one of her best stories, and she'd liked it so much that she'd asked me to co-author her next fic, and obviously I'd agreed, because who wouldn't, right? Not only would it be fun, but also, what better way to get more readers than to start writing with someone as popular as Soleil? But then we'd actually started talking about more than just fandom stuff, and we had everything in common, and—

Well, we had *most* things in common. Not everything. Because she was apparently part of the ninety percent of people who always knew what to wear.

"Nessie? Are you okay?"

I blinked. Somewhere in there, Soleil had stopped laughing. Now she was watching me like she was afraid I might faint or throw up or something else totally dumb.

"Yeah," I said, giving her a no-big-deal shrug. "I just . . . I didn't know there'd be rules."

Saying so made me feel about five years old, but it was the truth, and Soleil and I were nothing if not truthful with each other.

Her face brightened, and she came over and grabbed my biceps with surprisingly strong hands. "Don't worry about it. Look, I didn't mean to make you feel bad, okay? I'm just all hyped up from the flight and from meeting you and from standing in that ridiculous registration line! Oh my god, you've gotten your badge already, right? Isn't it such a madhouse over there?"

"It so is!" I said, instantly feeling a million times better now that we were on common ground again. "I mean, I was expecting the cosplayers, but did you see all the fake animals? I think there are like twelve conventions happening at the same time."

"Four," said Soleil. "I checked. And they're not fake; they're part of a taxidermy convention."

"Are you kidding me?" I said. "That's an actual thing?"

"Can you even believe it?" she said gleefully. "And as far as I can tell, it's a hundred percent white, cisgender, rich, middle-American men who think *feminist* is the worst *F*-word there is."

And there she was. The Soleil I knew and loved. The girl who went on biweekly message-board diatribes against the dangers of the gender binary and why monogamy was an outdated concept and the importance of diversity in fiction. Especially diversity in race and sexuality, both of which I had pretty strong feelings about, because *obviously*.

"Morons," I said. "Let us go forth and avoid them like the plague."

"Absolutely," said Soleil. "But first, we don our armor."

She darted over to the giant black suitcase she'd put over in the corner, and when she opened it, a huge tangle of clothes spilled out—far more clothes than would ever be necessary for a convention that didn't even last a full week.

She considered for a moment, then reached in and pulled out a shiny midnight-blue thing and unfolded it and held it against her body. "How about this one?"

It was a dress. A seriously *short* dress, with black lace along the neckline and straps so thin that they looked ready to snap.

"Too much?" she asked.

"*Is* it too much? You're the one who knows the rules. Not me."

She shrugged, letting the dress sag as she dropped her arms again. "Well, *rules* is maybe an exaggeration. But there's a sort of . . . *expectation* that the welcome dinner on the first night is where everyone dresses to the nines."

"I thought the welcome dinner was for the cosplayers to show off their costumes," I said.

"But we're not cosplayers, now, are we?" said Soleil.

My stomach did a little flip. "No, but . . . um, see, I didn't bring any fancy clothes."

"Ohhhh." Soleil looked me up and down for a second, all quietly and thoughtfully and still not sexily but soon, soon, hopefully soon. "Well, we're probably the same size, right? Or at least close enough? I mean, I brought enough dresses to feed an army."

"Not to mix metaphors or anything," I added, and smiled with relief and, oh good, Soleil was smiling back. "Really, you'll let me borrow something?"

"Nessie, oh my god, of course I will!"

With her newfound mission alight in her eyes, she tossed the lace dress aside and crouched in front of her suitcase and rifled through her clothes like a raccoon through a trash can.

"Try this on," she said, tossing me a bundle of red fabric.

I caught it, then froze. Was I supposed to change in the bathroom, or right here in front of her? Before I could decide, though, Soleil pulled her top off, and then her boots and jeans, and then she was standing just a couple feet away from me in a pink bra and matching underwear, like it was nothing, like she did this all the time, and—

And, just, holy *crap*, she was so pretty.

But if she could act like this kind of intimacy was no big deal, then so could I. I undressed, too, and put on the red dress while she tried on a yellow one, and we zipped each other up, and I tried not to shiver at the feeling of her fingers against my back, and mostly I actually succeeded, which, go me.

We looked in the mirror, and Soleil said what we were both thinking:

"Nope."

I laughed, and we took off the dresses and tried on different ones. I tried not to think too hard about being almost-naked in front of her. I tried not to notice if she was checking me out.

Twenty minutes and several changes later, Soleil and I stood side by side in front of the full-length mirror. She was in the midnight-blue dress, which hugged her figure in a way that managed to be both inviting and intimidating. And me? I was in a shiny black dress that had beaded blue flowers strewn across the bodice, and a halter top that actually made my boobs look kind of great, and a skirt that flared out when I twirled. She'd even done our hair and let me borrow some eyeliner and given me some of her bright pink lip gloss to wear for the evening.

We looked like we were about to go to prom.

"You likey?" she asked.

"Me likey," I replied.

"I'm glad it fits you." She gave my dress a fond look. "I bought that last month, for the Easter party where I met my boyfriend's parents."

"Wait, what?" I said, turning to look at her face-to-face instead of face-to-reflection. "You have a boyfriend?"

"Dave, yeah." She frowned a little as she met my eyes. "Oh wow, have I not told you about him?"

I shook my head and wiped my hands on my hips and willed my palms to stop sweating. "How, um, how long have you been, you know . . . together?"

"Only a little while. Like, not even three months." She smiled, kind of tentative, kind of worried. "Sorry, I thought I told you already."

I breathed out, long and slow, and instructed myself not be jealous of this Dave person. There was no reason to be jealous, because I'd known all along that Soleil didn't believe in monogamy, and I knew that meant she and I weren't exclusive, even if I, personally, had no interest in dating anyone else.

Besides, she'd just said *three* months. She and I had been together for almost four, which meant I had a full month on Dave, plus, hey, maybe the fact that she hadn't bothered mentioning him to me meant that he just kinda wasn't worth mentioning. Right?

Right.

So I swallowed down my stupid jealousy. "Cool. Dave. Okay."

"The point is," she continued, "his parents love me. And it all started at that party, with this dress. So it's got, like, positive karma all over it. You get me?"

Oh, now I got it. The dress had positive romance-karma, so *obviously* she was loaning it to me, which was maybe a little weird, sure, but also totally sweet.

"I get you," I said, and offered her my arm. "Shall we go dazzle everyone with our fabulousness?"

"Let's!"

Soleil took my arm, and together we emerged from our hotel room like butterflies from a cocoon, and it didn't matter that Soleil was part of the ninety percent. It didn't matter that she had a boyfriend she'd never told me about or that we hadn't kissed yet. The only thing that mattered was that I was finally breathing the same air as the person I cared about most in the world.

CHAPTER FOUR

PHOEBE

Beep! Bee—

I snatched my phone off the nightstand and silenced the alarm with a swipe. Next to me, Christina stirred a little. Grabbing my backpack, I crept into the bathroom and quietly closed the door before turning on the light.

The counter was covered in, like, a half dozen different tools to dry or straighten or curl hair, along with a bunch of makeup tubes and brushes. The warm-up room for the snare soloists opened at 8:00, and I'd been on enough band trips with these girls to know how to avoid being late. Shower at night, wake up early, and get the hell out of there before the bathroom beautification rituals began. Sometimes they'd try to drag me into it, like at IPAC freshman year when Amy offered to rub some beige liquid goo on my face to "cover up all those freckles." Other times, the torture was more bodily function related. Like last year in Orlando, when I nearly peed myself thanks to Nuri's *Lord of the Rings*–length morning shower.

Maybe I hadn't fully woken up yet, or maybe it was the hot

water, but the pain in my palms didn't register until I soaped up my hands and held them under the faucet. Wincing, I wiped them on a towel before examining the cuts. Nuri's mom, one of our chaperones, had helped me clean and bandage them last night. I'd pulled the Band-Aids off before going to bed, and it had only stung a little. Now they felt sore, though. No blood, but the skin around the cuts was dark pink and kind of puffy.

Carefully, I pulled on jeans and my *More Cowbell!* T-shirt and left the bathroom. Nuri was still sound asleep. Amy hadn't budged from the fetal position, but she had her phone close to her face. I could see her Instagram feed reflected in her glasses.

Christina was fiddling with the little one-cup coffeemaker next to the TV, her super-short black hair sticking up in every direction. She glanced over when I muttered *sharks* under my breath.

"What's up?"

I dropped my backpack on our bed and wiped my stinging palms on my jeans. "Nothing."

"Are your hands still hurting?" She flipped on a lamp, and Nuri groaned in protest. Ignoring her, Christina squinted at my cuts, then reached for her bag. "Here."

She tossed a tube of Neosporin at me. I caught it, frowning. "It's fine; Mrs. Hwang said they're not infected."

"Yeah, but your solo's this morning. Drumming isn't exactly going to make them heal faster." Christina dug out her smiley-face Band-Aids and handed me a few. I noticed she had one wrapped around the middle finger of her left hand. "Rubbed off a callus yesterday during 'Big Top,'" she explained with a grin, waggling the bandaged finger. "You're not the only one who's hardcore."

I laughed. We all had calluses, but Christina practiced more obsessively than any of us, so hers were thick and hard as rocks. When they rubbed off, it was extra gruesome.

She had a point about my hands, too. They might not be bleeding now, but who knew what shape they'd be in once I started playing. As I smeared ointment on the cuts, Amy stood up and stretched.

"Geez, Phoebe," she said, her voice hoarse with sleep. "Are you gonna be able to play? That's got to hurt."

"It's no big deal. Thanks for these," I added to Christina, tossing the Band-Aid wrappers into the trash can.

Standing, Amy held her phone up in front of Christina's face. "Jorge texted me a list of incredibly insulting band name suggestions. Which one of us should kick his ass?"

Christina's lips twitched as she read. "I don't know, maybe we *should* consider The Menstrual Cyclists."

Nuri, who was apparently awake after all, snort-laughed into her pillow. That set Christina and Amy into a fit of giggles. Smiling tightly, I double-checked my backpack for my sticks and practice pad, then grabbed the taxidermy bag and headed to the door. "See you guys down there."

"Oh, hey, good luck!" Christina called.

"Thanks!"

They were still laughing as the door clicked closed behind me.

After waiting in a Starbucks line that included a Katniss, a stoned-looking girl wearing a green sleeping bag like a dress, and two bearded guys having a heated debate about doing stuff to a goat that I dearly hoped was taxidermy-related, I found room B-2. A woman with an IPAC badge stood outside the door with a clipboard. She squinted at my badge.

"Phoebe Byrd," she said, checking my name off. "You're on at 9:25. I'll come get you at 9:20."

Inside, I did a quick scan of the room and spotted Jorge in the corner. He glanced up from his practice pad, lifting one stick in a quick wave before continuing his warm-ups.

"Hey," I said over the muffled, chaotic sound of several dozen drummers hacking away at their flat rubber practice pads. That noise always drove my parents nuts at home, but I found it comforting, like heavy rain hitting a rubber roof. "What time are you on?"

"Eight fifty-five," he replied, stretching his arms over his head. I caught a whiff of the spicy cologne he always wore a little bit too much of. "Scott's right after me."

After sucking down half of my iced mocha, I opened the recorder app on my phone. This was a ritual I'd started freshman year, when my English teacher had suggested I write an essay about IPAC for the school newspaper. I'd given it a shot, but it didn't come out great. No words could adequately summarize the experience. But audio recordings could. I'd edited the clips into a pretty cool two-minute mix, and it ended up on the newspaper's blog instead.

I got a ten-second clip of the racket and labeled it *IPAC Snare Solo—Warm-Ups.* Then I pulled my sticks and practice pad out of my backpack. My pad was gray, with a Weird Sisters sticker in the center and a bunch of faded Sharpie signatures—my friends in band, guest artists at our concerts, clinicians—that I'd started collecting freshman year.

The nerves were starting to kick in now. I'd done a snare solo at IPAC last year, too—sixth place out of a few dozen, not bad for a sophomore. Scott had been fifth, and Jorge had been second. Everyone fully expected Jorge to win this year, especially since last year's winner had graduated. I just wanted to crack the top five.

Okay, that was a lie. What I really wanted was to kick Scott's butt. Our scores had only been half a point apart last year. And a little vengeance for the scalpel incident wouldn't be the worst thing.

I warmed up slowly, trying to adjust to the odd sensation of the bandages separating my palms from the sticks. After a few minutes, the Band-Aids loosened a little, rubbing against the raw cuts. By the time Scott and the other guys showed up, my palms were burning.

"Yes." Scott swiped my iced mocha and took an enormous slurp. I shot him a withering look but said nothing. Nick and Devon immediately pulled their pads out and started to warm up. Scott took his time, as if to demonstrate how not nervous he was. But as

he drummed, he kept stopping to stretch his arms: his telltale sign of anxiety.

Scott and I had been friends since sixth grade beginner band, when our fight over who got the snare part to "Frosty the Snowman" at the holiday concert had ended with him stomping on my foot and me shoving my stick up his nose. Our director had given Christina the part while Scott and I got detention, and we were cool after that. We'd even gone to Homecoming together last fall. I'd found out later it was only because Amber Tanner had backed out on him. Which, whatever—it's not like I'd *wanted* it to be a romantic thing.

Scott stopped and stretched his arms again. His face lit up when he noticed the taxidermy bag next to my backpack. He grabbed and unzipped it. "This thing is like a serial killer's tool kit. *Fleshing knife, toe probe, lip tucker* . . . oh my god, this one's called a *membrane separator!*"

I snatched the bag back and zipped it up, glancing at the moderator near the door. "Pretty sure it's not cool to be walking around here carrying *knives*, so let's maybe not wave them around. And my hands are fine, thanks for asking."

I flashed my smiley-face Band-Aids at Scott. Jorge glanced up and winced.

"Why'd you make her play with scalpels?" he said, smacking Scott's arm with a stick.

"I didn't *make* her do anything," Scott retorted. Devon leaned over to take a closer look at my hands.

"You knew she needed those mallets for the xylophone solo,

though," he pointed out. "Taking them for your part was kind of a dick move."

Scott rolled his eyes. "How was I supposed to know she was going to use them?"

"What else would I use?" I said, leaning back against the wall. "My fingers?"

Before Scott could respond, the moderator called out: "Jorge Ramirez?"

We all wished Jorge luck as he headed to the door, sticks tucked under his arm. A few minutes later, Scott was up. Devon and Nick hacked away at their pads, their faces intent; this was their first IPAC, and they both looked a little nervous.

I would've been a lot less anxious if it weren't for the stupid cuts on my hands. It wasn't the pain; I'd drummed through plenty of busted blisters and blood vessels. It was the weird numbness from the Band-Aids, the way I couldn't feel the sticks touching the skin of my palms. I wasn't in control anymore. And the more I played, the worse it got: crushed diddles, popped flams, uneven rolls.

When the moderator called my name, a weird, buzzy ringing started in my ears. I grabbed my stuff and headed to the door, barely aware of Nick and Devon wishing me luck. The solos were next door in room B-1, which was a bit bigger than the warm-up room. But it was still no more than a hundred or so seats, about half of which were currently filled. Honestly, I would've preferred playing on a stage in front of a packed auditorium so dark I couldn't see all the staring eyes. Performing in a brightly lit room with a bunch of friends sitting a few feet away was about a million times more intimidating.

Scott whistled from the second row when I stepped up to the snare and started adjusting the stand for my height. I did a quick assessment of faces: Jorge sat next to Scott, and behind them were Nuri and Amy, along with Mrs. Hwang and the other parent chaperones. Mr. Mackey was a few rows back, sitting with another director. I saw a bunch of kids I vaguely recognized from Bishop not far behind them.

Brian sat front and center with Christina, already taking video on his phone. He gave me a thumbs-up, and I tried to smile back, but it probably looked like more of a grimace. The announcer began to introduce me, and my heart started pounding so loudly it drowned him out. I was about to royally suck in front of everyone because of these freaking bandages.

Turning around, I ripped the Band-Aids off my palms and shoved them in my pockets. Then I faced the chairs, picked up my sticks, and started to drum.

The pain was immediate. The cuts, all raw and open from the ointment and my warm-ups, stung so hard I gasped. I stared down at my hands, trying to focus on the fact that now I could at least feel the sticks as I played. But after less than a minute, the ache was so intense that tears pricked my eyes.

Nope. No. Absolutely no way in hell was I crying in the middle of my solo. Not happening.

Desperate to finish, I sped up, and then sped up some more. Someone let out a whoop, but this wasn't the good, adrenaline-induced kind of tempo change. It sounded like nothing but amateur nerves: flashy and fast, but total crap quality-wise. When I finished, I blinked a few times to make sure my eyes weren't wet before looking up. I smiled as everyone cheered, nodded at the judges, then hurried offstage.

I grabbed my backpack and crammed my sticks inside before anyone could see the blood, then quickly put on my hoodie so I could shove my hands in the pockets. Yesterday this had been funny. *Hardcore.* But now . . . I wasn't sure why, but I didn't want anyone to see.

"Nice job," Brian whispered when I sat down next to him. On his other side, Christina nodded in agreement.

I shrugged. "Thanks. The last half was pretty rough, though."

"Nah, you sounded great." He glanced up from his phone and adjusted his glasses, peering at me more closely. "You okay?"

"Yeah."

All I wanted to do was go back to my room and stick my hands in a bucket of ice. But I sucked it up and watched the next six soloists, which included Nick (good, but a little nervous) and Devon (pretty badass for a freshman) before ducking into a restroom and putting on new bandages. Then we headed as a group to the exhibit hall for a few hours of free time before we had to face the awards ceremony for yesterday's ensemble catastrophe.

The exhibit hall was my favorite part of IPAC. A massive room filled with every percussion instrument imaginable, some of which I didn't even know the names of. And everyone could try out whatever they wanted. The cacophony was incredible; within a minute of walking in, we passed a guy thrashing away at a drum set, a group of kids trying out Japanese taiko drums, an elderly man in a slick suit playing jazz chords on a set of vibes, a woman thumping out a samba on a Brazilian pandeiro, and a guy slapping at a set of congas with such intensity, my own hands stung even harder in sympathy.

For me, this was what IPAC was all about: the total chaos that could only come from a giant room filled with drums from all sorts of cultures and a few thousand musicians obsessed with banging on them.

I had my phone out and recording app on again, capturing clips of each new sound. Scott and Jorge made a beeline for some of the marching drums, Nick and Devon right behind them. Within seconds, it had devolved into a testosterone-fueled competition of who could play the loudest and fastest.

Christina hurried off with Nuri and Amy, and I thought I heard one of them say something about recording equipment. For The Menstrual Cyclists, I assumed, and felt a twinge of irritation. To qualify for IPAC, all percussion ensembles had to submit a recording in the fall, and this year Mr. Mackey had let me help him mix ours. I'd learned a little bit about sound engineering, and Christina and the others knew that. But they hadn't asked me for advice or anything, even though none of them knew the difference between a condenser mic and a dynamic mic.

I pocketed my phone and sighed. Brian was studying his map of the hall, his eyes shining behind his glasses. He was planning on majoring in music and becoming an orchestral percussionist after college, so being surrounded by all these pros always made him giddy. Last year, he'd literally spent two hours at a booth that sold triangles, having a deep discussion with the company's very enthusiastic representative about the effect beaters of various lengths and girths had on timbre. I'd honestly never heard so much unintentional sexual innuendo in one conversation.

But between my terrible solo performance and my aching hands, my current mood was a little less "stand in a noisy hall discussing the importance of the shape of a drumstick tip" and a little more "watch cartoons and eat vending machine junk food in a dark hotel room, alone." Luckily, I actually had a legit excuse for sneaking out, at least for a little while.

"I promised Mackey I'd find that taxidermy girl and swap our bags," I told Brian, patting my backpack. "I'll text you later so we can meet up, okay?"

He nodded. "Sure!"

Relieved, I left him looking for the triangle booth and headed straight for the exit. The chaotic scene in the hotel lobby took a few seconds to register.

A mob of women and little girls surrounded the reception desk. None of the girls looked older than five, but I could have sworn a few were actually wearing makeup. And costumes. Disturbingly sexy costumes.

"Beige! Beige, get off of there!"

A woman dragging an enormous purple suitcase hurried over to the fountain in the middle of the lobby, flapping her free hand. Her daughter—*Beige*, apparently—had climbed up on the edge and was now singing at the top of her lungs and shaking her hips in a way no toddler should even know how to do. I stood there and gaped, not even bothering to hide my horror. Because this little girl was dressed like Sandy from *Grease*. And not good girl Sandy. Tight black leather, bright red lipstick, blond hair teased up with a can of hairspray Sandy.

"*You're the one that I want!*" she crooned. "*Ooh-ooh-ooh!*"

Taking a few steps back, I tore my gaze away from Beige and finally noticed the sign above the reception desk.

Welcome
LITTLE MISS CITRUS

Oh sweet merciful cats.

Turning, I walked as fast as I could toward the elevators. Tracking down the taxidermy girl would have to wait. Hell, if this hotel was going to be swarming with crazy pageant moms, I might not leave my room for the rest of the convention.

CHAPTER FIVE

VANESSA

When our alarms woke us up the next morning, the very first thing I said was, "Hey, can I borrow something to wear?"

Because, okay, Soleil had been totally right about the dresses. I guess I'd been planning on going through the convention like I went through the rest of my life—quiet and backgroundy and unobtrusive—but as soon as I'd put on that dress and walked into the banquet hall arm-in-arm with Soleil, everything had changed. People had stared at us, and I mean not just her, but actually both of us. They'd stared, and they'd smiled, and—this was the best part—Soleil kept shooting me these conspiratorial grins, as if to say, *Sure, all these people think we're hot, and obviously they're right, but they don't even know the half of it.*

In other words, the kind of grins that promised kissing later.

Not that there *had* been kissing later. After an evening of stuffing our faces and dancing till our feet were sore, neither of us had really had the energy to do anything more than come back to the hotel room and face-plant on our beds. Our *different* beds. I'd thought about crawling into Soleil's bed so we could fall asleep with our arms touching, or even with her back pressed against my front or vice versa, but by the time I worked up the courage to ask if I could, she'd already started snoring.

But that was okay. We'd get there eventually. Just like she would kiss me eventually. She was probably just waiting for the right moment. She'd probably waited for the right moment with Dave, too.

"Hey, Soleil?" I said, when she didn't answer. Sheets rustled in the other bed, and she murmured something unintelligible. "Soleil! We should get up. Your panel's in an hour."

"An hour?" she said, sitting bolt upright. "Ugh, no, I'm late."

I pushed the covers aside and fumbled for my glasses. "You're not late. You have an hour, like I said."

"But I have to shower and eat and drink all the coffee in the universe and I don't even know what I'm going to wear and—wait, did you ask me something?"

She was already zooming around the room, checking herself in the mirror and grabbing things out of her giant suitcase and rubbing the sleep out of her eyes, as I sat on my bed and watched her. I felt like a tree in the middle of a hurricane.

"I asked if I could borrow something to wear."

"Oh!" she said, with a breathy little laugh. "Sure, yeah, anything you want. You don't mind if I take the first shower, right?"

"Sure," I said. She was already closing the door behind her.

I took my time getting ready, stretching and yawning as Soleil buzzed around me, angling herself this way and that in front of the mirror in order to get her makeup exactly right. Personally, I thought she looked great no matter what she did, but I didn't say anything. I just kept myself out of her way as I swabbed deodorant under my arms, put on my jeans and the red blouse I'd found in Soleil's suitcase, and dotted concealer over my zits.

Despite Soleil's insistence that she was going to be late, we actually arrived in room A-21 about fifteen minutes early. There were only six other people there, and they were all clutching cups of coffee. Three of them were girls, all pale and wearing similar costumes: dapper suits with purple shirts and purple ties, bulky headphones looped around their necks, and eyes drawn on their foreheads. One was a dark-skinned guy in a bloodstained prom dress, and two were a white guy and an Asian girl dressed in regular clothes and, unlike last night, none of them gave Soleil or me a second glance when we walked in.

We claimed a pair of seats on the side of the front row, and Soleil rubbed her hands frantically on her thighs, wrinkling her skirt and smoothing it out again, over and over.

"You'll be fine," I said. "You'll be great. Haven't you done, like, a million of these before?"

She let out a strained laugh. "Maybe ten, tops. But those were just panels. This is different. I've never read my stuff out loud before."

Our stuff, I wanted to say—but stopped myself, because Soleil's nervousness was genuine, which meant this was not the time to argue semantics. So I just repeated, "You'll be fine."

"Thanks, sweetie." She reached over to squeeze my hand.

"You're the best. You know that, right? Ooh, there's the moderator. Beth! Hey!"

And with that, Soleil shot out of her seat and threw her arms around a petite black girl in a Ravenclaw tie. Beth, apparently. Maybe they knew each other from previous conventions. I felt a little pang of jealousy at the thought . . . but that was dumb. It didn't matter how long they'd known each other, because whatever kind of relationship Soleil had with Beth, it had nothing on her relationship with me. If I could make myself not be jealous of Boyfriend Dave, then I could do the same thing with Moderator Beth.

So instead of staring at them as they talked, I pulled out my schedule and went over my plans for the rest of the day. After this panel—Your Fandom's Best Fiction, Volume One—Soleil and I were going to the *Wonderlandia* meetup at eleven thirty. Then lunch. Then we would go to a panel about diversity in young adult fiction, and then this book-to-movie panel, where a bunch of Soleil's favorite fantasy authors would be talking about film adaptations of their work. After that, we could either get in line for the main-stage costume contest or do our own thing.

Personally, my vote was for taking advantage of the massive swimming pool on the roof of the hotel.

"Are these seats taken?" asked a voice that definitely wasn't Soleil's.

I looked up, and there, looming above me, were three girls in Harry Potter costumes. One was in a floaty dress accessorized with a bunch of scarves and a pair of round glasses that magnified her eyes: Professor Trelawney, obviously. One wore dark green robes over a black dress, accompanied by a classic witch hat and a scowling expression: clearly Professor McGonagall.

Both costumes were great, but the third girl, the one who'd actually spoken, was wearing probably the best costume I'd ever seen. She was dressed as Professor Snape. But not the black-robed Snape that I'd already seen ten times over since registration—or, for that matter, the almost-naked Snape who'd started shouting things like "Death to the Mudbloods!" while running drunkenly around the convention center. This Snape was dressed in a woman's coat and a hat with a bird on it—which was to say, Snape in Neville Longbottom's grandmother's clothes, straight out of that one scene in *Prisoner of Azkaban*. Boggart Snape.

She smiled and raised her eyebrows, which was when I realized I'd been staring. And not answering.

"Sorry! Sorry, didn't mean to be a creeper." I shifted Soleil's purse to the floor beside my own bag. "Go ahead, sit down. Sorry. It's just, you know, your costume. It's awesome."

"Aw, hey, thanks," said Snape, taking the seat next to me. "I'm Merry. That's Jaya, and that's Tiff."

The two professors waved; I waved back. "I'm Vanessa. Call me Ness."

"Nice to meet you," said Merry, as Jaya and Tiff paired off into a separate conversation. "You here alone?"

"Actually, no. My, um, roommate. She's a panelist."

"Ah." Merry looked up at the tiny stage at the front of the

room. There was one long table with five chairs behind it, all of which were full. "Which one's your roommate?"

"Blond hair, pink shirt," I said, pointing. "Her name's Soleil."

Merry's eyes widened. "Wait. You're friends with Soleil? *The* Soleil? 'I Knew You Were Trouble' Soleil?"

"Yup!" I said, suddenly all kinds of giddy because I so, so wanted to tell her that Soleil and I were way more than just friends. I wanted to tell her that I was wearing Soleil's shirt right now, and that Soleil had dressed me up and taken me out last night and everyone had stared at us as she whirled me around the dance floor after dinner. I wanted to tell her. But I didn't. Somehow, that information seemed too private to share.

"Oh wow," said Merry. "Oh . . . just, wow. She's actually the one I'm here to see. Wait. Soleil does use *she*, right?"

"Yup. Why?"

Merry gave me a nervous smile. "I just like to try and be respectful. Because—you know." And she pointed to a button on her chest. It was small, and it was formatted like one of those *My Name Is* stickers. Except instead of *My Name Is*, it said *My Pronouns Are*. And underneath that, in a font that was clearly supposed to look like handwriting, the words *They/Them/Their* were printed.

"Oh!" I said. "Sorry, I didn't see. You're . . . gender-fluid?"

"Gender-neutral." Merry's smile loosened a little. "You?"

"Just a plain old girl," I said. "*She* and *her*. Sorry."

Merry laughed. "Why are you sorry? Being a girl is awesome. Some of my best friends are girls." She gave a quick nod toward Jaya and Tiff, who were both wearing *My Pronouns Are* buttons, too.

"No, I mean, I'm not *sorry*," I said. "I just . . . never mind. I don't know what I mean. But yeah. I'm a girl."

"Cool," said Merry, and looked back up at the stage. "Seriously, I've been fan-crushing on Soleil like crazy ever since that StraightFlush thing. God, remember that?"

"StraightFlush?" I echoed with a frown.

"Yeah," Merry said. "Were you not around for that whole thing? Some dude named StraightFlush got all up in Soleil's business, being like, 'God, why is everything you write so gay? Ugh!'"

"Ohhh, right, yeah, I think she told me about that," I said. "That was, what, a year ago? We didn't know each other yet, back then. What happened?"

"What happened is Soleil totally reamed the guy out!" Her eyes—*their* eyes, rather—were alight with admiration. "She wrote this huge post about how important it is to have diverse representation, and about how everyone *knows* Five and Seven are actually gay in canon, despite that idiotic hetero-fantasy ending, and—I mean, god, *all* her posts are amazing. Did you read the one about how being in fandom gave her the courage to come out to her parents as pansexual?"

I nodded. "Actually, that was the post that got *me* to come out to *my* parents."

Suddenly, Merry's gaze was laser sharp. "Oh, yeah?"

"Yeah," I said. "I'm gay. Or—well, mostly gay, I guess? Or homoflexible. You know. Mostly I like girls, but you never know what's gonna happen."

And omigod, how amazing was it to just be able to *say* that stuff? Out *loud*? To someone wearing a button saying what their pronouns were? It was like my little fandomy corner of the internet had come to life, in the best possible way.

"Same, actually," said Merry, giving me this weirdly secretive look. "Only I usually just say I'm queer. Fewer syllables, more bases covered."

"Nice," I said, and meant it. Soleil called herself queer, too, whenever she didn't feel like explaining what *pansexual* meant.

Merry's eyes lingered on me just a second longer, then they cleared their throat and looked up at the stage again. "Anyway! Soleil!"

"Soleil, yeah," I said. "Have you read that one *Wonderlandia* fic? 'Carry Me Home'?"

"Ooh, yeah," said Merry. "The one where Seven is gender-fluid instead of male, right? That one's gorgeous."

My entire face was about to go up in flames. This was the actual literal best day of my life, or maybe the worst, because I was definitely about to die.

"Well, the reason I asked is, um—I actually wrote that one with her."

Merry looked at me like they were about to faint. It was identical to the way they'd just looked at Soleil, and oh my god, oh my god, oh my *god*.

"I totally forgot she had a co-author on that one," they said, reaching over to squeeze my forearm. "Seriously, you two are amazing."

"Thanks," I said, or squeaked, or something. "Actually, 'Carry Me Home' is the one she's doing for the reading."

"Really? You must be so excited."

I was actually kind of petrified but also kind of giddy, and between the anticipation of Soleil pointing me out as her co-author and the memory of how fabulous we'd been last night, my entire stomach was turning into a sea of bubbles, but that was a lot of information to give to a total stranger, so I just nodded.

"Yeah. Pretty excited."

That was when Beth the Moderator tapped her microphone. The room fell quiet, and everyone looked at the stage, and Soleil looked over at *me*. She winked, all traces of nervousness gone from her demeanor. I flashed her a smile.

"Hey, guys, welcome to the fourth annual We Treasure Fandom convention!" said Beth, surveying the room from her chair at the very end of the table. "Wow, not a bad crowd for ten in the morning."

Understatement of the year. The room was on the smaller side—maybe two hundred chairs, at most—but it was full to bursting. People stood along the walls and crowded in the back, straining their necks for a view of the stage. I was very glad I'd gotten a seat. My own little oasis of space in the crowd.

"So," she continued, "welcome to Volume One of Your Fandom's Best Fiction! I started this series because—well, there are so many fandoms being represented at WTFcon, you know? I've never even heard of half of them! So I figured, why not put together a series of panels where we can all share our fandoms with each other? Right?"

The panelists nodded, and the audience responded with claps and cheers.

"Thought so," said Beth, eyes sparkling as she grinned. "And thus was born Your Fandom's Best Fiction. We've asked a representative from each of WTFcon's most popular fandoms to read a few pages of fanfic they've written. Then I'll ask them some questions—and then you, my fine audience, will ask questions, too. Sound good?"

More clapping. More cheering. Beside me, Merry stuck their fingers in their mouth and let out a wolf-whistle.

"Great!" said Beth. "And if you like this panel, we've got Volume Two at four o'clock this afternoon, Volumes Three and Four tomorrow, et cetera. It's all on your schedules, and you know how those work.

"But for now, without further ado, here are our four panelists for Volume One. Representing *Welcome to Night Vale*, we have Tricia from Tennessee, better known on FicForAll as 'Cecil's Dead Mom'!"

Clapping and cheering, mainly from the girls dressed in purple, who were sitting right behind me.

"Representing *My Little Pony: Friendship Is Magic*, we have 'The Artist Formerly Known as Todd,' all the way from Toronto!" More cheering, this time for a guy who looked kind of familiar. And kind of hungover. "Representing *Frozen*, we have 'Ice Princess

Sally' from San Francisco!" More cheering. I twisted my hands together as my stomach tried to turn itself into a pretzel.

"And finally, representing *Wonderlandia*, we have 'Soleil' from New York City!"

This time, I joined in the cheering. Up on the stage, Soleil beamed.

Beth turned to her panelists. "Soleil from New York City, why don't you start us off? Tell us a little bit about your fandom, and read us some of your fic."

"Sure thing," said Soleil, her voice all peppy as she leaned closer to her mic. She smiled out at the room, picked up one of the notecards she'd prepared, and said, "So, if you plug *Wonderlandia* into a search engine, you'll find a website with the following description. Ahem.

'Wonderlandia is your loveliest daydream. Wonderlandia is your worst nightmare. Wonderlandia is a wonderland with no Alice, where caterpillars smoke up all day, cards make experimental art, queens think fondly of all the people they'd love to behead if only they could summon the energy, and nobody likes that rabbit who's always in a hurry. Nobody.'

She put the notecard down and smiled at the room again. "What it doesn't say is that the series was made by a bunch of friends who'd just graduated from college and basically had no idea how a video camera works. Let alone costumes. I mean, the Caterpillar's costume is basically a green sleeping bag. You get me?"

A low tide of laughter rippled through the room, and she went on: "But the series isn't all low-budget weirdness-for-the-sake-of-weirdness. At its heart, it's got one of the best love stories I've ever seen. It's not only really unique, but it's also a great example of positive queer representation in media, which is so, so, *so* important to me. Well, at least, it was a great example until the end of the show, when it got all messed up because they were angling to get picked up by a network. Can we say 'forced heterosexuality' much? It was almost as bad as Cap and Sharon Carter in *Civil War*."

More laughter. Beside me, Merry leaned forward in their seat, nodding and nodding and, yeah, I got that. Soleil had that effect on people.

"But anyway," Soleil continued, "the romance is between the Five of Spades and the Seven of Hearts." She described the trajectory of the relationship between Five and Seven, just enough to give her audience a context for understanding the story she was going to read. When she was done, she picked up a few pages and said, "And that's where my story begins. It's called 'I Knew You Were Trouble,' and this is the first chapter."

My whole body went still. She wasn't supposed to read "I Knew You Were Trouble." She was supposed to read "Carry Me Home." The one she'd written with me. I'd even helped her pick out a good section.

Soleil's reading voice, silky and melodic and totally unlike her speaking voice, washed over us, with sentences that I practically knew by heart. I'd read this story over and over when she'd first posted it, and eventually written a sequel to it, which had basically started our entire friendship. I *loved* this story.

But why had she changed her mind?

Everyone around me cheered when Soleil put her pages down. Merry whistled again. I clapped kind of halfheartedly—and when Soleil looked over at me, she must've seen the disappointment on my face, because she actually started looking kind of worried.

It was a good panel, full of well-written fanfic and interesting questions from both the moderator and the audience. *Why did all of you choose to write slash pairings instead of hetero pairings? How do each of you feel about how outsiders seem to perceive your fandom? Would any of you ever want to write original fiction instead of fanfiction?* Stuff like that.

And when it was over, people actually asked the panelists for autographs. Seriously. Autographs. Soleil looked like her face was about to explode from smiling so hard.

"Hey, girl!" she said, bounding over to me when the crowd started to disperse. "Hey, listen, hope you didn't mind the last-minute story switch."

"Yeah, uh, I did notice that," I said. "I thought we said chapter two of 'Carry Me Home' would be—"

"I know," she interrupted, "but see, here's the thing. And I didn't realize it until just a few days ago. The point of this panel isn't to show off your best writing. It's to convert new people to your fandom. And you have to have so much more context to understand 'Carry Me Home.' 'I Knew You Were Trouble' stands more on its own."

I thought about that. She did have a point, but . . .

"You decided a few days ago?" I asked. "Why didn't you say anything?"

"Because I'm a forgetful moron," she said with a self-deprecating laugh. "I thought I told you. I didn't realize I hadn't until I saw you looking all sad over here. I'm so-so-so sorry, Nessie. Forgive me?"

A smile tugged at my lips. "Well, obviously, I forgive you."

"Aw, yay! You're the best." She leaned in, all conspiratorial. "So how'd I do?"

"Totally great," I said.

"Amazingly great," added Merry, beside me.

Soleil blinked at Merry, clearly thrown by the sudden presence of a third person in our conversation. As was I, actually. Caught up as I was in wondering why Soleil had switched stories, I'd forgotten that Merry might want me to introduce them to Soleil. I looked around for their professor friends, too, but apparently McGonagall and Trelawney had already left.

"Aw, that's sweet of you," Soleil said, in this weirdly different voice. The kind of voice that sounded like her perfume smelled. "What's your name?"

"Merry." They stuck out their hand, and Soleil shook it. "I was telling Ness here that I'm a huge fan of your writing. I especially like all the stuff you do with gender in your stories. It's nice to see people writing about identity-exploration that way, you know?"

Soleil's eyes flicked up to the badge on Merry's chest—and

immediately, her whole face brightened. "Ooh. You're a 'they'? That's so super cool. Good for you."

Merry blinked, and their lips twisted into a wry smile. "I mean. Sure. Yeah, good for me. Woo."

Apparently missing Merry's sarcasm, Soleil went on: "You're *exactly* the audience I was trying to reach with those stories. I'm so glad you found my stuff. Yay. Hey, do you want an autograph? Apparently we're doing autographs. I mean, isn't that so crazy? I'm just a fanfic writer!"

She dug in her purse and pulled out a pen.

Merry's expression turned kind of unreadable, and their gaze flicked over to me, then back to Soleil again. "Uh, no, that's okay. But are you guys going to the house meetups next? You're Hufflepuffs, too, right?"

I was about to ask how they knew that, but then I remembered: I'd put a Hufflepuff ribbon on my badge this morning. One more example of why this convention was infinitely better than real life.

"This one is," said Soleil, gesturing to me. "But I'm Gryffindor all the way, baby."

"Aha," said Merry, and turned back to me. "Well, how about you? Hufflepuff meetup? Jaya's already saving me a seat, and I could text her to save one for you, too."

"We're going to the *Wonderlandia* meetup," said Soleil, before I could answer. "Sorry. Actually, Nessie, we should get going. Want to make sure they still have seats, you get me?"

"I get you," I said.

Soleil hooked her arm through my elbow and started steering me toward the door—but Merry followed us. "Also, hey. Ness. Any chance you're coming to the costume contest tonight?"

Soleil and I looked at each other. "Dunno yet," I said. "Why, are you entering?"

"You bet," said Merry, fondly touching the brim of their black hat. "So it'd be super cool if you came. I mean, no pressure or whatever, since we just met. But, you know. It'd be cool."

"It is officially under consideration," said Soleil, even though the question had been firmly directed at me. She tugged at my arm again. "But we really have to run, okay? See you later!"

This time, as we darted out into the hallway where hundreds of other con-goers were taking pictures of each other's costumes and lining up for panels and meetups in other rooms, Merry didn't try to stop us.

"*It'd be suuuuuuper cool if you came,*" said Soleil, her voice going high and snotty as she echoed Merry's words. "Come on. If you want people to cheer for you, bring your own friends. Don't try and steal mine."

She squeezed my arm, which made me feel about a zillion things at once. I mean, on the one hand, she'd just proven my specialness, my belonging-to-her-ness, with a single gesture, and what could possibly be more awesome than that?

But on the other hand: "Come on, don't be mean. Merry's got friends. They just went ahead to save seats at the Hufflepuff meetup. Besides, Merry came to this panel specifically to see you, so maybe we should return the favor. Show some support. Fannish solidarity, you know?"

"Oh, please," said Soleil. "I'm not about to show solidarity with someone whose costume sucks."

"Are you kidding?" I said. "That was the best costume ever!"

Soleil raised an eyebrow. "In what universe? Isn't Boggart Snape supposed to have a *vulture* hat? That was, like, a bluebird or whatever."

"Maybe they couldn't find a stuffed vulture," I said. "And that's a pretty tiny detail coming from someone who told me, not even twenty-four hours ago, that Harry Potter is over."

"Oooh, there's that biting Nessie wit," said Soleil. I couldn't tell whether or not she was being sarcastic. "Anyway, didn't you want some pool time tonight?"

That was true. I definitely wanted some pool time. Not to mention some one-on-one time, because literally everything we'd done so far had either involved being in a crowd, getting ready to be in a crowd, or talking about having just been in a crowd, and don't get me wrong, all that stuff was *fun*, but if Soleil was planning on kissing me? It wouldn't be with a bunch of people around. We'd need to be alone.

"Yeeeaaah," I said, hesitating as we reached room A-16. They were about to open the doors for the *Wonderlandia* meetup. Yet another crowd. "Yeah, screw the costume thingie. Let's do the pool."

CHAPTER SIX

CALLIE

There was nothing in the world more boring than grooming an entire flock of wild turkeys with tweezers. The cerulean warblers were already in the judging room, perched on the Non-Game Birds table in the Master Division, and my dad was going over the ibex one last time with a penlight, a fine-toothed comb, and a can of compressed air. Last time we were here, he'd talked to me while I'd helped groom the competition mounts, making jokes and teaching me tricks for how to fix each tiny imperfection. But today he was so focused on the animals that it was like I wasn't even here. Between this morning's talks and workshops and Dad's epic networking session last night, we'd barely spoken since yesterday afternoon. He'd left me alone in the room before I'd even had time to suggest my people-watching-and-burger-eating plan.

"Dad," I said, but he just kept humming tunelessly to himself as he fluffed and sprayed. I tapped his shoulder. *"Dad."*

"Hmm?"

"Remember two years ago when that guy entered the sculpture for the Interpretive Division that was half bison and half VW

Bug?" Mom and I had stuck our heads into the judging room about five times a day to giggle at the bison-car. We had named it Sven, for some reason.

"Mmm." Dad lifted the ibex's tail and inspected it with the penlight.

"Did you see the guy go by earlier with the giant steampunk bear with all the clockwork in its face? So weird."

"Mmm," Dad said again. I wasn't sure he was even processing the things I was saying.

I sighed. "I think the turkeys are done. Do you want to check them?"

That finally got through to him. "In a few minutes." He glanced at his watch. "The trade show's open. Head over to the Van Dyke booth and pick up all the glass eyes I need before they sell out, okay?" He pulled a handwritten list out of his jacket pocket. "Be sure to get the AFE2 series for the hartebeest eyes, not the AFE series. Get the less-dilated pupil for the cheetah eyes, and the bobcat eyes should be the sixteen-by-twenty-one milli-meter. All the rest are self-explanatory. I'll meet you over there and pay for everything after these guys are installed in the judg-ing room."

I shoved the list into my back pocket without looking at it. "Yeah, okay." I hung around for another minute, waiting for a *thank you*—I'd done a really good job on the turkeys, and even if he wasn't going to bond with me, a tiny bit of praise for my assis-tant skills would've been nice. But Dad just went right back to the ibex, so I left him alone.

I picked my way through the grooming area extra-carefully—tensions ran high before judging started, and I didn't want to risk bumping into someone's mount. I passed a woman crying over a detached antelope ear and a man grooming a scarily convincing saber-tooth tiger he'd made for the Re-Creations category. There were three wolf heads stuck to a pole by their tongues, which their owner was spritzing with fake animal spit called Jaw Juice to make them look extra wet and shiny. Near the end of the hall, a middle-aged woman in bifocals and a glittery kitten shirt was grooming her wild boars, one of which was on top of the other. As I walked by, she winked at me and whispered, *"They're doing the dirty."* I gave her a tight smile and sped up.

The trade show floor was already surprisingly crowded. A group of small children ran past me, dressed in matching shirts that read, *PETA: People Eating Tasty Animals*, and I wondered how many of them would grow up to be vegetarians. The Van Dyke booths were right at the front, their giant sign flanked by yellow polyurethane deer and bear manikins waiting to be covered in pelts.

And there, next to the sign, sorting through a bin of glass eyes, was Jeremy. Finally—a chance to interact with someone who didn't think harmless socializing was grounds for a lecture about professionalism.

Jeremy was absorbed in the eyes, so I crept up behind him, my sneakers silent on the hideous teal-and-red-swirled carpet. There was a box of pale gold sheep eyes with horizontal pupils near the front of the booth, so I grabbed two of them and held them up in front of my own eyes. When I was inches from his back, I growled, "Judge Jeremy Warren, I presume?"

Jeremy whipped around, and a few eyes flew out of his hand and pinged across the booth. The Van Dyke representative glared at us over his giant handlebar mustache.

"Oh my god, you scared me," Jeremy said. "My, Callie, what creepy eyes you have."

"The better to creep on you with, my dear," I said, and he laughed. I dropped the sheep eyes back into their bin. "What're you looking for? Or are you just browsing?"

Jeremy opened his hand and showed me a bunch of cat eyes. "I'm doing a big restoration project for the Field Museum. A tiger, a cheetah, and two of the lynxes need work."

"The Field Museum? Wow, congratulations. That's a big deal."

"Yeah. I feel a little out of my depth, honestly. The tiger's so faded that I have to hand-paint the entire thing. Your dad recommended Luscious Mango hair dye. This whole thing would be a piece of cake for him."

"But they picked *you*. I'm sure you're going to do great."

"Thanks." He smiled, then retrieved his fallen eyes and handed his credit card to Mustache Man. "Do you need any eyes?"

"Yeah, I've got a list. Will you wait for me?"

"If it's quick, yeah. Then I have to head over to Skin It Yourself! and pick up some frozen raccoons."

I pulled my dad's instructions out of my pocket, expecting only the three items he'd mentioned, but the list was *way* longer than that. *Ten pairs BioOptix II whitetail deer, 30mm, light; six pairs coyote, 16/21mm; turkey, ten pairs each 12mm, 13mm, 14mm; three pairs AFE2 black bear, 18/22mm.* There were at least forty items, all printed in letters as tiny and neat as the stitches my dad used to sew up his birds. It would take me forever to find all this stuff.

"Can we meet up after you get the raccoons?" I asked. "This might actually take a while."

Mustache Man handed Jeremy his receipt, and he carefully folded it into his wallet. "Probably not. I've got a judges' meeting, and there are still a couple of things I need to do to prepare for it. And then judging starts at eight and goes until late. I'm sorry."

This might be my only opportunity to catch up with Jeremy without my dad looming over us, and there was no way I was going to pass it up to hang around the Van Dyke booth. "Okay," I said. "Just give me one second."

I stepped up to the representative and flashed him my prettiest smile. "Hi. I'm Hamish Buchannan's assistant. He loves working with Van Dyke products; he buys from you exclusively." I had no idea if that was true, but Mustache Man started looking a little friendlier, so I held out the list. "Mr. Buchannan would like to place a large order. Would you mind packing up these items for me? I'll be back to get them in a little while."

"Sure thing," the guy said, and for the first time in eight hours, I was free.

"What are the raccoons for?" I asked as Jeremy and I headed across the trade show floor.

"I'm doing a hands-on skinning demonstration for kids on Friday. You would've been all over that when you were little, huh?"

"Totally. Remember when we used to race to see who could flesh out possums faster?" I asked.

"How could I possibly forget the shame of losing to a third grader?"

I laughed. Openly talking about taxidermy with someone I liked and respected was such a weird experience. All my friends at home thought my dad's job was gross, and I'd stopped inviting people to my house altogether after The Fateful Seventh-Grade Sleepover. Emma Perkowitz had walked into the spare bedroom, reached for the light switch, and accidentally grabbed the snout of the warthog head mounted on the wall. She had screamed like she'd touched a hot stove for a solid five minutes, and it only took another half hour for all the rest of the girls to fake sick and call their parents.

"So, you're your dad's proper assistant now, huh?" Jeremy asked. "That's really impressive, at your age. He must be proud."

I shrugged. "I don't think he even notices me most of the time. He hands me a task, I do it, I hand it back. He rarely even says thank you. It's not like it was before—" I suddenly remembered that Jeremy didn't know about Mom, and I broke off just in time. "Before . . . when you were around," I finished lamely.

"You should take the silence as a compliment. It probably means you don't need a lot of instruction. He barely left me alone for one second during my internship."

"Maybe. I guess." Most of the noise in the studio back then didn't come from my dad critiquing Jeremy's work; it came from the three of us shout-singing along to Bruce Springsteen. But he didn't seem to remember that, so I didn't remind him.

"Do you think you'll continue with it in college?" Jeremy asked. "Study zoology or anatomy or something? You must be pretty into it if you're putting in all that time."

Part of me wanted to tell Jeremy the truth—that since my mom left, the studio was the only place my dad seemed to see me at all; that I only kept working there because I didn't want to exist in a completely separate world from him. But that seemed pathetic.

"I don't think so," I said. "I actually want to work in radio. Like, at NPR, maybe." I suddenly felt shy. The last time I'd tried to run this idea by my dad, he'd brushed it off like it was just a phase or a hobby, not a real goal.

But Jeremy said, "Ooh, that would be awesome. You have a good voice for radio."

"I do? Thanks. I never thought about doing the actual broadcasting, but I think I could be good at the behind-the-scenes stuff. Like being a producer, maybe."

"Definitely. That would be cool, too. I bet you'd be good at either."

We walked by a booth that specialized in animal teeth, one that sold artificial throats and tongues, and one offering discounts on freeze-drying your deceased pets. Farther down were two booths staffed by middle-aged guys who looked like twins; one was selling odor remover, and the other was selling bottles of deer, coyote, and fox urine. Near the end of the row was the Bug to the Bone Skull Cleaning Service, where a sealed terrarium full of dermestid beetles were eating away at the remaining flesh of what looked like it had once been a ferret.

We finally arrived at Skin It Yourself!, where Jeremy bought three large frozen raccoons. "Can you hang on to one of these for me?" he asked the guy manning the booth. "I can't carry them all at once. I'll come back for the third one after my meeting."

"I can help you take them upstairs now," I said.

"Really?" Jeremy asked. "That would save me a ton of time. Your dad doesn't need your help with anything else?"

"I don't think he'll be done for a little while. He was still finishing up with the ibex when I left. I should have time to run upstairs and pick up the eyes at the Van Dyke booth before he gets here."

"Wow, that would be so great. Thanks, Cal."

We headed toward the trade show exit, stopping every once in a while so Jeremy could say hi to friends and colleagues. Even though I hadn't seen him in years, we'd known each other so long that being with him felt incredibly easy. Having him here reminded me of a time when my family was whole and happy, and I finally relaxed for the first time since I'd gotten here.

And then we passed the Van Dyke booth, and I almost ran smack into my dad.

"Hey, Hamish," Jeremy said. He raised one of his raccoon bags in the approximation of a wave.

"Hi," my dad said, and then he turned to me, his face stony. "Callie, where were you? And where you are going?"

"I was helping Jeremy," I said. "I'm just going to carry this raccoon up to his room, and then I'll be right back, okay? The Van Dyke rep is packing up your eyes—I gave him the list."

His eyebrows scrunched into that furrowed V-shape I had seen all too many times. "I asked *you* to pack them up for me."

"I'm sure he's doing a much better job than I would've. They should be ready in a minute."

My dad sighed like he was carrying the weight of the world. "That's not the point. The Van Dyke employee doesn't need the practice. You do. Why am I paying you to assist me if you're just going to wander off and socialize?"

His words hit me like a slap. Dad reprimanding me when I messed up was nothing new, but I hadn't even done anything *wrong* this time. Not to mention that he was embarrassing me in front of Jeremy and all the other Van Dyke customers. I felt my cheeks go pink.

"I'm not socializing," I said quietly. "I'm just helping a friend for a few minutes."

"I'm really sorry about this, Hamish," Jeremy said. "I didn't know you needed her."

"Don't be silly. This isn't your fault. I'm sure she told you she wasn't busy." Dad turned back to me. "Callie, I brought you here because it's a great opportunity for you to *learn*, but you're not going to get anything out of it if you don't take some initiative. This convention only comes around once every two years. I need you to do the work I ask of you, and when that work is done, you should be familiarizing yourself with new materials and techniques. That's what the trade show is here for."

"I've been in sessions with you since ten a.m.," I said. "I've been learning all day. And the turkeys looked good, right?"

"What?"

75

"The turkeys. I did a good job grooming them, didn't I?"

"Yes, they looked good. But doing something right doesn't give you license to slack off."

Jeremy took a step back; he looked intensely uncomfortable. "You know what, I'm going to take the raccoons myself. Thanks for offering to help, Callie, but I can handle it."

"But you can't carry all these at once, and you don't have time to make two trips before your meeting," I said.

Jeremy looked back and forth between my dad and me like he had no idea what to do, and Dad finally sighed. "Just go. But from now on, make sure I don't need you before you run off to help someone else, okay?"

"*Okay*," I said. "I'll be right back." I just wanted to get out of this room as quickly as possible. "Come on," I said to Jeremy.

We left the trade show and headed toward the bridge to the hotel in silence. "You really don't have to carry that all the way upstairs," he said when we got to the elevators. "I'll figure something out. I don't want to get you in trouble."

"It doesn't matter," I said. "I'm in trouble anyway. It kind of feels like I'm always in trouble."

"Yeah, but maybe—"

A little kid dressed in a tiny pleather catsuit came barreling out of nowhere, shrieking at the top of her lungs, and dashed right in front of Jeremy. He stopped short, and we both stared. A woman who must've been her mom chased after her, wielding a can of hairspray. "Beige, if you don't get back here this instant, there will be no dessert tonight!" she shouted.

I watched until they were out of sight around the corner, and then I said, "Um . . . what the holy hell was that?"

Jeremy blinked. "I think there's one of those baby beauty pageant things going on in D-wing."

Sure enough, there were a couple more little kids in the hotel lobby, all dressed in sparkles and lace. Every one of them had ringlets so perfect they didn't even look real. Then one kid reached up and scratched—*under* her hair.

"The toddlers are wearing wigs," I whispered to Jeremy.

"That kid was named *Beige*," he whispered back, and we both burst into horrified laughter.

By the time the elevator arrived, Jeremy and I were wiping tears from our eyes. Two teenage girls with badges for the fandom convention got in with us. One of them had a whole bunch of colored ribbons stuck to the bottom of her badge, one of which sported a tagline I recognized: *Someday, your worst memory could be your best story.*

"Hey," I said. "Do you listen to *A Thousand Words*?"

Her eyes lit up. "Yeah! Do you?"

"It's my favorite! I listened to it almost the entire twelve-hour drive here." I turned to Jeremy. "It's this really cool podcast. You should check it out."

"You're coming to the workshop tomorrow, right?" asked the girl.

"The what?"

"They're going to explain their whole process, all the behind-the-scenes stuff, and answer questions and everything! And they're going to broadcast the whole thing live on their website. Haven't you heard them talking about it on the last couple of episodes?"

She was right—the hosts of *A Thousand Words* had been talking about a live show at something called WTFcon for weeks. "Oh my god, I didn't realize that was here!" I said. "Maybe I could get away for a few hours? How hard do you think it would be to sneak in? I'm not registered for WTFcon."

"Aw, that sucks—they're actually been pretty strict about checking badges. Are you here for the drumming thing?"

"No, the taxidermy championships," I said.

"Eew," the girl said, and she and her friend both giggled.

It shouldn't have mattered to me—I was never going to see them again—but it still gave me seventh grade flashbacks. I dropped my eyes to the floor. When the elevator opened on fourteen and Jeremy said, "This is us, Callie," I gave the girls an awkward half wave and followed him out. I was relieved when the doors closed.

Jeremy unlocked room 1418 and let me go in ahead of him. My mom and I always used to unpack all our stuff when we stayed in hotels to make the space feel more like ours, but aside from a suit hanging in the closet, a pair of shoes on the floor, and a laptop and binder on the desk, his room looked untouched. Jeremy started loading the raccoons into the mini-fridge he'd brought, and I pulled open the curtains, revealing an air shaft and the side of an office building.

"Nice view," I said.

"Oh yeah. I've got some seriously classy accommodations."

"Well, you are *super* important. All those master turkey-stuffers are counting on you." I sat down on his bed, which was covered in the same ugly fleur-de-lis spread as mine.

Jeremy shut the fridge. "You should probably get back downstairs."

"Ugh, don't make me." I flopped backward onto the mattress. "Can you believe how crazy-controlling and uptight my dad was being? I was literally with him the entire day, and then I do a nice thing for someone else for ten minutes, and he completely flips out! It's not like I was sneaking away to buy drugs or something. I thought he brought me to this convention because he actually *wanted* me here, and he's been so rude to me the whole time. Did you know he *yelled* at me after we saw you at registration yesterday because I was 'mocking him in front of a judge'? As if you're going to take points off his turkeys because I made a dumb joke. You made a dumb joke, too! I'm sure he didn't think *you* were being unprofessional."

Jeremy smiled, but it looked a little pained. "I'm sorry."

"Do you think you could maybe say something to him? Tell him I'm actually working really hard and he should be nice to me? We used to have so much fun at these things, and this time . . . well, you saw."

Jeremy rubbed his hand over his close-cropped hair; I'd forgotten how he always used to do that when he was embarrassed or uncomfortable. "This is between you and your dad, Cal. I really can't get involved."

"But he actually listens to you. You're like family."

"That's kind of what he's saying, though, right? I can't be family right now because I'm judging his work. I have to stay impartial. It sucks that you guys are fighting, but I can't be in the middle of it."

I shouldn't really have expected him to stick up for me, but it still stung a little. "Fine," I said. "I get it. But can I just stay here for, like, ten more minutes while you prep for your meeting? I won't bug you, and I promise I'll go back downstairs when you have to leave. But I just need a little more time away from him."

Jeremy sighed. "Listen, I want to hang out, too. But now isn't a good time, and I'm not going to hide you. I really am sorry, but you've got to go deal with this, okay?"

There was this sinking feeling in my stomach, like a gaping pit was opening up and swallowing my organs one by one. I'd had such high hopes for this convention, and nothing was going right, and I wasn't even allowed to *complain* about how nothing was going right to the one person I thought was on my side. I was on my own, just like always.

"Yeah, okay," I said. "I understand."

"Come on," said Jeremy. "I'll walk you to the elevator."

The door shut behind us with a final-sounding slam, and as we walked down the hall side by side, all I could think of was the *A Thousand Words* ribbon on the WTFcon girl's badge.

Someday, your worst memory could be your best story.

Maybe that was true. But right now, everything just sucked.

CHAPTER SEVEN

VANESSA

When Soleil flashed her name tag at the *Wonderlandia* meetup, pretty much everyone recognized her. Most people were as chill about meeting her as Merry had been—except this one trio of girls. They basically pounced on Soleil and started bombarding her with praise, and then showed up at the next panel we went to *and* the one after that, and *now*, as we left the book-to-movie panel seven hours later, they were still following us.

I asked Soleil if she thought it was creepy. I mean, stalkers, right?

But she smiled beatifically and said, "Nah. They're just nervous. Working up the nerve to talk to us again, probably."

Us, I thought. *Us, us, us.*

As we approached the walkway that linked the convention center to the hotel, she added, "Bet you a dollar one of them asks us to hang out."

I thought about this. It'd been seven hours. The whole time, they'd been glancing at Soleil—and, by extension, me—every four seconds or so. Like they wanted to make sure we were still there. But none of them had said anything since the meetup this morning.

"You're on," I said.

But as soon as we shook on it, I heard the distinct sound of walking-footsteps becoming running-footsteps.

"Told you," muttered Soleil under her breath. "Get that dollar ready."

"We'll see," I said, just before a hand reached out and tapped Soleil on the shoulder.

"Oh, hey!" she said, turning around with this look on her face like she was totally surprised to see the three girls there. "What's up?"

"Um, well," said the girl who'd done the shoulder-tapping. Her hair was almost as blond as Soleil's, and her cheeks were bright red. She looked older than me, and maybe even older than Soleil. Her two also-probably-older-than-me friends hung back a few paces, watching us. "Well, so. Soleil and"—a quick glance at my badge—"Vanessa? We were wondering if maybe you wanted to, you know, maybe have a drink with us? Or maybe have dinner? Or whatever? Our treat, obviously, because . . . you know . . ."

Soleil smiled broadly, her eyes softening. "That's so sweet of you."

The blond girl—*Aimee, Rochester, NY*, said her badge—blushed even harder. "So you'll come?"

Soleil glanced quickly at me, but I didn't have time to weigh in before she said, "Well, Nessie and I are still figuring out our game plan for tonight, actually. And whatever we do, we have to head back to the room to freshen up first. So—"

"Wait," said one of the other girls, a brunette whose name tag said *Danielle, Buffalo, NY.* "Nessie? As in the Ness who wrote 'Carry Me Home' with Soleil? That's you?"

My face—no, my entire body—was on fire. But in a good way.

"That's me!" I managed to reply.

Danielle from Buffalo looked back and forth between Soleil and me, eyes shining like she was about to cry. "Oh man, I didn't know. I'm sorry, I should've— Okay, I know this is creepy, but I read everything you guys post on the boards. I ship you guys *so hard*."

"Awww!" said Soleil, and slung an arm around my shoulders. "Hear that, Nessie?"

I was going to explode from sheer joy.

"And 'Carry Me Home,' right?" Danielle continued. "Just, that story! *That story!* It was . . . gah! I have so many questions to ask you guys!"

"Like what?" Soleil asked eagerly, as Danielle's friends exchanged a knowing look behind her.

"I mean, there's the gender stuff, obviously," said Danielle. "Seven being gender-fluid was just so, so well done. But it was actually Five that really got to me. The part in the beginning, right? Where he goes to the Caterpillar's dance club with all those other Spades, but he ends up just drinking in a corner by himself the whole time because he feels so awkward because he doesn't know how to do the normal-social-person thing because he over-thinks everything all the time? That part."

"Aw, yeah, that's one of my favorite scenes," said Soleil.

This time, when I didn't reply, it wasn't because I was too happy to form words—it was because I'd written that scene. With the Five of Spades in the Caterpillar's club. And I'd basically based it on how I felt every day at school. Hanging off to the side, not really talking to anyone, not understanding how other people seemed to feel so comfortable around each other and, sure, maybe drinking in the corner of a dance club wasn't *exactly* the same as eating lunch in the school library—but it wasn't exactly *not* the same, either.

"Was all that social anxiety stuff from, you know, personal experience?" said Danielle, lowering her voice.

"Dani, come on, that's not something you can just ask," said the third girl. *Marziya, Buffalo, NY.*

"No, it's fine," said Soleil, giving Marziya a dazzling smile. "And yeah, it was."

I gave her a sidelong look because, yeah, it was definitely personal, but it was personal for *me*, not her. I took a deep breath, trying to work up the nerve to claim credit for that scene—but by the time I got there, Danielle was already talking again.

"I knew it!" she said. "Nobody writes stuff like that so well unless they've, you know, *been there*. Listen, you guys *have* to come for dinner with us, okay?"

"Maybe," said Soleil. "Like I said, we're not sure what the game plan is. But how about if you tell us *your* plans, and we'll come if we can?"

"We were going to that fancy-looking Mexican place in the lobby," said Aimee. "El Sol? Say seven o'clock?"

"El Sol," repeated Soleil, smiling widely. "You know that means *sun* in Spanish?"

"Oh, ha, like your name," said Danielle.

I snort-laughed; Soleil didn't seem to notice.

"Yup," she replied. "So, okay, El Sol, seven o'clock. We gotta run, but hopefully see you there!"

"Hope so!" said Danielle.

Soleil looped her arm through mine and steered me rapidly onto the walkway. "One dollar, Nessie. I win."

"You don't win." Hey, look, apparently I was capable of speaking again, now that it was just me and Soleil. "The bet specifically said they'd ask us to hang out. At no point did any of them use that exact phrase."

"Oh, stop being nitpicky," said Soleil. "I totally won that bet."

I rolled my eyes and dug a pair of quarters out of my bag. "You half won. So here's half a dollar."

She pocketed the quarters. "Close enough."

Only when we were safely inside our hotel room, with the door firmly shut, did I say, "We're not really meeting up with them, right?"

Soleil, who'd been beelining for the mirror, stopped dead in her tracks. "You mean you don't want to?"

"You mean you *do* want to?"

"Hello, free dinner," she said. "And I don't know about you, but I'm not exactly rolling in cash."

Neither was I. Sure, I had my mom's credit card, but I would have to pay her back for anything over a hundred and fifty dollars. That wasn't the point, though.

"I just thought we were going to the pool tonight," I said.

"We can go after."

"It closes at nine."

She shrugged, grabbed an eyeliner pencil, and started applying it to her left lid. "Then we can go another night. Do you want some of my mascara?"

"No, thanks," I said. "But wait: The pool tops cheering for Merry's costume, but letting your fans buy you dinner tops the pool?"

"Merry?" she said absently. "Oh! Oh. The Boggart Snape person. Right. Well, obviously, yeah. Here, you should try some of this blue liner. It'd look so great on you."

I sat on the bed, wondering if she'd notice my complete disinterest in her makeup tips. "Well, I still think the pool's the way to go. It'd give us time to hang out, just us, you know?"

"Mmm," said Soleil. "True."

She didn't seem too convinced, though, which meant clearly it was time to pull out the big guns. "Also . . . it would give us time to start thinking about our Creativity Corner project."

The Creativity Corner was the super dumb name of the fan-works competition that would happen on the last night of the convention, three days from now. Anyone could enter, and the entry could be anything at all—a play, a reading, a drawing, whatever—as long as (a) it was original and (b) it contained a tribute to something made by someone else.

Soleil and I had entered under my name, because hey, if there was one thing we both knew, it was that we worked super well together.

Her eyes widened in the mirror at the reminder, and she spun around to face me. "Ooh. Yeah. I've been meaning to tell you, I had an idea for that!"

Well, this was promising. "What's the idea?"

"A dance piece," she said.

"A . . . what?"

"A dance piece! Like a parody one! We dress up as characters that everyone knows, preferably characters that everyone *ships*, and we do a totally overwrought dance of, like, epic unrequited longing. You get me?"

"That's kind of genius," I said. "So, like, Five and Seven doing a pas-de-deux?"

"Exactly!" she said, clapping her hands together. "Except not Five and Seven. *Wonderlandia*'s fandom isn't that big, so people might not recognize them. You don't want to do something for a fandom that even the *judges* might not know, right?"

"Right. So we have to think bigger," I said. "Like Frodo and Sam or something."

"Exactly!" said Soleil again. "Or Finn and Poe from *Star Wars*. Or Dean and Castiel from *Supernatural*."

"Or the Doctor and Rose from *Doctor Who*."

"Or the Doctor and the *Master* from *Doctor Who*."

"Which version of the Master? Dude or lady?"

"Like it matters," she said. "Either way, the audience will eat it up."

"So let's get choreographing!" I said. "After we swim, I mean."

"Oh, come on, not tonight," said Soleil. "I already said I wanted to meet up with those girls."

All the energy drained right out of me. "Really?"

"Like I said: free dinner. Plus, that one girl with the black hair— Crap, what was her name?"

"Danielle."

"Right! Danielle. She wanted to talk about *our story*!"

"My club chapter in our story," I added quietly.

"Yeah, exactly! Don't you wanna hear what she has to say about it?" Then she paused. Looked over at me. "Oh, shoot, Nessie. Are you mad that I didn't say it was yours?"

I looked down at my feet, clicking the toes of my red shoes together. "Well, not *mad*. I just. I would've said something myself, but—but you guys were talking so fast. I dunno. I've never actually talked, like face-to-face, with someone who's read my stuff."

Well, except Merry, this morning before the panel. But talking to Merry had been different, somehow. Easier.

"So you can say something when we're at dinner." She reached out to give my shoulder a squeeze. "How often is it that you get to hang out with fans? Besides, it's Mexican food!"

"So?"

"So . . . well, you're Mexican, right?"

I cringed, because oh my god, what in the world was up with her? She was never this thoughtless online. "Uh, half Mexican. Also half Irish. So."

"So we'll see if they have corned beef and cabbage. Whatever."

"Hey, come on. Don't be . . ." I hesitated because, well, this was *Soleil*. The fandom queen of calling people out on stuff exactly like this. "Don't be stereotype-y," I said, and slightly hated myself for it. I was the worst social justice warrior ever.

"Oh. Sorry." Before I could figure out if she was *actually* sorry, though, Soleil went back to her makeup. "But you should still come. It'll be fun."

The problem was, she was right. It *would* be fun. They'd buy us food and shower us with compliments, and we'd talk about "Carry Me Home" and eat enough guacamole that we'd maybe die of avocado poisoning, and it would be surreal and wonderful and everything I'd come to WTFcon to do.

But it would also be a whole lot of attention, and what if it ended up being just like before? When Soleil and Danielle had done all the talking before I could even think of what to say? I didn't want that again. Right now, all I wanted was some alone time with Soleil. I wanted space to be all flirty with her like I was online, and I wanted her to be thoughtful and kind, the way *she* was online, and more than anything I wanted her to *kiss me already*.

"Nessie?" said Soleil, who'd started on her lipstick while I'd been sitting here, considering what to say.

"You go." My voice came out kind of wobbly. "I'm gonna go to the costume contest."

Soleil's eyebrows shot up—but she wasn't nearly as surprised as I was. What I'd meant to say was, *I'll stay here and order room service and go swimming by myself.* But now that I'd said the other thing, I found that it was a pretty appealing idea. Maybe I didn't want to watch Soleil soak up even more attention from her fans, even if some of that attention was technically aimed at me—but I also didn't want to be the pathetic loser who waited alone in a hotel room for her girlfriend to come back. If she was going to do something cool, then so would I.

"Is this because I said the thing about Mexican food?" she said. "Listen, that was dumb of me. Like, Microaggressions 101 level dumb. But I already said I was sorry, okay?"

"It's not that," I said, even though maybe, yeah, it was a little bit that. But what I said out loud was, "Merry asked me to come."

"Oh, right, *Merry*," said Soleil, rolling her eyes.

I frowned. "What's wrong with Merry?"

"Nothing at all." Soleil shrugged and turned back to the mirror again, poking at her already-perfect eyebrows with an index finger. "Do what you want, and we'll catch up later. I was just hoping we could spend some quality time together, that's all."

I was hoping the same thing, I thought—but obviously didn't say it out loud. Murmuring a quiet goodbye, I patted my pocket to make sure my hotel key card was still there, then headed for the elevator.

Only once I'd reached the lobby downstairs did I realize something very important: I'd left my bag in the hotel room.

I swore under my breath, which made this nearby woman shoot me a look. The kind of look that made me want to swear again, louder, just to see how angry I could make her. Except she had a little kid with her, and my family, while not anti-swearing in general, was absolutely anti-swearing-around-small-children.

Besides, the sight of this particular small child stole any lingering swears right out of my mouth.

She couldn't have been older than five or six, and she was dressed in what could only be described as . . . well, a disco ball. Except dress-shaped instead of round. There was a matching silver barrette in her blond hair, and gobs of silver eye shadow that shone gaudily against her pale skin. And she was wearing heels. Tiny, silver, little-girl *heels*.

When she saw me staring at her, she gave me a pink-lipsticked smile that looked a hundred percent practiced.

The woman, seeing this, took the little girl's hand. "That's a stranger, Delancey, honey. Remember what Mommy said about strangers?"

"Ignore them!" said the disco ball, in a voice like lollipops and sunshine and newborn puppies.

"That's right," said her mom, shooting me another look. "Save your pretty smile for the judges."

I fled.

Despite the thick crowd in the lobby, nobody joined me in the elevator, which meant it was an express ride back up to the fifteenth floor. The doors slid open and I started marching back toward 1502 . . . but slowed down as I got closer to the room.

I hadn't been gone that long. Soleil was probably still in there, fixing flaws in her makeup that only she could see. And did I really want to see her again so soon? While I was still kind of annoyed at her, and probably vice versa?

I thought about heading back toward the elevators, but there were faint voices coming from that direction now. Girl voices. Soleil hadn't given our room number to the Fangirl Trio, had she? I couldn't remember. And encountering them again, right after she'd chosen them over me, was the very last thing I wanted to do.

For a second, I felt this primal urge to *escape*. To go into my room, lock the door, and wait for Soleil to meet me online so we could talk, the way I did almost every day after school, except I obviously couldn't do that now, and what in the world did people *do* when even the internet wasn't an escape option?

Right between 1506 and 1508, there was a little doorless room with a vending machine and a thingie for ice. It wasn't much, as far as hiding places went, but it was something. So I slipped inside.

And promptly sank to the floor, because what was I even doing?

Seriously, after all the effort I'd put into begging my parents for registration money and time off from school? All that time poring over the WTFcon schedule and making plans with Soleil? All that stuff for all those months, and this was where I'd ended up: sitting on a cold, tiled floor in front of a vending machine.

On top of that, I'd given all my change to Soleil, so I didn't even have money for Doritos, which were literally the only food in the universe that never failed to make me feel better.

"Oh," said a voice from somewhere above me. I looked up, totally prepared to ask Soleil, very politely, to leave me alone—but it wasn't Soleil.

Hovering in the doorway, looking at me with no small amount of surprise, was a girl I didn't know. Pale skin. Wavy reddish hair. Tall. Her gaze flicked from me to the vending machine, then back to me again, which made me realize that I was basically blocking her path. Politeness warred with the desire to stay exactly where I was. And instantly lost.

"You can step over me," I said. "I don't mind."

"Oh," she said again. "Cool, okay."

But once she'd stepped over my knees and given the machine a quick once over, she looked down at me again. "Are you all right?" She said it kind of like she felt she *should* say it, not like she really wanted to know.

"I'll probably live." Wow, what a stupidly melodramatic thing to say. "Sorry. Yeah, I'm fine. Don't mind me."

"You don't look like you're fine," said the girl.

Ugh, this sucked, this *suuucked*. I was so pathetic that strangers stopped to take pity on me. "Totally fine. A hundred percent fine."

A pause. "Then why are you on the floor?"

The answer slipped out before I could actually decide whether I wanted to give it: "Because I'm waiting for my girlfr—uh, my roommate to leave, so I don't have to see her when I go back to get my bag, which I forgot in our room, and which contains my wallet, which I need in order to get dinner."

And then my stomach growled, like it wanted to prove a point. It growled so loudly that the redheaded girl actually laughed. It was kind of rude, but it also made her look a lot friendlier.

"Sorry," she said immediately. "I didn't mean . . ."

"It's fine," I said.

"God," she said, slumping against the vending machine. "I swear, Mercury's gotta be in retrograde or something. Your life sucks, my life sucks, everything sucks. I bet even if I hide in my bed for the rest of the night, that'll end up sucking somehow."

I straightened up again. "Your life sucks, too? How come?"

"No reason. It's nothing. Never mind." Her face closed off, and she shook her head sharply and shoved her hand into her pocket. "Sorry. You look like you have enough problems. You shouldn't have to deal with my craptastic life."

As she pulled a bunch of loose change from her pocket and started slotting coins into the machine, it occurred to me that I actually kind of *wanted* her to tell me about her craptastic life. But only kind of. Because this wasn't some FicForAll forum, where I could just be like, "Rant away!" and she could be like, "Here are all my problems!" and I could be like, "Sending hugs and virtual cookies!" and we could go back to talking about Five and Seven and their epic romance.

It didn't work that way in real life. Or maybe it did. But that was just the thing: I had *no idea* how it worked in real life. It wasn't like I was drowning in friends, and I was the baby of my family, so I didn't really have much experience comforting people face-to-face.

So I kept quiet and watched her as she punched in the numbers for the snack she'd selected.

The machine whirred, and a bag of Doritos fell from its row.

Doritos.

Suddenly, I was sure that I was about to cry.

It must've shown on my face, because when the redhead turned back to me, she suddenly looked all concerned. "Seriously, you're not okay, are you? Hey, you want me to get you some of these, too?" She held up the chips.

"Oh god, no," I said. "I don't need Pity Doritos. I'm really okay. Thanks, though."

She considered me for a moment, then she settled down on the floor beside me. "Have some of mine," she said, ripping open the bag. "That way they're Friend Doritos, not Pity Doritos, *and* I don't have to go back downstairs yet."

She shoved the bag at me, and I really wanted to refuse, because of politeness or something—but the smell of all that fake cheese was too much to resist.

I took a chip and ate it. So did she. For a moment, we both crunched in reverent silence.

"Thanks," I said.

"I'm Callie," she said, holding the bag out to me again.

"Good to meet you," I said, taking another chip. "I'm Vanessa. Call me . . . actually, no, just call me Vanessa."

CHAPTER EIGHT

CALLIE

After getting snapped at on the trade show floor and totally dismissed by Jeremy, all I really wanted to do was take my fake cheese products back to my room, listen to old episodes of *A Thousand Words* under the covers, and pretend my dad wasn't waiting for me downstairs. Talking to total strangers in the hallway definitely wasn't on my agenda. But for some reason, looking at Vanessa's downcast expression was actually kind of helping. It was nice to have proof that I wasn't the only miserable person in this hotel.

Besides those beauty pageant girls, obviously. Those kids were going to need so much therapy when they grew up.

I wanted to hear more about Vanessa's roommate drama, but I felt weird asking outright, so I started with, "Which con are you here for?"

She flipped her badge around and held it up. It was a WTFcon one with a bunch of ribbons stuck to the bottom, like the girl in the elevator: a couple of Harry Potter ones, one covered in spades and hearts and the words *We're All Mad Here*, and a bright green one that said, *All Hail the Glow Cloud*. She didn't have one for *A Thousand Words*.

"Cool," I said. "You're a Hufflepuff?"

"Yeah!" Her face lit up. "Are you? Were you at the meetup earlier? I didn't get to go."

"I'm not here for WTFcon. But I think I'd be a Ravenclaw."

"Oh," Vanessa said. "That's cool. My older sister's a Ravenclaw. Well, *she* says she's a Ravenclaw, but I'm pretty sure she's actually a Slytherin. Anyway. Which con are you doing?"

Annnd I'd totally set myself up for that one. If I told her the truth, she'd probably react like the last girl, and I'd ruin any chance I had of making a friend. Then again, making a friend here seemed pretty unlikely regardless, so what did it really matter? Even the people who were supposed to care about me weren't on my side these days.

"I'm here for the taxidermy championships," I said, and then I waited for Vanessa to laugh or scoot away like I had a contagious disease.

She didn't do either. She just stared at me, eyes huge behind her green tortoiseshell glasses. "Wait, seriously?"

"Yeah? I'm not, like, obsessed with it or anything, but my dad pays me to be his assistant."

She shifted a little, obviously uncomfortable. "Isn't that . . . I mean, I'm not saying anything about *you* as a person, but . . . isn't it kind of cruel? Killing all those animals?"

"Most of them die of natural causes, actually," I said. I

constantly had to explain this to people who thought taxidermists were animal-murdering psychos. "He does a little bit of work for hunters who eat the meat—deer and turkeys and stuff—but mostly he works for natural history museums. Like, a snow leopard will die in a zoo, and he'll mount it for a display so people can learn about how awesome snow leopards are and why we need to protect them. He's done work for the Smithsonian and the American Museum of Natural History in New York and stuff."

"Oh," Vanessa said, visibly relaxing. "That's way better. But . . . do you have to, like, touch organs and stuff?"

"Yeah, sometimes."

She shuddered. "I could never do that. I'd probably faint. I mean, *organs*. I can barely stay upright when I get paper cuts, you know? I'd be the worst vampire ever. Um, what I mean is . . . that's pretty badass."

I shrugged like it was no big deal, but I *was* feeling a little bit badass all of a sudden. That definitely wasn't a feeling I'd had since I'd gotten here. "You get used to it," I said.

My phone buzzed, and I dug it out to find a text from my dad. Almost here? Jeremy said he sent you back down five min ago. I stuffed it back in my bag without answering, the badass feelings evaporating in an instant.

"So, what happens at a taxidermy convention, exactly?" Vanessa asked. "Are there people cutting up dead animals everywhere?" She looked nervous, like she was worried she might stumble upon a zebra bleeding out in the hallway.

"Not really. There are demonstrations and seminars and a trade show and stuff, but the main thing is the competition. Everyone puts their best work in this huge ballroom, and a bunch of judges score it. It's pretty amazing, actually. It's like an entire museum all crammed into one room."

"Huh. That actually sounds cool." A little crease appeared between her eyebrows. "Wait, a taxidermy trade show? What do they sell?"

"You don't even want to know."

She laughed and took another chip. "Yeah, I probably don't."

"So, what do you do at a Harry Potter convention? Where's your costume?"

"We don't all wear costumes," she said. "And it's not only Harry Potter—it's a multi-fandom thing. I'm mostly here for the fic stuff. Harry Potter, definitely, but also *Wonderlandia* and *Yuri On Ice* and *Sherlock*, at least before it sucked, and that old show *Slings and Arrows* and, ooh, recently I started writing Alanna fic. You know, those Tamora Pierce books? And—"

"Wait," I said. "Did you just say you write . . . 'fic'?"

Vanessa suddenly looked nervous again, and she pulled her curly ponytail over her shoulder and started twisting the end around her finger. "Yeah? A lot of people think it's all sex stuff, but it's really not, I swear. Mine is mostly—"

"No no no," I said. "I don't . . . what's fic?"

She stared at me. "Fanfic? Fanfiction?"

"I have no idea what that is."

"*Oh.*" Her whole body relaxed, and she wiggled her feet a little, the sides of her bright red flats bumping together. "It's when you take someone else's characters and write new stories about them. I wrote this one Harry Potter fic where Luna steals a thestral and takes Neville hunting for magical creatures all over Scotland. Stuff like that."

"People do that?"

She laughed. "Yeah. Tons of people. It's kinda my entire life."

"I mean, it sounds cool. I would totally read that Luna and Neville thing. Do you write stuff with your own characters, too?"

Vanessa shrugged and looked down. "Sort of. I mean, I've started writing about nine different novels over the past year, but . . . I dunno. I always get bored after a chapter or two. Plus there's nobody reading it, you know? With fanfic, I post my stuff chapter by chapter, and people are all like, 'Hey, gimme more!' in the comments, so it keeps me moving."

"Instant gratification," I said, and Vanessa nodded. "So you have fans online?"

"Oh yeah," she said. "Especially since I started co-writing with my roommate. She's basically a fanfic celebrity. *Everyone* reads her stuff."

"The same . . . um . . . *roommate* you're hiding from?" I was pretty sure she had started to say *girlfriend* before, but I wasn't positive.

"Yeah."

"How come you're avoiding her?" The chips were gone now, and I tipped the remaining crumbs into my mouth and crumpled the bag into a ball.

"I'm not avoiding her, really. It's . . . complicated." Vanessa sighed. "Okay, so here's the thing. She's not just my roommate. She's kind of . . . she's my girlfriend. Except we only met in real life for the first time yesterday. And things have been so crazy since we got here that we haven't really gotten to hang out at all, just the two of us. So we were going to go to the pool tonight and start planning our project for the end of the con and, you know, have some alone time. But then these random people started fangirling all over her, and they invited us to dinner, and she went, and I . . . didn't."

I blinked at her. "You're dating, but you only met each other for the first time *yesterday*? Is that even a thing?"

A defensive look came over her face. "Of course it's a thing. We've been together for four months."

"And you've seriously *never* seen her in person before?"

"She lives in New York. I live here. We have school, and plane tickets are expensive. It's not like we can just take off and visit each other all the time." She looked down at her shoes again. "Plus, it's romantic."

"Okay, but . . . your girlfriend, who met you for the first time *yesterday* and only has a few days to spend with you, ditched you to hang out with total strangers?"

Vanessa squirmed. "No, it's not like that. She didn't *ditch* me; she wanted me to come, too. I just didn't feel like it. So technically, I guess it was me who ditched her? But the point is, those other girls were gonna buy her dinner and spend all night flailing about her writing, and how can you turn that down?"

"No offense, but I'd be *pissed* if someone did that to me. If you didn't want to go, she should've stayed with you."

"I don't really blame her," Vanessa said, like she was trying to convince herself. "She's just not used to everyone paying this much attention to her in real life. So she's basking in it because it's new and exciting, you know? I'd probably do the same thing if people started treating me like I was J. K. Rowling."

"No," I said. "I've known you, like, five minutes, and I'm pretty sure you wouldn't."

"I dunno. Maybe not." She toyed with her rubber Hufflepuff bracelet, printed with two badgers and the words *JUST AND LOYAL*.

We were both quiet for a minute, and then I said, "Okay, I know it's not really my business, but . . . you're sure you guys are *actually* dating, right? Not just internet-dating?"

Vanessa looked up at me again. "It's the same thing. Dating is dating."

"Well, it's not *really* the same. And leaving you alone in a hotel doesn't really sound like something a girlfriend would do. Has she acted more normal the rest of the time you've been here? Like, holding your hand and kissing you and introducing you to people as her girlfriend?"

"Not yet," Vanessa said. "But like I said, we've been in crowds basically every second since we got here. And she's pretty private about her relationship stuff. She's not going to start making out with me in front of a million people, you know? Hence the need for alone time."

"Doesn't sharing a hotel room count?" I asked. "Or are you sharing with other people, too?"

"No, it's just us," Vanessa said, going a little pink. "But I think she hasn't been in the mood to start anything yet."

"So why don't *you* start something? What do you have to lose?"

Vanessa shook her head. "No. No way. That's not . . . I'm not . . . I don't *do* that. It'd be too—I dunno. But if either of us is gonna do anything, it'll be Soleil."

This was getting weirder by the second. "Her name is *Soleil*?"

"Yeah."

"Like *Cirque du Soleil*?"

"No, it's French for 'sun.' It's pretty." Vanessa cleared her throat and straightened up. "Hey, I told you why my day sucks. How about it's your turn now?"

"We need more chips if I'm going to think about that," I said. I dug around in the bottom of my purse until I found a few loose coins and got up to put them in the machine.

"I'm really going to owe you," Vanessa said as I sat back down and pulled the bag open.

"Who says I'm sharing this time?" She reached over and took a chip without asking, then smiled at me with bright orange teeth. I smiled back. "Sorry," I said. "I didn't mean to pry into your business or anything."

"It's okay. But seriously, what happened to you? I mean, you don't have to talk about it if you don't want to, obviously. But if you do, I can listen."

As if on cue, my phone buzzed with another text from my dad. Where are you???

I thunked my head against the vending machine, and it made such a satisfying sound that I did it again. "My dad is being a total dictator, and when I asked for help from this guy Jeremy, who's literally my only friend here, he totally blew me off."

Vanessa took another chip. "That sucks. What's he being a dictator about?"

"Long story short, I offered to help Jeremy with something really quick when I was supposed to be doing something else for my dad, so he got mad and yelled at me right in front of Jeremy and all these random strangers, which was awesome for my self-esteem, let me tell you. And then instead of just sucking it up, I asked Jeremy to talk to my dad for me because he never listens to anything I say. And Jeremy was basically like, 'No, dude, I'm not getting involved in your family crap, deal with it yourself. Oh, look at the time, gotta go hang out with some dead ducks, see you never.'"

"Oof," Vanessa said. "I'm sorry."

"Thanks." I scrubbed at my eyes with the heels of my hands. "Ugh, my dad's still waiting for me downstairs at the trade show, and I just *cannot* with him right now. I'm sick of getting snapped at when I didn't even do anything wrong. I wish I could just go home. Or hide out at your con. The hosts of *A Thousand Words* are doing this live show tomorrow morning, and it's my favorite podcast of all time, but I'm going to be stuck in a seminar about stuffing weasels instead of learning about the thing I actually want to *do* with my life."

"You want to make podcasts?" Vanessa asked. "That's so cool."

"Something in radio, yeah. I know it's dorky."

"It's not dorky. I love podcasts. *Night Vale* and *Thrilling Adventure Hour* and *The Heart*, especially. What's *A Thousand Words*? I've never heard of that one."

"It's basically a storytelling podcast. There are these two hosts, Anica and Rafael, and every week they pick a question—something really vague, like, 'What are you worried about right now?' or 'What's the last thing that made you laugh?'—and then they go around and collect stories from strangers. And when they chop them up and edit them together, they end up making a totally *different* story, and it's just . . . really cool."

"Nice. I'll check it out." Vanessa took the last chip and crunched it slowly. "What if you ditched your dad tomorrow and went to the podcast thing instead?"

"That would be awesome, but I really shouldn't. He's pissed enough at me already. And isn't your con really strict about checking badges?"

"Yeah, but . . ." Vanessa reached up and pulled her badge over her head. The yellow lanyard got caught in her ponytail, and the buttons she'd pinned to it—*We Need Diverse Books* and *Ovaries Before Brovaries* and *#yayhamlet*—clanked together as she struggled to untangle herself. When she finally managed to pull it free, she held it out to me. "You can borrow this, if you want."

I blinked at her. "Seriously?"

"Yeah. There's some stuff I want to go to in the afternoon, but you can have it for the morning. I kind of want an excuse to lie low tomorrow anyway."

The workshop was only an hour and a half. My dad would be in sessions all morning; it wasn't like he'd need me for anything. I could just say I was going to a class in a different room, and as long as I met up with him afterward and spouted some taxidermy facts, he'd never know the difference. The family bonding I was hoping for clearly wasn't going to happen, and neither was the fun hangout time with Jeremy. Maybe I deserved to do this one thing for myself to make coming all the way to Orlando worth it.

"You would give me your badge?" I asked Vanessa. "Fifteen minutes ago, you didn't even know me."

She shrugged. "I know you now."

And the thing was? I kind of felt like she did.

CHAPTER NINE

PHOEBE

We didn't even rank in the competition. There were a total of thirty-four schools, and they only announced the top ten percussion ensembles at the awards ceremony. By the time the announcer got to sixth place, everyone from Ridgewood knew we didn't have a shot.

In a completely non-shocking turn of events, Bishop won.

Mr. Mackey got the full results after the ceremony. "Twelfth," he told us, in what was probably supposed to be an encouraging tone. "Still in the top third. Not bad, all things considered."

I flinched when he looked at me, even though I knew he meant it in a positive way. After all, if I hadn't used the scalpels, the xylophone feature would've been missing entirely, and we would've ranked way lower than twelfth.

Still. Watching all the Bishop kids scream and hug when they won wasn't exactly the best feeling.

I was trying to get myself into at least a semi-decent mood for that night. Devon had brought his Xbox, and Mr. Mackey had given us permission to order pizza and hang out in Devon and

Nick's room until the curfew at eleven. (And we all knew if we could convince Mackey to sit in on "one more game" when he came to break up the party, we could easily push curfew till at least midnight. The guy was a Halo fanatic.)

But when we walked out of the last clinic of the evening—a killer tabla session with this guy from Mumbai—the snare solo results had been posted.

We joined dozens of kids from other schools crowded around the list. A few seconds later, everyone was high-fiving Jorge and clapping him on the back. He'd won, of course. Scott had gotten fourth. Devon was sixth.

I was eighth.

Two rankings lower than last year. Only one above Nick, who was a freshman. And four below Scott.

I congratulated Jorge and hung back a little from the group. After a minute, Brian and Christina joined me.

"Still really good, out of twenty-one," Brian said. I gave him a withering look, and he laughed a little. We both knew it was crap. Christina's sympathetic smile vanished, and she glared at someone behind me.

I glanced over my shoulder as Scott walked up, and automatically shoved my hands in my pockets. "Nice job," I told him.

"You too."

I snorted. "Yeah, not really."

He gave me a smile that was part teasing, part pity. "Hey, eighth's pretty badass for someone with shredded hands."

I tried to smile back, but I could do without the placating. In fact, I kind of wanted him to be an aardvark about it so my anger would still be justified.

Which was stupid. There wasn't any point in being angry, really. Scott had been thoughtless, swiping the timpani mallets. But it wasn't like he put the scalpels in my hands. I wasn't sure what I was so pissed about anymore, to be honest. All I knew was I didn't want to hang out with anyone right now.

"I'm gonna call my mom before the pizza gets here," I told Brian. "Save me a few slices if I'm late, all right?"

"Yeah, all right." Brian studied me. "You sure you're okay?"

Scott rolled his eyes. "No, she's devastated. You know what a crier Phoebe is."

Brian and I laughed, while Christina shook her head. No one ever saw me cry. Not when I dislocated my kneecap during band camp freshman year, not when I tripped during a halftime show and my drum went rolling across the field in front of the whole stadium, not when my little brother Neil's evil hamster bit a chunk out of my arm. I *never* cried in front of anyone. Especially not in front of the guys.

I pulled out my phone and waved as Brian-and-Christina headed over to the hotel, but Scott hung back.

"You'll definitely come up later, right?" he asked, nudging my elbow.

"Yeah . . . ?" I looked at him questioningly, because he had this weird little smile on his face. "What?"

"Nothing!" His mouth shifted back to its regular smirk. "Just want to make sure you aren't using those cuts as an excuse to stop me kicking your butt at Halo."

"You wish." I faked a grin back at him before turning and heading to the exit, phone to my ear.

But I didn't call my mom. I'd definitely have to sometime tonight; my parents would have lots of questions about how both competitions went. I just didn't feel like pretending to be okay with it at the moment. Once I saw Scott step into the elevator, I did a 180, opened the recording app on my phone, and started wandering the conference center, getting audio of anything and everything.

No sexed-up toddlers in sight, to my relief. I found two girls sitting cross-legged outside of the closed IPAC exhibition hall and recorded one playing a cool little thumb piano called an mbira. I walked around C-wing and captured about a minute of a burly, leather-jacketed dude talking about how to remove the scent glands from a dead skunk. Then I decided to check out the fan con in A-wing.

I was looking down at my phone as I walked, labeling my audio clips, when someone up ahead yelled: "Todd, hurry up!"

A guy wearing a gaudy Christmas sweater and what was obviously a fake mustache burst out of one of the bigger ballrooms, some sort of trophy hanging at his side. I could hear the excited chatter of a huge crowd coming from inside. A second later, a tall, thin guy strutted out, looking quite pleased with himself. He seemed familiar, but it took me a few seconds to place him. His longish dark hair was gelled and curled, and he was wearing a suit. A very, very tight suit. I gawked shamelessly.

Undies-Snape cleaned up *good*.

Judging from the look on his face, the shorter guy with the trophy clearly agreed. I wondered if he was the cotton-ball-twinkly-lights person from last night. No tackling now, though—he took Todd's hand, and they set off together down the hall, fingers interlaced. I watched them go, because . . . well, like I said. That suit was *seriously* tight.

The ballroom doors flew open again, and more costumed people poured out. I pressed myself against the wall, flipping my recorder app on. I already knew what I'd be labeling this audio clip. *Awesome Geek Parade.*

I recognized some of the costumes, like the woman in the flowery dress and sweater-vest pushing the food trolley from the Hogwarts Express, and the guy walking around with a giant Azkaban *HAVE YOU SEEN THIS WIZARD?* poster framing his face. But there were a bunch of costumes I didn't get at all. Like the dozen or so girls all carrying flashing silver pen-thingies, but wearing different, distinct outfits: one had a long, rainbow-striped scarf, one had a trench coat, and one looked like a magician with a cape. Another had a bow tie, and she winked at me as she straightened it.

I got some pretty hilarious audio clips, too. "I got shafted!" ranted one guy, pushing off the hood of his black cape. "I'm a freaking Ringwraith, how could they not see it?" Then there was the bearded dude in battle armor, wielding both a sword and a trophy and arguing with his friend: "But I'm *not* Ned Stark, I'm Boromir!"

As the last of the crazy fan parade filed through the doors, my eyes fell on one costume in particular. Conservative green coat and skirt, fur stole, giant red purse. Oily black hair, stuffed bird perched on her hat.

"Boggart Snape!" I exclaimed. "Oh my god, best costume *ever.*"

Boggart Snape was deep in conversation with Professors Trelawney and McGonagall, but she glanced up at the sound of my voice. Then she smiled and waved.

"Hey, thanks!" she called.

McGonagall nudged her. "See? Told you! The judges are morons."

"Eh, I guess," Boggart Snape said with a shrug as they continued down the hall. "I still think it's this dumb bluebird, you know?"

"Yeah, but where're you gonna find an actual vulture?" I heard Trelawney say right before they rounded the corner.

Snickering, I trailed behind them all the way back to the elevators in the hotel lobby. Bluebird aside, that costume was seriously cool. I thought about taking a picture of her to show Christina but figured that'd be a pretty creepy thing to do. Although maybe if I asked her . . .

But just as I opened my mouth to call after them, the elevator doors slid open and Scott stepped out.

"Hey!" I said. "What are you doing down here?"

"Looking for you," he said. "I've got something for your hands."

"Ah." Well, there went my alone time. "What about Halo?"

He shrugged, following me back onto the elevator. "No fun without you."

My neck suddenly felt warm, which was annoying. Scott could get flirty every once in a while, but it didn't mean anything. My brain knew that by now, but the rest of me sometimes responded to it against my will. "Is Mackey playing yet?"

"Not yet," Scott said, punching the button for the sixth floor. "We'll sucker him into it when he tries to pull curfew."

I smiled. "Yeah."

The elevator was empty, but our shoulders kept bumping together the whole way up. As soon as we stepped into the hall, I could hear the sounds of Halo 5 coming from Devon and Nick's room. But Scott led me into the room next to it. I pointed questioningly at the *Do Not Disturb* sign, and he shrugged.

"Brian put it there this morning. He got all paranoid about that missing bag and spread the other mallets out to count them, and he didn't want housekeeping moving anything."

"Ah." I closed the door behind me and wrinkled my nose. "Whoa. Smells like coffee. Coffee and . . . something else." Something sickly sweet.

"Oh yeah, Jorge made some last night." Scott pointed to the pot on the little shelf next to one of the beds, which was filled to the top with alarmingly black liquid. "He used the bag from Devon's room, too, so it'd be extra-caffeinated. Oh, and Mountain Dew instead of water."

"Why?"

"We were going to stay up all night, but we fell asleep before it finished brewing."

I rolled my eyes. Morons.

Scott started rummaging through his backpack while I surveyed the room. Poor Brian. He was the neat and organized type, while Scott and Jorge were . . . not. Brian's suitcase was zipped up and tucked away in the corner, while the contents of Scott's and Jorge's suitcases appeared to have been the victims of a minor in-room tornado. Shirts, jeans, and boxers were strewn all over one of the beds, the night table and the chair in the corner. A lone black sock dangled from the lamp. Crumpled receipts and gum wrappers littered the carpet, no doubt pulled from pockets and mindlessly released as if the floor was some sort of trash-eating void. (I'd witnessed them do this many times.)

The other bed, the one closest to me, was covered in sticks, mallets, and triangle beaters, all neatly organized by type and size. Behind me, a wad of hand towels sat on top of the wardrobe that held the TV. They seemed to be wrapped around something. I did not want to know what that something was.

I heard a yell of despair through the wall, followed by triumphant laughter. I wondered if Christina was hanging out with them.

"Here, hold out your hands."

I turned to find Scott right behind me. Eyeing him suspiciously, I held my hands out, palms up. "Not really in the mood for the hand-slap game, just so you know."

He smiled, peeling off the bandage on my right hand, then my left. It was that same weird little smile from earlier. I watched as he squeezed gel from a little tube into both my palms. "This stuff is amazing," he informed me. "My mom orders it online."

Scott tossed the tube and bandages onto the floor—I mean, into the magic trash void—then cupped his hands under mine and started very, very gently rubbing the gel into my palms with his thumbs. All thoughts of Brian and Christina flew out of my mind.

What was happening right now.

I stared at Scott, completely caught off guard. The gel was minty and cool on my aching cuts, and his hands were warm and his fingers were just as callousy as mine, and *what even was happening right now.*

"Um." I struggled to keep my tone even. "Thanks?"

Scott shrugged again, keeping his eyes on my hands. "Sure." His thumbs stopped moving for a second. I held my breath. "Sorry about your solo," he said. "I know you'd've done better if it wasn't for this." He resumed the thumb massage, and I exhaled.

"So are you finally going to apologize for making me play with scalpels?"

"I didn't *make* you."

"You took my mallets."

"Which is not the same as putting scalpels in your hands."

"What else was I going to use?"

"How about anything but knives?" He was laughing, and I tried not to smile because I could tell he was messing with me. And sure enough, a few seconds later: "Fine. I'm sorry. Okay?"

"*Thank* you." I injected as much weariness into those two words as possible. It wasn't very effective, though. Because now that I'd finally gotten my apology, my full attention was back on the thumb massage, which was making me feel many things that weren't remotely weary. I wondered briefly if he'd used this move on that senior from Bishop last year. Then I decided I didn't care.

"I'm going to be useless at Halo," I heard myself say. "It's not like I can really hold the controller."

Scott was quiet for a few seconds. "Hmm. So . . . wanna hang out in here for a while?"

"Guess so."

I moved closer, just a little, ignoring the voice in my head saying, *No, seriously, Phoebe, what the actual hell are you doing?* Then the voice shut right up, because kissing. Kissing was happening now.

Very soft, tentative kissing, which was amazing for about two seconds until it freaked me right out because *soft* and *tentative* were two words I'd never associated with Scott. Or myself, for that matter.

Screw that.

I grabbed his shirt and yanked him closer with probably more force than necessary. He seemed briefly taken aback, then responded so eagerly I bumped into the wardrobe. He kissed me harder, and his hands slid up my waist just as the giant mystery wad of damp towels fell and hit my head. I gasped at the shock of cool liquid running down my neck.

"What the—" Then the scent of spice and pine trees hit me so hard I nearly gagged. Scott stepped back, and we both looked down at the now-empty bottle of Jorge's cologne by our feet, surrounded by the hand towels. I grimaced, running my hands through my sticky hair. "Why the hell was that up there?"

"It broke in his suitcase," Scott said, as if that were a perfectly logical reason to wrap it in towels and set it precariously on top of a wardrobe.

"Whatever." I paused for a second. I'd fooled around with precisely two guys before but never in a hotel room. Never in a situation where it could really escalate. Not that it *had* to escalate.

Maybe I wanted it to escalate, though.

Maybe I needed to stop thinking and start kissing again.

So I moved in, but after a moment Scott pulled away. "What?" I asked, trying not to sound freaked out. Was he reconsidering now? Was he backing out?

"Nothing, just . . ." He squinted at me. "It's kind of weird doing this when you smell like Jorge."

"Oh. Well . . . get over it?"

Scott blinked a few times. "Okay."

Easy.

Nothing tentative about his mouth this time. My hands were still too tender to be useful, but my fingers danced lightly along the back of his neck and pulled at his hair a little. Which was apparently appreciated, judging from various audible reactions. And one increasingly prominent physical reaction, which, hello, this was new territory for me. He pulled me back a few steps—or maybe I pushed him forward?—and before I could decide whether or not I really wanted to, we'd toppled onto the bed.

I had this panicky moment of *Oh my god, you're on top of a guy, watch your knees, Phoebe, CAREFUL WITH YOUR KNEES!* as he wriggled back toward the headboard. Then his hands squeezed my elbows, and he gasped. "Stop!"

"What?!" I thought for sure I'd accidentally kneed him in the groin anyway. Then I sat up and realized we were on the wrong bed. The one covered with sticks and mallets. Scott's eyes were bugged out in . . . not pain, exactly. More like Extreme Surprise. "What's wrong?"

"Triangle beater! It's . . . ah . . ."

Arching his back, he pushed away a bunch of sticks and a gong mallet from under his butt, then shoved his hand down the back of his jeans.

Horrified, I scrambled off the bed, slipping on several sets of timpani mallets. I backed into the shelf and my elbow knocked over the coffeepot. *"Sharks!"* I whirled around and barely caught the pot before it hit the floor. But not before the lid flipped open, sloshing the entire pot's worth of Mountain Dew coffee all down my front.

I straightened up slowly, shaken, and turned to face Scott. We stared at each other. Him, sitting awkwardly on a pile of sticks, the freed triangle beater in one hand while his other held the gong mallet over his lap in a pretty ridiculous position, given the circumstances. Me, my hair sticky with cologne, empty pot in my hands, my shirt and jeans soaking wet and stained a color Crayola would probably call Toxic Sludge.

His lips were twitching like he wanted to laugh but was waiting to see if I did, too. And I did, because this was beyond ridiculous and I could feel coffee seeping into my underwear and oh my god *what* would Brian say if he knew where that triangle beater had been, and before I knew it I was slumped against the wall, laughing so hard my sides hurt.

Scott cracked up, too, and when he clumsily scooted off the bed and knocked a bunch of sticks to the floor in a clatter, it only made us laugh harder. Then he knelt down next to me and took the coffeepot from my hands, and I had the sudden, horrifying realization that I was about to cry. And not tears-from-laughter crying. Tears-from-confusion-and-regret-and-humiliation, what-the-hell-am-I-even-doing crying. *Girl* crying.

No way could I let Scott see this.

I shot to my feet so fast I got a head rush. "Okay. Yeah. I'm gonna go back to my room."

"Wait, Phoebe . . ." Scott stood, too, still holding the coffeepot. "Are you okay?"

"Of course!" I faced him, lips pressed together, trying to keep the tears back through sheer force of will. "I mean, I could use a shower. But otherwise, fanfreakingtastic." *Definitely not about to bawl my eyes out. I'm not one of* those *girls.*

"Right." Scott smiled a little. "But are you— Will you come back?"

I exhaled slowly. "I don't know. I mean, this wasn't . . . It didn't mean anything, right? Why'd you even ask me up here?"

His smile faltered, and I felt a twinge of guilt. "I don't know. Because you looked really upset when the solo results went up, and I . . . I felt bad."

"Yeah, I *was* upset." I shrugged and attempted a good-natured grin. "So we fooled around because we both felt sorry for me. Ha."

"Phoebe, hang on—"

"It's fine!" I called, already halfway to the door. "Seriously, no worries. See you later, okay?" The door clicked closed before he could respond. I hurried down the hall, reeking of cologne and stale, too-sweet coffee. A tear rolled down my cheek, and I barely made it back to my thankfully empty room before losing it completely.

CHAPTER TEN

VANESSA

I didn't go to the costume contest. Not because I didn't want to see Merry win—and *obviously* they'd win—but because my brain was full to overflowing with what Callie had said about me and Soleil in the ice room, and there was no space left for anything else. Not costumes, not Merry, and definitely not crowds. So after Callie left, I went straight back to the hotel room. I called my mom, because I'd promised to do that at least once a day so she'd know I hadn't been murdered by an internet creeper. Then I changed into my bathing suit and headed for the pool. And, joy of joys, there was a hot tub! I climbed in. And I asked myself a very serious question:

Did I have the guts to make the first move on Soleil?

The answer, terrifyingly, was yes.

Yes because it *had* to be yes; I was willing to bet that she and *Dave* had done plenty of kissing, and even though I totally-definitely-one-hundred-percent wasn't jealous of him, I couldn't let him keep all that Soleil-kissing for himself. Yes because being together with someone meant stepping out of your shy-little-wallflower comfort zone; years and years of reading first-kiss fanfic had already taught me that much. And yes because, as Callie had said, we were already a couple, so what did I have to lose?

Problem was, I had no idea how in the world you were actually supposed to go about making that kind of move. My characters were always so good at it, but actual real-life *me* . . . ?

When my hands started turning pruney in the hot tub, I went back to the hotel room, pulled up FicForAll on my laptop, and started reading through my own stories. And Soleil's stories. And the one we'd written together. I skipped right to the kissing scenes in each one, and I studied all the descriptions we'd written of the characters' body language. It was all pretty vague stuff, like *moving closer* and *leaning in* and *drawn together like magnets*. Not helpful at all.

Except maybe it was. All those descriptions implied characters who were just so into each other that they couldn't *help* getting up in each other's faces, so hey, maybe that was the answer. Maybe I had to stop overthinking it and just follow my instincts.

When Soleil got back that night, I was lying on my stomach, reading the FicForAll message boards on my laptop—specifically, looking at all Soleil's old posts, filling my head with everything I liked about her in anticipation of the First Real-Life Kiss that was about to happen. I'd spent the past hour or so, ever since the pool had closed, scrolling back through every message StraightFlush had ever left. The initial incident was exactly as Merry had described it: some guy being all homophobic about her fanfic, and Soleil generally being a rock-star badass as she put the guy in his place.

"Oh, Nessie." Soleil sat beside me and put her hand on my back, right below my neck. Eeee. "I really wish you could've come had drinkies with me. Those girls are so cool, and Danielle and I had such a great conversation about 'Carry Me Home.' You would've loved it. Hey, whatcha reading?"

Kiss kiss kiss, I thought, twisting around to stare at her lips. This was supposed to be easy. It was always so easy in our stories. *Okay. Relax. Stop overthinking. Just do it.*

"Nessie?" She leaned over me to read my screen, and her hand was still on my back, and I wanted her to leave it there forever.

Then I remembered she'd asked me a question.

"Oh!" I said. "I'm, ah, catching up on FicForAll. Hey, did you see that StraightFlush douchebag is back? He's harassing a different Five/Seven shipper now."

I pulled up the page in question, and Soleil frowned down at it. "Yeah, of course I saw. I wrote a post about it last week. It got, like, a million hits."

"Oh, I guess I didn't see it yet."

"That's fine," she said. "It's the same stupid stuff as last time. You don't have to read it. You've heard all my rants already."

"Sure, but I'll definitely read it anyway. Just not right now." I shut my laptop and sat up to face her, all beautiful and confident and way more relaxed than me. She smelled like perfume and alcohol.

Kiss her, I told myself, because it needed to happen, and it needed to happen *now*.

Kiss her, I thought, and didn't move.

"Uh, Nessie?" said Soleil, frowning at me. "Something up? You look like you're about to puke."

And, okay, that was almost *exactly* what Seven had said to Five in "Carry Me Home," when Five had decided to tell Seven how he felt but couldn't figure out the right way to do it. If that wasn't a sign, I didn't know what was.

I leaned forward, and I put my hand on her cheek to keep her right where she was, and . . . I kissed her. We were *kissing*. Oh my god oh my god oh my god.

And then—then we weren't kissing anymore. And Soleil was giggling. It was almost identical to how my mom giggled after she'd had a couple glasses of wine.

"Aw, Nessie!" she said, patting my cheek as she leaned back. "Guess I'm not the only one who had a few drinkies tonight, huh?"

"Whuh?" I said dully, all kiss-dazed and stupid and, just, Soleil, Soleil, *Soleil*. I'd kissed Soleil. I'd broken the seal, and now we'd move on to the *real* kissing, with tongue and teeth and hands in each other's hair, which was totally terrifying in the best possible way, and I was ready. I was so infinitely ready.

Except—that drinkies comment. What was that supposed to mean?

She leaned in again, just for a second, and gave me another peck on the lips. Not a real kiss, like the one I'd just given her. More like the kind my weird aunt Rosa gave me whenever she came over. It even ended with a "Mwah!" sound. And then she stood up and stretched her arms over her head, yawning broadly. "God, I'm beat."

Okay, I was definitely missing something.

"Um," I said slowly, hesitantly. "Um, sorry, but—"

"Oh my god, don't apologize," Soleil said with another giggle, as she pulled her hair back and wrapped an elastic band around it. "I get super cuddly when I'm drunk, too. Just ask Dave. God, just ask Dave's *roommates*. Just ask *my* roommates. The things you learn about yourself in college, right?"

"But—but I'm not—"

"Ooh, right, right, you're not in college yet," she said, pulling her shirt off over her head. "Whatever. You'll see when you get there."

"Not that." I took a deep breath. "I was gonna say I'm not *drunk*."

Soleil paused, T-shirt crumpled awkwardly in her hands. She was wearing the cutest polka-dot bra underneath, and I tried not to stare at it. Or at, you know, her boobs. She stared at me plenty, though. But not sexy staring. Staring like she was trying to figure out what I meant.

"I'm completely sober," I said, even though, duh. "I'm not . . . what you said . . . I'm not getting cuddly because I'm drunk. I'm . . . I mean we're . . ." I gestured from her to me and back again. "Aren't we?"

As soon as I asked the question, I immediately wished that I hadn't. Because I could see the answer in the confusion on her face. Followed by the surprise. And then the . . . whatever that was. The little smile and the softening in her eyes as she sat back down on the bed with me.

"Aren't we what?" she asked in this really soft, really serious voice.

Oh god, did she actually want me to say it, now that I knew I was wrong? Except—wait—how *could* I have been wrong? All those emails, all those texts, all those message board posts, out there in the open for anyone with a FicForAll account to see. Over and over again, the same two words.

I made myself say them again now: "Internet girlfriends."

Soleil's smile brightened, and she looked almost relieved. "Well, obviously we are! But that doesn't mean— Oh. *Ohhhhh*." Her eyes widened, and she actually pressed a hand to her mouth for a second. "Oh, Nessie, *no*. I never meant—like not—not in real life . . ."

Not in real life.

My throat was made of concrete. I was about to suffocate and die and, let's face it, that would probably be for the best.

"I'm so sorry if I made you think that," she went on, "but I say that all the time! The girlfriend thing. Julie's my concert girlfriend. Yvette's my French class girlfriend. Anna's my gym girlfriend." She bumped my shoulder with hers. "And Nessie's my internet girlfriend. You get me?"

Oh my god. Oh my god.

"But . . . you were all flirty and . . . and I know you have that boyfriend, but you keep talking about how monogamy is stupid, and . . ."

"That's just so Dave and I can make out with whoever we want at parties," said Soleil. "We don't, like, actually *date* other people."

She didn't date other people. She wasn't dating *me*. And here I was, thinking I'd been in a long-distance relationship for the past four months.

I was the stupidest person alive.

"Hey, Nessie. Sweetie. You okay?" She tried to slip an arm around my shoulders, but I shied away and, thankfully, she took the hint. "Okay, well, listen, we don't have to talk about it, if you don't want. We can just pretend it never happened. Okay?"

It wasn't okay, and I *did* want to talk about it, but the problem was, as usual, I had no idea what to actually say. So I stayed silent, my eyes squeezed shut because I couldn't even think about looking at her.

After a moment, Soleil said, "All right. Message received. I'm gonna wash up, okay?"

She headed into the bathroom, leaving me on my bed. I'd spent all evening thinking I was about to star in a real-life version of one of our stories. We'd kiss, and we'd compare our feelings and find the parts that matched up, and we'd look into each other's eyes and confess our deepest secrets, and we'd fall backward onto the bed in a tangle of passion. All the stuff that had happened in "Carry Me Home."

Or the parts that *hadn't* happened in "Carry Me Home." Like me telling her that this had been my first kiss.

"Hey, Nessie?" called Soleil. "Is my contact lens case out there?"

"I don't see it," I called back, without even looking.

"Oops, found it!" There was a pause. "So, uh, hey, what are we doing tomorrow? I know we decided on the panel about gender in *Doctor Who*, but before that there's still the choice between the vlogger thing and the presentation about Snape's heroism. Oh, and the panel on lady superheroes. Which one—"

"Actually, I have to get my badge replaced tomorrow," I said loudly.

"Wait, what? You lost your badge?" When Soleil poked her head out of the bathroom, she looked totally horrified.

"Yup. I have to go to the registration desk for a new one. So I can't go with you to the morning stuff."

"Oh man, that sucks so hard," she said, looking all crestfallen.

It didn't suck, the idea of not spending the morning with Soleil. It should have, but it didn't. Not after everything that had just happened between us.

"Yeah," I lied. "It totally sucks."

Soleil went back into the bathroom, muttering something about the horrible texture of the towels.

I got out my phone, tucked myself into bed, and turned off my light. Then I downloaded the first episode of *A Thousand Words*. I'd never listened to it before, but Callie's enthusiasm had piqued my curiosity, and I was desperate for a distraction from The Kiss. I plugged my earbuds in and listened, pretending to be asleep so I wouldn't have to talk to Soleil again.

Eventually I fell asleep for real, to the sound of at least ten different voices talking about the difference between obsession and love.

* * *

The next morning, Soleil was gone before I even woke up. She'd left a handwritten note on my side of the dresser, though:

> *Morning, Nessie! Left early 4 the Lady*
> *Superheroes panel @ 9 & didn't want 2 wake u*
> *since u have to get yr badge 1st anyway. Txt me*
> *when yr back @ WTF!*
>
> *xoxoxo*

And she'd signed it, not with her name, but with a drawing of a smiley-faced sun.

There was nothing at all in there about last night. Sure, there was the "xoxoxo" at the bottom—but that was it. Maybe she was doing exactly what she'd said she would. Pretending it never happened.

But maybe that was for the best, all things considered. Maybe that would make it easier for us to stay best friends, even if I'd been wrong about the dating part.

On today's schedule were a whole bunch of kick-ass panels, a writing workshop for which both Soleil and I had submitted stories, and the Karaoke Extravaganza at the end of the day. Soleil had already signed up to sing "Defying Gravity." I'd promised to be the Glinda to her Elphaba. But before all that even started, I was going to check out the taxidermy convention. Callie had given me her badge in exchange for mine. I hadn't been sure whether I'd pick dead animals over alone time in my room, but curiosity had won.

So when I finished showering and getting dressed—in another one of Soleil's shirts because, well, she *did* have really good taste—that was where I went. Toward B-wing, where a mass of people in flannel and camo and trucker hats were all milling around under a banner that read:

Welcome to the World Taxidermy & Fish Carving Championships!

Fish carving?

Okay, then.

A bunch of people were headed upstairs on the escalator, so I followed them, painfully aware of how much I stood out. I mean, I wasn't just a sore thumb. I was a sore hand. An entire sore *arm*. I wondered if my badge would get inspected. I wondered if someone would call me out as a fraud and I'd get kicked out or, like, skinned and stuffed. But when I got to the top, the security guy waved me through with a glazed expression and barely a glance at my badge.

Yeah, apparently people sneaking in wasn't a huge concern over here.

The room was pretty big, but not nearly as big as the WTFcon marketplace room, which I'd visited yesterday with Soleil. It looked like a museum. A museum so crowded with displays that you almost couldn't walk, but still.

There were lions. There were foxes. There were wolves and zebras and this giant shaggy cow thing, guarded by a super proud-looking guy dressed in a button-down American flag shirt. There were a couple of animals I was pretty sure didn't even exist any-more, like a saber-tooth tiger, and I wasn't a hundred percent sure if they were fake or not. Someone had sawed a baby deer in half and replaced its midsection with a fancy dollhouse—the title plaque below it read *This Faun Is Not a Metaphor*, whatever that meant. And right beside it were two enormous boars, one humping the other. I stifled a laugh as I moved past the display.

Just beyond it was a long table crowded with birds, all arranged in what I guessed were supposed to be their natural habitats. I zeroed in on a red-winged blackbird with spread wings, and leaned closer for a better look.

As I inspected the bird's tiny feet, a male voice said, "No touching, young lady." I jumped back. The flannel-clad guy who'd spoken pointed to a sign pasted onto the table.

DO NOT TOUCH, it said. A zillion other signs, pasted in front of pretty much every other display, said the exact same thing.

"I wasn't going to," I said.

A few feet away from me, a pair of serious-looking men approached another display: a cute black-and-white monkey perched in a forked tree branch. Its long tail was curled around one of the branches, and its face was tilted upward a little, like it was curious about something.

Now I understood why those signs were there. I really, really wanted to pet the thing.

"*Cebus capucinus*," said one of the men as he peered under the monkey's tail with a penlight and one of those little mirrors they stick in your mouth at the dentist's. "Good pose. Has jizz, for sure."

Okay, what? I inched closer to the two men.

"The neck's slightly overstuffed," countered the second man. "And is it supposed to be climbing up or down? The direction of the gaze implies up, but the way the metatarsals are flexed indicates down."

The first man peered at a page in his binder, then at the monkey's leg. "You're right." He leaned in and sniffed the monkey's shoulder. Like, literally sniffed it. "Good odor, though."

They kept muttering to each other, pointing out flaws that I absolutely couldn't see. Uneven stitches along the inside of one ankle. Something about the paint color on the inside of its nostrils. And what in the world had they meant by *jizz*?

". . . nothing for sale at all?" came a voice that, thankfully, startled me right out of that train of thought. Mostly because it sounded young. Like, my age. I hadn't seen anyone in the entire B-wing who looked my age.

But there, standing between a slightly cross-eyed eagle and a really awkwardly posed lion, was a girl. White, dirty-blond ponytailed hair, seriously cute. She was talking to an older woman wearing a sweatshirt with a pug face on it.

"Sorry, sweetheart," said the woman. "None of the work here is for sale. Now, if you wanted to mount your *own* vulture—"

"No, no, that's okay," said the blond girl. "I'll just stick with my bluebird. Thanks, though."

That was, like, a bluebird or whatever, came the echo of Soleil's voice in my ears, and I instantly knew who the blond girl was. Wait, no. Not girl. The blond *person*.

"Merry?" I said, going over to them as the pug-sweatshirt woman wandered away.

They jumped a little at the sound of their name, then their eyes brightened with recognition. "Oh, Ness! Hey!"

Merry wasn't in costume, which was why I hadn't recognized them right away. Instead, they were just wearing baggy jeans, sparkly Chucks, and a T-shirt that said *Maximum Effort* across the chest, over a black-and-red circular logo.

"*Deadpool?*" I said, pointing at the shirt. "Nice. Good movie."

"The comics are even better," said Merry with a grin. "What're you doing over here?"

"Secret mission," I said.

"Ooh. Do tell."

"Well, it's not that secret. It's not even a mission. I just wanted to see the animals. How about you?" Then I remembered what they'd just said to the pug-shirt woman. "Something about a vulture? Are your friends here somewhere, too?"

"Nah, they're at a *Supernatural* panel," said Merry. "I gave up on that show in the middle of season six, so we split up for the morning. But yes to the vulture part. You remember my hat? From my Boggart Snape costume?"

"Absolutely," I said. "Hey, how'd the contest go? I'm really sorry I couldn't make it. Did you win?"

They rolled their eyes. "No. I wasn't *authentic* enough."

"Because of the bluebird? Come on, that's the tiniest part of the costume. And the rest looked amazing."

"I know, right?" Merry sighed. "But there was another Snape, and he . . . well, he was a *he*. So, you know. Authenticity!"

"Ew," I said.

"Whatever. It goes like it goes. But just in case the bird made the difference, I came over here to buy a vulture for next time—only it turns out none of this stuff is for sale." They looked furtively around, then lowered their voice. "It also turns out that these people are the absolute best kind of weirdos. Did you see that lady I was talking with before? She's a taxidermist, and she was trying to drag me over there to see what she made, which is, and I quote, 'a portrait of two boars who love each other very much.'"

I burst out laughing. "Oh, I saw that! They were humping!"

"Wait, seriously?"

"Seriously! Come on, I'll show you!"

But before we got more than a couple feet, I felt a tap on my shoulder, which made me jump. I turned, and right behind me was yet another girl who looked my age. Tall and brunette and freckled, she grinned at Merry, then at me, and said, "Hey, I'm trying to find someone, and please say you can help me so I don't have to talk to any of the trucker-hat guys?"

Merry shook their head. "Sorry. Don't know anyone here."

"We're stowaways," I added in a dramatic whisper. "We're actually with WTFcon."

"Ooh, really?" said the brunette. "Man, I tried to sneak into that one before, but they are total *dinosaurs* about checking badges."

Merry and I exchanged a look. I was pretty sure we were thinking the same thing, but I took point on saying it:

"Dinosaurs?"

"Oh, sorry." The brunette laughed a little. "My little brother discovered swear words last year, so my family's been trying to say different stuff instead. Mainly animals. There's a swear jar if we slip up, so. It's kind of a habit now."

"Foxing good habit," I said, as straight-faced as I could.

"Exactly," said the brunette, pointing at me as Merry burst out laughing. "Congratulations, you are now an honorary member of the Byrd family."

"Wait, wait," said Merry. "You use animals to swear, and your last name is *Byrd*?"

"It's a four-letter word." She grinned at us. "Ba-dum-ching."

"Womp womp," I said, and Merry groaned.

"Oh, shut up, that's the greatest joke I've ever made," said the brunette. "Anyway, my point is, it's impossible to sneak in over there. Way easier to sneak in here."

"Can't imagine why," murmured Merry.

"Excuse me, you three," said a man's voice. It was one of the judges, and he and his partner, still looking oh-so-serious, had apparently finished inspecting the monkey. "Would you mind not blocking the aisle? There's an aardvark over there that requires our attention."

We moved dutifully aside, and there was this suspended moment where I was hyper-aware of the ridiculousness of my surroundings, and I could tell Merry and the brunette were, too.

"*Aardvark* is definitely one of my brother's favorite code words," whispered the brunette, and all of us instantly cracked up.

"I'm Vanessa, by the way," I said, as soon as we'd all calmed down a little. "This is Merry. Should we call you Byrd, or do you have a first name?"

"I do, and it's Phoebe," said the brunette. "So, do you guys wear costumes or what? I saw a bunch of totally killer costumes last night. I think there was a contest or something."

"Nah, I'm just a fanficcer," I said, then tilted my head toward Merry. "But this one does the costume thing."

Phoebe peered at Merry. "Oh, wait, it's you! Weren't you wearing that Boggart Snape costume last night?"

"That's me," said Merry. "I think I remember you! We talked for a second, right?"

"Yeah, because I couldn't get over how *completely amazing* you looked," said Phoebe. "Seriously, it was like you stepped right out of the movie."

I noticed Phoebe's eyes flicker down to Merry's pronoun button as she talked. She didn't comment on it, though. Just sort of nodded to herself.

Merry grinned. "Thanks. So, you're not here for the taxidermy stuff, and you're not with WTFcon. Please tell me you're here with that baby beauty pageant thing."

"God, no," said Phoebe. "I'm here for IPAC. The percussion one."

"Checking out the other conventions on your downtime?" I said.

"Well, that and these babies." Phoebe held up a black case.

"Long story, but I have to give these back to, what is it, Buchannan Taxidermy? And get my mallets back."

I was about to ask what the long story was, when something clicked in my head. I'd tucked my badge into my shirt so nobody would call me out on not being Callie, but I pulled it out now and checked to be sure—and, yup, there it was. I held it up so Callie's full name was right there in plain sight. "You mean *this* Buchannan Taxidermy?"

Phoebe's brow furrowed in confusion. "But I thought you were here for the other—"

"Shh!" I hissed. "Not so loud. I swapped badges with this girl who wanted to see a panel about a podcast she likes. It's actually really good. The podcast, I mean. *A Thousand Words?*"

"Oh, that's one of my favorites," said Merry. "After *Limetown*. And *First Draft*. Oh, and *Welcome to Night Vale*, obviously."

"Ooh, I love *Night Vale*," I said. "Cecil and Carlos, am I right?"

"Carlos and his perfect hair!" said Merry, pressing a hand dramatically to their chest. "Hey, did you read that one fic where Cecil and *Earl* hooked up?"

"One fic?" I said. "Come on, there's, like, twenty-thousand fics of that."

"No, but I mean this one in particular where—"

"Um, just so you guys know," said Phoebe, "I have no foxing idea what you're talking about. Who's Cecil . . . ?"

"Oh, sorry! Fictional character." Merry shook their head with a smile. "Note to self: Make Phoebe listen to *Night Vale*."

"Anyway," I said, "Callie told me about the panel last night when I met her, and I had nothing to do this morning, so we swapped badges for a bit." That was when my bag buzzed. "Actually, that's probably her," I said, and dug my phone out from under all my crap.

That was AWESOME, said Callie's text. I totally owe you. Meet me by the weird cactus outside A-wing?

I knew the exact place she was talking about: a plastic cactus the size of a grizzly bear, standing outside A-wing for no reason that I could discern.

Cool, be there in 5, I typed back, and tucked my phone back into my bag.

"She wants to meet me outside," I said to Phoebe and Merry. "Come with?"

Merry beamed as they nodded. Phoebe's only reply, though, was "Aardvark."

Apparently that meant yes.

CHAPTER ELEVEN

CALLIE

As I left the ballroom after the podcast workshop, I was actually glad for the first time that I'd come all the way to Florida. Anica and Rafael had walked us through the production of an entire episode of *A Thousand Words*, from deciding on a concept to building narrative structure to post-production. They'd done a sample interview with an audience member and then shown us how her words could make us feel different things depending on what sound effects or music they played underneath. I was confident I could master the technical stuff if I got my hands on equipment like theirs, but I had no idea how I'd ever learn to craft a perfect story out of other people's experiences the way they could. They were just *so freaking good at it*.

When the workshop was over, fans swarmed to the front of the room to talk to Anica and Rafael. Part of me wanted to go up and say hi, too, but I needed to get back across the convention center before my dad realized I wasn't really in Hall 5C. Hopefully the information I'd learned from the duck taxidermy videos I'd watched on YouTube last night would be enough to convince him I'd been at the waterfowl demo all morning.

And then I pulled out my phone, and there on the screen were two missed calls and five texts from my dad.

> **Dad:** Where are you?
> **Dad:** In 5C but don't see you
> **Dad:** Talked to Harley and 3 other ppl. Nobody saw you in session
> **Dad:** Why aren't you answering my calls
> **Dad:** CALLIE CALL ME RIGHT NOW

Dad had been forced to tell his archrival that he'd lost his assistant? Oh god, I was in so, so much trouble.

I tried to remind myself that I hadn't really done anything wrong. It's not like my dad needed me to sit in sessions with him, and I deserved to do one small thing for *me*. But he must've gotten into my head, because instead of feeling defiant and self-righteous, I just felt awful. Maybe he was right about me after all; pretending I was learning to mount ducks and running off to another con was legitimately unprofessional. If I wanted to show him I deserved to be treated with respect, sneaking around behind his back wasn't exactly the best way to do that. There was nothing to do now but find him and own up to my mistakes.

Where will you be in 15 min? I wrote back. I'll come meet you. Then I texted Vanessa to come find me so I could return her badge, sat down against the wall next to this weird plastic cactus, and tried to prepare myself for the confrontation to come.

Four girls dressed as Ninja Turtles wandered by, deep in a discussion about postmodernism. A girl in an elephant-print romper struggled to carry a giant cardboard cutout of an actor from *The Vampire Diaries*. The woman behind her looked kind of familiar, but I couldn't place her until I noticed the little kid at her side. Today, Beige was dressed in a Viking helmet and leather breastplate with metal cones where her boobs would be a decade from now. Her platinum braids reached her butt, and she was clutching a fake sword.

"Now, sweetheart, remember not to give it all away on your first '*am Rande des Rheins zuhauf,*'" said her mom. "You have to save that beautiful instrument for the higher notes later on in the aria."

Beige nodded, her face completely serious. Was this kindergartener seriously going to sing opera? In *German*?

"You're going to kick Delancey's puny behind," her mom said. "Sweetie, what do we call Delancey?"

"My arch-ne-me-sis," Beige said, enunciating carefully.

"And what do we do with our archnemesis?"

Beige raised her foot-long sword in the air. *"We crush her!"*

After a few endless minutes, Vanessa finally showed up with two other girls in tow. "Hey!" she said, giving me a little wave. "Merry, Phoebe, this is Callie. Callie, my friends: Merry and Phoebe."

The taller girl came up and held out her hand—or, *their* hand, according to the button about pronouns pinned to their shirt. "I love your hair," they said. "Is that your natural color? There are so many great characters you could cosplay. Merida or Willow or Oz or Poison Ivy or *any* of the Weasleys . . ." I must've had a strange expression on my face, because they broke off all of a sudden. "Sorry! Rambling. Great to meet you."

I shook their hand. "You too." I turned to Phoebe, and then I realized I'd seen her before. "Hey, you're the one with the drums. Your friend ran me over with a xylophone." I pushed up my sleeve to show her the purple bruise on my elbow.

Phoebe winced. "A marimba, yeah. Sorry about that. My friends are morons. Anyway, I've been looking for you all over so I could give you this."

She held out a black leather case, stenciled with the words *BUCHANNAN TAXIDERMY*. But that didn't make any sense. My dad's tool kit was upstairs with all the other turkey demo stuff.

"Wait, how did you get that?" I asked. "I saw it in my room this morning."

"Actually, you've got the bag with all my drumsticks and mallets," Phoebe said. "It looks really similar."

"Oh *no*. What have you been using to play?"

"Um." Phoebe looked down at her palms, which were all bandaged up.

"Oh my god. Please tell me you didn't play the drums with my dad's taxidermy tools."

"It was an emergency. Scalpels don't actually sound that bad on a xylophone, as it turns out." She shrugged. "It's fine. I'll heal."

"Man," I said. "You're really hardcore. I hope you disinfected the crap out of your hands afterward. Some of those scalpels were, um, inside a badger on Monday."

Phoebe gazed at her palms in awe. "Sweet, I've got Hufflepuff hands!"

"So the podcast thing was good?" Vanessa asked, obviously desperate to change the subject.

"It was amazing. Thank you so much for letting me borrow this." I took off her badge and passed it over, and she handed mine back in return. "Did you like the animals?"

"Yeah! They were actually really cool! And we got to see some judging happen. Except, wait, okay. There was this one monkey, and I thought I heard a judge saying it had, um"—she leaned closer to me and lowered her voice—"*jizz*? Does that actually mean . . . ?"

I burst out laughing. "Oh my god, no. That means it's really lifelike. I don't know why they say that."

"Check out the Incredible Hulk costume over there," Phoebe said, totally deadpan. "Has some serious jizz."

"Tony Stark would agree," murmured Merry, and Vanessa giggled.

My phone vibrated, and my heart started pounding as I dug it out of my pocket. This was going to be so bad. "Hang on a second, okay?" I said to my new friends, then moved a couple of steps away before I answered.

"Hey, I'm so, so sorry," I started before my dad could say anything. "I have to run up to the room really quickly, but I'll come meet you right after that, okay?"

"Callie, where *are* you? Why haven't you been answering your phone?" He was already at an 8.5 out of 10 on the irritated scale, and it made me feel even worse.

"I went to . . . um . . . a class. Not a taxidermy one. I promise I'll explain everything when I see you, okay? I'm seriously so sorry. I just need, like, ten minutes, fifteen tops."

My dad made this huffing, sighing sound that I knew meant he had reached the end of his rope. "Meet me at the trade show entrance," he said.

"I will. I'll be there, I promise," I said, and the line went dead.

"Everything okay?" Merry asked when I rejoined the group.

I tried to rearrange my face into a neutral expression. "Yeah. I just . . . I have to go. Phoebe, you want to come upstairs with me for a second and swap bags?"

Before she could answer, a blond girl bounced up and wrapped her arms around Vanessa from behind. Even from a few feet away, I could smell the cloud of fake-flowery perfume that surrounded her. Phoebe turned away and let out a delicate little cough.

Was *this* the famous Soleil? I'd been picturing her as elegant and mysterious. This girl looked like she should be modeling for The Gap.

"Hey, girlie!" she chirped. "Where have you been? I thought maybe you'd make it back in time for Gender Roles in *Doctor Who*, but I guess not. But you got your new badge, right?"

"Wait, why did you need a new—" I started, but Vanessa shot me a quick, scared look, so I shut up.

"Yup," she said. "It took a little longer than I thought."

"Ugh, did they give you a hard time? The girl who registered me was a total bee-yotch."

"It was fine. Everything's fine," Vanessa said. She looked intensely uncomfortable. "Guys, this is Soleil. My . . . roommate. This is Callie and Phoebe, and you already know Merry."

"Oh, yeah. Hi." Soleil's eyes swept over Phoebe and me. "What're your fandoms?"

"We're here for the other conventions," Phoebe said.

"Oh." The girl's interest in us instantly evaporated, and she linked her arm with Vanessa's like she was trying to mark her territory. "So, I'm meeting Danielle and Aimee and Marziya for lunch at that place in the lobby. You have to come this time. I mean, as long as you're not *opposed* to Mexican food."

Vanessa squirmed. "Mexican food's fine."

"Great! Let's go. They're waiting."

"I—um, okay. Merry, do you want to come eat with us?"

"Actually, Merry, I'm *sooo* sorry, but I only made a reservation for five," Soleil said. "I'd see if they could fit one more, but the restaurant's gonna be super crowded right now, so." She gave a little one-shouldered shrug that made my skin crawl.

"I've got plans with my friends for lunch," Merry said. "Maybe we can meet up later, Ness?"

"We're going to the third fanfic reading this afternoon. Find me there, okay?" Vanessa turned back to Phoebe and me. "And I guess I'll see you guys later?"

I couldn't believe she was going to let this tiny, peppy monster drag her away right in the middle of a conversation. "Yeah, text me," I said.

Soleil tugged Vanessa's arm. "Nessie, come *on*. I told Danielle we'd be there five minutes ago." As they took off down the hall, Vanessa turned back over her shoulder and mouthed *Sorry* to us.

Merry left to meet their own friends, and Phoebe and I went to get her mallets. "So, taxidermy," she said as we walked across the bridge to the hotel. "You really skin animals?"

She sounded so excited about it that I wasn't nervous at all when I said, "Yeah, sometimes."

She gave me a huge smile. "That is *awesome*."

Okay, seriously, what were the chances of finding two girls my age in a row who didn't think taxidermy made me a freak? "Thanks," I said. "I was pretty into it when I was little, but now I mostly do it . . . um, for the money. I mean, it's fine. But if I never saw another scalpel, I wouldn't mind that much."

Phoebe looked down at her hands. "Yeah, me neither."

"I seriously can't believe you did that."

"It was pretty stupid. But sadly, it's not the stupidest thing I've done in the last twenty-four hours."

"Really? What was the stupidest?"

"Eh . . ." Phoebe wrinkled her nose. "Let's call it a hormonal mishap, the details of which are far too humiliating to share."

"Oh no. Sorry."

"Anyway." Phoebe shot me a sly smile. "*Soleil*, huh?"

"Oh my god, what is up with her? Why does Vanessa like her? She's *horrible*."

"Seriously," Phoebe said. "I don't get it at all."

I wanted to ask Phoebe if she thought Vanessa and Soleil were really dating, but I wasn't sure if she even knew about the internet girlfriend thing. So instead I said, "When I met Vanessa last night, Soleil had just backed out of their plans so she could hang out with a bunch of fans, and Vanessa was clearly upset, but she sat there and made excuses for her anyway. It's like she's brainwashed or something."

"I know! And she seems so cool otherwise. There are tons of great people here. Why would you choose to hang out with someone who doesn't even respect you?"

We were at the elevators now, and the doors opened as soon as I pressed the up button. "Also, can we talk about her *name*?" Phoebe continued as we got inside. "Who names their kid Soleil? Is that supposed to be like *Cirque du Soleil* or something?"

"That's exactly what I said! And Vanessa got all snippy about it."

"That can't be her real name. She's probably, like, an Ann or a Jane or something."

"Or something super old-fashioned and embarrassing, like Mildred."

Phoebe laughed. "I had a great-aunt Mildred. Once she threw her toast at my little brother because he cursed in front of her."

We were still laughing by the time we got to my room. Phoebe went straight for her mallet bag and swapped it for my dad's tools, and then she started inspecting the giant coolers against the wall. "What's in these?"

"Turkeys. My dad's doing this seminar tomorrow about turkey taxidermy. They're in different stages of being finished, like a cooking show."

"Oh my god, can I see?"

"I'm not supposed to open them and let the cold air out. The feathers start to fall out if they get too warm. But if you come back after the demo tomorrow, I guess I can show you."

"Okay," Phoebe said eagerly, and she gave me her number so I could text her. The moment I hit save, the phone rang, and my mom's picture flashed up on the screen.

My stomach knotted up just for a second, a Pavlovian response to her calls that was still ingrained in me from last year. I was fine with talking to Mom now, but I had refused to speak to her at all for the first four months after she'd moved across the country to "start over." That hadn't stopped her from calling me every day and leaving long, apologetic voicemails, most of which I deleted unplayed. Every single time her name popped up on my screen, I'd been assaulted by a wash of sadness and anger, and it stressed me out so much that I'd hidden my phone in my sock drawer and left it there for two months.

But after a while, it had started to feel like holding out was costing me more than giving in. My dad had withdrawn from the world even more than usual after Mom left. He'd spent most of his time in the studio since he started getting really big museum jobs when I was about eleven, but now that was the *only* place I ever saw him, and even there he never talked or joked with me like he used to. I ate dinner alone almost every night, he never asked about my life, and I needed one parent who was actually trying. Mom had done a seriously crappy thing, but at least she was putting in the work. We checked in a couple of times a week now, and our relationship was slowly creeping back toward normal.

"Do you mind if I answer this?" I asked Phoebe. "It's my mom. We keep missing each other."

"Go ahead. Do you want me to leave?"

"No, it's fine." I clicked the talk button. "Hey, Mom."

"Cal! I finally got you!" I could hear the smile in her voice, and it made me miss her. "How are you, sweetheart?"

"I'm okay," I said. "We're in Orlando."

"Oh wow, I forgot that was this weekend. How is it going?"

I sigh. "It's . . . going."

"That good, huh?"

"I don't know. I guess I thought things with Dad would be better here? Like, maybe we could actually have a good time together? But everything's just . . . the same as it is at home." I felt kind of weird saying this stuff in front of Phoebe, but when I glanced over at her, she was absorbed in the taxidermy supply catalog on the desk.

"I swear we used to have fun at these conventions," I said. "I'm not crazy, right?"

"No, you're not." She sounded sad. "Our animal guessing game, and our room service nights . . ."

"And Sven the bison-car," I reminded her.

"Yes! That was so funny!" She laughed. "I miss you so much, Cal. I'm counting down the days till you come out here. Just six more weeks. I was thinking maybe we could go to Willow Canyon the first weekend and camp for a couple of nights. How does that sound?"

"Great," I said. "It sucks that I can only stay for a month. I wish we had longer."

It was totally silent on the other end of the line, and I wondered if the call had dropped. "You still there?" I asked.

"I'm here. But . . . sweetie, did you just say you *want* to come out here for longer?"

"Yeah. It's okay, I know the court only gave you four weeks during the summer. I just wish—"

"Cal, didn't your dad talk to you about this?"

"What about it? I mean, we booked my ticket and stuff."

"No, I mean . . . You guys didn't have another conversation? Recently? Like a week ago?"

"No," I said. I couldn't remember the last time my dad and I had a conversation about anything that didn't involve my professional attitude or passing the tail splitter.

My mom sighed loudly. "God, I could kill that man."

A cold dread crept down my spine, the same feeling I used to get when I heard my parents yelling at each other. "What? What happened?"

"I called him last week and said I wanted you to come out here for the whole summer, and he said he needed you in the studio. I told him I'd pay for him to hire someone else, so he said he'd talk to you. But then he called back the next day and said you only wanted to be here for a month, and if I wanted extended visitation rights, I'd have to take you guys to court. And obviously I wasn't going to force you to be with me if you didn't want to."

I suddenly felt a little wobbly, and I sat down hard on the edge of the bed. "He didn't even ask. He never said anything about it."

My mom gave a breathy laugh. "Well, that's kind of a relief, honestly. I thought you and I were in a pretty good place right now."

"We are."

My heart was suddenly racing, and I pressed a hand over it. Dad had spent all this time and effort pointing out how everything I said and did was wrong, and I had legitimately felt like a terrible person for going behind his back. And all that time, he'd been going behind *my* back, keeping secrets about things that were much more important. Skipping out on ninety minutes of a convention wasn't great, but rerouting my life without even asking? That was an entirely different level of awful.

A ball of white-hot rage gathered in my stomach and started spreading outward, up my throat and into my arms and down my legs. "I want to stay with you the whole summer," I said. "Is that still okay? Or is it too late now?"

"Of course it's not too late. I want you here as long as possible. But if you can't get him to give his permission, I can't take him to court right now. I can't afford any more legal fees. I'm really sorry."

"I'll make him say yes." My voice was trembling, and I realized the rest of my body was, too.

"Great. That's great. I'm thrilled you want to come." My mom sounded so relieved, like a huge weight had lifted off her chest. I felt like it had settled right onto mine.

"I have to go," I choked. "I'll call you soon, okay?"

"Okay, sweetheart. I love you."

"Love you, too," I said, and she hung up.

I stared at the CALL ENDED screen and tried to breathe, but every lungful of air felt ragged and shallow. For the first time in more than a year, I had a parent who wanted *more time* with me. And my dad had prevented me from knowing about it.

"You okay?"

I nearly jumped out of my skin; I had forgotten Phoebe was in the room. "Yeah. No. I don't know."

"Well, that's . . . specific," Phoebe said, and I managed a tiny laugh that sounded more like a cough.

"It's a long story," I said. "Basically, my parents are divorced, I live with my dad, and my mom lives in Arizona. And I just found out she wants to see me more, but my dad told her I didn't want to go, except *he never asked me about it.*"

Her eyes widened. "Dude, seriously? What a shark-head."

"A . . . what?"

"Ha, sorry. We have a swear jar at home, so I say animals instead of curse words. Anyway, sorry, I probably shouldn't call your dad a shark-head."

"No, you're right. He is." I dug the heels of my hands into my eye sockets until I saw swirling colors. "How am I even supposed to react to this? How am I supposed to go back down there and face him right now? I just want to, like, *break* something."

Phoebe eyed the turkey armature boxes. "You could, you know."

"Not really. It would feel great for about three seconds, and then I'd have to clean up a huge mess, and my dad would probably spend the entire night screaming at me."

"You wouldn't have to clean it up if you did it in *his* room. Or outside. Or . . . ooh! What if you rigged one of the turkeys to explode during his presentation or something?"

"That's . . . not really possible," I said, but maybe she was onto something. Even without an explosion, there were lots of ways to make a demo go wrong. After what he'd done to me, he totally deserved to have the thing *he* cared about most fall apart right in front of him.

"I could sabotage the demo, though," I said slowly. "But that would be too much, right? There are going to be, like, five hundred people there."

Phoebe shrugged. "He's basically trying to sabotage your life. That's *way* worse."

She wasn't wrong.

"I don't know," she said. "It's your call, obviously. But think about it."

"Yeah," I said. "You know what? I definitely will."

CHAPTER TWELVE

VANESSA

"I can't believe it," said Soleil, clutching at her short purple skirt as she leaned against the wall. A few feet away, literary agent Wendi Scherer emerged from the same room Soleil and I had just left. Soleil glared as she walked by, and raised her voice a little: "I can't *believe* she didn't like it."

Wendi Scherer kept walking, eventually disappearing into the crowd. I don't think she noticed us there at all.

"Well, she didn't exactly say that," I said, leaning against the wall beside Soleil. "She just said it wasn't marketable."

Soleil sniffed. "She said it was derivative. Derivative means bad. Bad means she didn't like it."

"Nooo," I said. "Derivative means it reminds her of something else. Which is probably fair, since you literally submitted the first chapter of 'I Knew You Were Trouble' with the character names changed. So if she's a *Wonderlandia* fan, which she said she was, then obviously—"

"So you hated it, too?" said Soleil, her voice suddenly small.

I laughed at that, because *what*? She knew I loved her writing.

"Fine, whatever," she said. "I knew doing the workshop was a bad idea."

It had actually been Soleil's idea for us to submit our stories to the writing workshop, but this seemed like a bad time to point that out, so I just shrugged and said, "I thought it was fun. I learned a lot."

"Learned a lot about what?" Soleil said flatly. "Stuff like how I'm a terrible writer?"

"No, god, no," I said. "I mean all the stuff she said about *my* chapter."

The workshop had been an hour and a half long, and they'd capped registration at ten people. Everyone had sent in either a short story or the first chapter of a novel for Ms. Scherer to read and critique, and today we'd all gone over her critiques as a class. The eight minutes we'd spent on my chapter had gone by so quickly, and I tried to remember everything she'd said about it.

Soleil raised an eyebrow, clearly impatient for me to keep talking.

"You know," I said. "That thing she said about how the seed of my entire book should be present in the first chapter. Remember? She said all my dialogue was great, but it needed to be *aiming* for something instead of just meandering around."

"Oh, come on, Nessie. I gave you that note like two months ago. Tenth chapter of 'Carry Me Home.' Remember your first draft of that? Five and Seven were just talking in circles for three pages, and nothing actually happened."

I stared at her. I mean, sure, she'd definitely said that to me—and she'd definitely been right, which was why I'd changed it—but the context had been completely different. That had been a downtime-after-a-fight-scene chapter in a fanfic. This was supposed to be the first chapter in a completely original *book*.

Soleil rolled her eyes. "But hey, I guess if Super Awesome Famous Agent Wendi Scherer says it, then suddenly it's worth listening to. Especially since she thought your characters were *soooooo* original and *soooooo* unique and whatever."

"She didn't say that," I said. "She said they were *interesting*. That was literally all she said—you know, before she started drilling me on what the plot of my book was. And hey, at least you didn't have to admit that you didn't actually *know* what your plot was."

"I guess," she said sullenly.

"Come on, Soleil. It was just a workshop. The whole *point* was for her to tell us what was wrong with our chapters."

A moment passed. As Soleil took long, deep breaths beside me, I watched the crowd—some costumed, most not. Two guys passed by, dressed like Sherlock Holmes and John Watson from the BBC *Sherlock* series, and they were holding hands.

"Look." I nudged Soleil as I nodded at the couple. "So adorable, right? And the one guy kind of even looks like Benedict Cumberbatch."

She squinted at him. "No, he doesn't. His face isn't weird enough." A pause, as she watched them disappear into A-17. "Definitely adorable, though."

I let out a quiet breath. Her bad mood was ebbing away. This was good.

"Hey, sorry for snapping at you," she said after another moment. "I'm . . . I don't know. Not used to people being so harsh about my writing."

"Sure you are," I said. "StraightFlush, remember?"

"Ha!" she said. "Well, that was different. That dude was just being . . . well, you know. A *dude*."

"True enough," I said. "And hey, she wasn't that harsh. She pointed out the stuff in your story that she liked. There was a lot of it."

Soleil nodded slowly. "She did like my plot."

"See?" I said. "You're good at plot, and I'm good at dialogue. We were destined to be co-writers."

Soleil smiled and looped her arm through mine, hugging me close, which, yay. "I wouldn't have it any other way. And anyway, who cares if our stuff is derivative, right?"

"Our stuff?" I said. It was only her story that had been called derivative. Not mine.

"Yeah! Who cares, if we're just gonna be writing fanfic anyway? Fanfic is inherently derivative. And it's not like either of us actually wants to write a whole original book and get published for real."

"We don't?" I said, looking sideways at her. Because the thing was, I *did* want to write original stuff. I liked creating characters, and I liked building worlds from scratch, and I liked the idea of seeing my name—my real name, not my screen name—on the spine of a book one day. That was the main reason I'd agreed to submit a chapter to Ms. Scherer's workshop.

"God, no," said Soleil. "I mean, have you read those FicForAll threads where people post about trying to get published? You have to write to, like, five hundred agents. And once you get an agent, which, okay, odds are you won't, then your book gets sent to another five hundred editors. They always say no. Writing original stuff is like ninety-nine percent rejection."

"True," I said, even though I kind of didn't mind all that stuff. Sure, it would probably suck a little, but it would be worth it in the end, right?

"Fanfic is so much better," she said, nodding to herself. "You post whatever you want, and everyone loves it. And if they don't love it? Screw them."

"Definitely. Screw them."

What I didn't say was, why did it have to be fanfic *or* original writing? Why couldn't a person just, you know, write both?

What I did say: "Hey, the karaoke thingie starts in half an hour. Want to go make sure we get a good spot?"

"You mean the Extravaganza?" said Soleil, making jazz hands that were probably supposed to be ironic. "Yeah, I guess. I just . . . ugh."

"What?"

She slumped against the wall again. "I'm not sure I'm in a 'Defying Gravity' kind of place right now. You know. Emotionally."

"Oh, sure you are," I said. "I mean, the whole song's about

Elphaba saying 'screw you' to the Wizard, right? So imagine you're singing to that agent instead."

"*Deriiiivative*," sang Soleil, to the same tune as "unliiiiimited" in the song. I cracked right up, and she grinned and continued: "*You called my stuff deriiiivative.*"

"Ooh, you have a great voice!" said someone off to my left, startling me out of my laughter. It was Danielle from lunch earlier today, with Marziya and Aimee not far behind her and, oh god, I was so not in the mood for the Fangirl Trio right now.

"Aw, thanks!" said Soleil, instantly snapping back into social-butterfly mode. She pushed herself off the wall and hugged each of them in turn.

"Are you going to the Karaoke Extravaganza?" asked Danielle.

"Like we'd miss it," said Soleil. "We're doing 'Defying Gravity' from *Wicked*. I'm Elphaba, and Nessie here is my Glinda. How about you?"

"The three of us are entering together, actually," said Danielle, gesturing at her friends. "And guess what we're singing?"

Before Soleil could answer, Marziya said, "Taylor Swift! 'I Knew You Were Trouble'! And we're gonna dedicate it to you!"

The namesake of her most famous story, sung by her very own fans, dedicated to her. Soleil looked about five seconds away from melting out of sheer happiness and, yeah, let's be real, I should have guessed that all it would take to improve her mood was a shower of compliments.

"What are you guys doing afterward?" Danielle went on, as our group of five began moving toward the escalator.

"Actually," I said, "tonight Soleil and I were going to work on our project for the Creativity Corner."

"Ooh, lucky," said Marziya. "I wanted to enter that, but we forgot to sign up in time. Now there aren't any slots left. And I had this great idea for a multi-fandom painting, see, because all three of us are artists—"

"Oh my god!" said Soleil, almost slipping in her excitement as she stepped onto the escalator. "I have the best idea. What if you guys joined *our* project?"

I frowned. The Fangirl Trio girls were nice and all, but this project was supposed to be just Soleil and me. "Wait a sec—"

"We'll need backup dancers, right, Nessie?" she continued. "And you've already registered, but nobody's asked how many people are in our group."

"But . . ."

"But what?" said Soleil, eyes alight as she looked . . . not at me. At the person next to me. Danielle.

"That's an awesome idea," said Danielle.

But it was supposed to be the two of us, I thought. *Nobody else.*

Although, yeah, that was before last night and The Kiss. Had I really screwed things up so badly between us that Soleil didn't want to be alone with me anymore?

"Then it's settled," said Soleil. "You lovely ladies are with us. Come on, let's sing some karaoke!"

She practically leaped off the escalator. We dashed toward the ballroom, which was already full of people, and made our way toward the front. There was a line of people trying to sign up last-minute, but we moved past them and checked in at the DJ booth. Well, Soleil and Aimee checked in. The rest of us hung back, and I scouted the place for somewhere to stand.

I pointed to a small gap in the crowd. "There's a spot over there."

"Marz, can you go stake it out?" said Danielle.

"We can all—" I began, but Danielle grabbed my arm and shushed me. And then waited until Marziya was gone. Pushing up my glasses from where they'd started sliding down my nose, I said, "Hey, what's going on?"

Danielle licked her lips, looking suddenly nervous. "I, uh . . . wanted to ask you something. See, I don't want to do anything if you're not okay with it, but . . . um . . ."

"But what?" I asked.

"Um . . ." Danielle looked over at the DJ booth, I guess to make sure Soleil and Aimee were still in line. "See, it's about Soleil. She's been kind of, you know, flirting with me? Like, *all day?*"

All my internal organs shriveled up. This could not be happening.

"Uh, really?" I said.

"Really really," said Danielle. "She keeps, you know, *looking* at me. I can't tell if it's supposed to be flirty or not, but then she kind of linked her pinkie with mine at that panel a few hours ago, so I started thinking maybe it was?"

"Oh," I said faintly. I hadn't noticed any of that. Sure, I'd noticed Soleil sitting next to Danielle at the panel—Houses, Factions, and Districts: The Perks and Pitfalls of Narrow Self-Definition—and nothing had happened that I could see.

But there were those five minutes when I'd run out to find the bathroom, so maybe she'd done the pinkie thing then?

"I mean, thing is," she said, fiddling nervously with a lock of her black hair, "she's basically a solid ten on the smartness scale *and* the hotness scale *and* the awesomeness scale, and we're both from New York, and . . . well, she keeps talking online about how she doesn't believe in monogamy? But even if she *is* trying to be flirty, I don't want to do anything without talking to you first, because . . . well, you know."

"I know what?" I said.

Danielle shrugged. "Because you're her girlfriend. And you seem cool. And I don't want to step on anyone's toes."

I took a deep breath. And then another. I was not going to cry right before the karaoke competition. I was not, I was not, I was not.

"Why, um. What makes you think I'm her girlfriend?"

Danielle scrunched her eyebrows together. "Uh, everything? Why? Wait, are you guys *not* together?"

Without meaning to, I reached out and grabbed her arm. "No, I'm serious. You thought we were dating. Why did you think that?"

"Uh," said Danielle again. "I dunno! I mean, every time you guys join a thread on the FicForAll message board, it's literally all flirting, all the time. Like, oh, what was that one from last week? When that other girl was like, 'Come on, ladies, get a room!' and Soleil was like . . . wait, what was her reply? Hold on. Let me just find it again . . ."

She fished her phone out of her purse, tapped the screen a few times, then held it out to me. Sure enough, there was the exchange on FicForAll.

> **xKatsudonErosx:** Enough with the PDA, ladies! Get a room lol!
>
> **Soleil:** Hate to break it to you, but we already have one . . . at WTFcon next week! I'd give you our room number, but the place'll be rockin' so don't you dare come a-knockin'. :D :D :D

I read it again. Then one more time, just to be sure. Okay, yeah, if I squinted, I could see where Soleil might have been joking. But on the other hand, how could she possibly be surprised that I'd taken her seriously? She'd been saying stuff like that for months. Stuff like *I wish you were here so I could kiss you all over your pretty little face* and *I'm so lucky to have you* and . . . well, and *I love you*.

I'd told her I loved her, too.

"So, um," said Danielle slowly. "You're saying you guys *aren't* dating?"

I shook my head, handing her phone back. "No. Just, um, online flirting. In real life we're just . . . you know. Friends."

"So I should totally go for it," Danielle murmured.

"She's got a boyfriend," I said.

Danielle blinked. "Oh. Huh. Is he here, too?"

"No," I said. "And they're more monogamous than she wants people to think."

Danielle frowned, but before she could ask me any more questions, Soleil and Aimee found us again. Aimee and her friends were scheduled to go second, and Soleil and I were fourth. Marziya waved from the spot she'd claimed, right between a group of Slytherin-robed tweens and a group of exceptionally tall hobbits.

The lights dimmed. The DJ welcomed us to the Extravaganza and then called the first contestants up on stage: Todd Something and Noah Something-Else. Cheers erupted as they took the stage—the same two guys I'd seen a little while ago. They were still dressed as Sherlock Holmes and John Watson.

"Aw, yay!" said Marziya. "I saw those guys last night at the costume contest. They won Best Couple."

"Well, obviously they did," said Soleil. "Look at them. What I wouldn't give to be the meat on *that* sandwich. Am I right, ladies?"

I wanted to run away, or I wanted to throw up, or maybe I wanted, just a little bit, to punch Soleil right in the mouth. But then the music started.

It was "Bad Romance" by Lady Gaga. And there, up on stage, were a very dapper Sherlock and an ugly-sweatered John, grinning their faces off as they sang directly to each other.

Within seconds, everyone in the room was screaming their approval like their lives depended on it. And I screamed as loudly as any of them. Partly because it was a great distraction from feeling whatever I'd been feeling a second ago—and partly because these two guys were *awesome*. Neither of them could really sing, but it didn't matter. They were having so much fun up there, hips swiveling and hands clawing in motions that I vaguely recognized from the old "Bad Romance" music video. But then—

"Shoot! Nessie!" came Soleil's frantic voice, right in my ear.

"What?"

"They don't have the lyrics projected anywhere," she said, looking kind of terrified. "They're singing from memory."

"So?" I said—and then realized what she was getting at. "Ohhh, do you not have 'Defying Gravity' memorized?"

"Well, of course not! Every karaoke bar I've ever been to, they have a TV or something with all the lyrics." I raised an eyebrow; this wasn't a karaoke bar. This was WTFcon. What had she expected? "Arg. Do *you* have it memorized?"

"Just my own part, but yeah."

"Arrrrg," she said again, rubbing her hands on her thighs.

"Walk, walk, fashion baby," sang John, as Sherlock swung his mic around by the cord and strutted across the stage like it was a catwalk. Aimee, Marziya, and stupid Danielle all howled their appreciation.

"You could pull up the lyrics on your phone?" I suggested.

She made a face. "One hand for my phone, one hand for the mic. I'd look like an idiot up there."

Something inside me thrilled at the idea of being more prepared for this than she was—but I didn't show it. With a shrug, I said, "Either that or we drop out. Your call."

Up on stage, Sherlock was wailing about how he *don't wanna be friends*—and then they were on the weird French part of the song.

Soleil clutched her hair like she was about to rip it out by the roots. She looked totally terrified and, once again, totally stressed.

"Here," I said, "I'll look up the lyrics, okay?"

She gave me one single, worried nod, and I pulled my phone out of my bag. And turned it on just in time to see the battery run out. Ugh.

"Hey, mine's dead," I said. "Can I use yours?"

She rummaged around in her purse, found her phone, entered her password, and handed it to me.

Her texting app was open, but I closed it before I could see anything personal. I was no snoop. Then I tapped her browser open—and immediately recognized the website it was on. A header image that compiled snippets of fan art from at least twenty different fandoms. The words *All For Fic & FicForAll* superimposed over the image.

And there, right under the header, were the following words:

Welcome back, StraightFlush!

I blinked, and blinked again, but it was still there. Even though it couldn't be. StraightFlush was the guy—and it had definitely been a guy, right?—who'd attacked Soleil because her writing was "too gay."

But here was the very same screen name, logged in from Soleil's phone.

Maybe I was remembering it wrong. Maybe the guy's name had been StraightFlush with letters or numbers after it, and I was only remembering the main part, and maybe Soleil had registered another version of the same screen name in order to . . . I dunno. Reclaim it? Or something?

Yeah, maybe that.

Because the alternative was that Soleil herself had been StraightFlush all along. And that wasn't possible, because it just *wasn't*.

"Hey, girlie-girl, any luck with those lyrics?" said Soleil, making me jump.

Up on stage, Dapper Sherlock and Ugly Sweater John were taking a bow and waving at the crowd. As they left the stage, the DJ made some stupid joke about how bad their romance actually was, and then introduced Aimee and her friends, who were no longer standing with us. I hadn't noticed them leaving.

"Um, yeah," I said. "Just a second. Connection's slow."

I did the search and pulled up the lyrics, then handed the phone to Soleil. "Thanks, Nessie. You're the best."

"No problem," I said.

The spotlight shone on Danielle, who was holding the mic to her mouth. "This song," she said, "is dedicated to our favorite *Wonderlandia* fanficcer, and the hottest lady in this room. You know who you are."

The DJ started the song, and Danielle, Aimee, and Marziya began to sing.

Everyone cheered. Beside me, Soleil cheered more loudly than anyone.

This time, I didn't join in.

CHAPTER THIRTEEN

PHOEBE

My sore-as-hell Hufflepuff hands weren't enough to get me out of the mallet technique workshop before dinner.

"It'll still be educational," Mackey told me, holding the door open. "Even if you can't play. And hey, you remember Giovanne Clark?"

"Who?" I'd just noticed Scott and the other guys heading down the hall, and I edged to the side so that the door hid me from their view.

"Sound engineer, record producer? Those jazz fusion CDs I loaned you last semester when you had all those questions about analog versus digital recording, she was the—"

"Oh, right!" I nodded, pressing myself against the wall. "Yeah, I remember." I heard Scott's voice getting louder, and I held my breath.

"She's here, recording the showcase concert tonight. I might be able to introduce you—she'd have better answers to your questions than I did, for sure."

Through the gap between the door and the doorjamb, I saw

the guys enter the room. None of them noticed me hiding like a complete wuss.

I exhaled loudly. "That'd be so cool! Thanks!"

"Sure thing."

"But, um . . ." I fidgeted nervously. "Is there anything else going on right now that I could maybe check out instead of this marimba clinic?"

Mackey squinted at me. "I already said you don't have to play. Is something going on, Phoebe?"

"What?"

"Are your hands getting worse? I thought Mrs. Hwang was—"

"No, my hands are fine, I swear," I said quickly. "I'm just . . . tired."

He rolled his eyes. "You should try sleeping."

"Yeah, that's why I—"

"At *night*." Mackey gestured for me to enter the room. "Props for asking if you can skip a class to take a nap, though. That's a new level of guts even for you."

I forced a laugh. "Yeah, well. I tried."

Keeping my eyes fixed to the floor, I walked inside, headed straight to the back row, and slid into the chair on the end. The room was maybe three-quarters full, and Christina was already standing behind the marimba, which almost made me smile. She *would* be the first to volunteer. To my relief, Scott and everyone else were on the other side of the room. Everyone except . . .

"Hey."

I jumped as Brian squeezed past me and sat down. "Oh. Hey."

"He's one of the judges for the timpani solos tomorrow," Brian whispered, jiggling his leg nervously. At the front of the room, I saw a man with a shock of white hair and a paunch now talking to Christina. "Richard Rogan, Oberlin Conservatory of Music. I heard he's pretty tough."

"Ah."

Richard Rogan chose that moment to start the workshop, saving me from further conversation. After introducing himself, he asked Christina to play a chorale so he could critique her technique. I leaned back in my chair and watched her with a weird mix of pride and envy. I'd participated in a bunch of IPAC clinics in the last two years, and they'd all been amazing. I'd played surdo in a Brazilian band led by a samba master, kempul gongs with an incredible gamelan ensemble from Bali, and chekeré in an Afro Cuban music workshop. Even though we lost the competition every year, I always left Orlando really in love with being a percussionist.

This year, though, I'd just be leaving with Band-Aids on my hands.

It was hard not to feel bitter. Our ensemble ranked a record low, my solo was a total disaster, and now I couldn't participate in any of the workshops. I couldn't even bang on stuff in the exhibit hall—my palms were still too sore. All I could do was walk around getting audio clips of everyone else making music and being awesome.

Oh, and hooking up with guys, then running out of the room crying. I was a pro at that.

"He's on the scholarship committee, too," Brian whispered, tapping his mallets on his still-jiggling knee. "Mackey told me after lunch. I'm kind of freaked out, you know?"

His mallet bag was leaning against his leg, neatly filled with all the sticks and mallets that had been spread out on his bed last night. Including the triangle beater that had been to the dark side. I carefully kept my gaze averted, but my face and neck still felt flushed with residual embarrassment.

"Yeah . . ." My phone buzzed in my pocket, and I shifted in my chair to reach it and read the text.

> **Callie:** Hey, it's Callie. Moving forward with the sabotage . . .

"I wasn't all that nervous about my solo before," Brian was saying. "But now I am, a little. Or maybe a lot."

I glanced at him, taking care to keep my phone at my side so he couldn't see it. When I looked back down, Callie's second text popped up.

> **Callie:** Wanna help me ruin some turkeys?

I pressed my lips together hard to keep from laughing as I typed my response.

"Not like tomorrow's a scholarship audition or anything," Brian continued. "But I mean, first impressions and all. It's kind of scary. At least it's early—nine thirty."

This is both the best and weirdest text ever. Also, hell yes. I pressed send, then looked up to find Brian staring at me. "Sorry," I said quickly, tucking my phone under my leg. "Wait . . . why are you scared?"

Brian frowned. "Because I want to go to Oberlin? But I can't afford it without a scholarship?"

"Oh." I looked over at Richard Rogan again. "Brian, you don't have to worry about college auditions for another year. I doubt he's going to remember everyone from this workshop a year from now."

"Yeah, but he'll probably remember the timpani soloists. Especially the *good* ones." I stared at him blankly, and he sighed. "He's one of the judges tomorrow, like I said."

"Oh! Right. Sorry."

Brian ran his hand over his hair. "Are you okay?"

"Yeah! I'm sorry," I said quickly. "Just out of it today, I guess." At the front of the room, Christina headed over to sit next to Nuri and Amy while some guy I vaguely recognized from Bishop took her place behind the marimba.

My gaze drifted to the second row, where Scott sat with Jorge and the other guys. He'd texted me five times before lunch asking how I was doing, then given up. I felt guilty for not responding, but really, what was there to say? *Hey, that was fun until it was mortifying. I tried to wash the Mountain Dew sludge out of my underwear but they're pretty much ruined, so housekeeping is in for a treat when they empty the trash next to the fourth floor elevators. How's your butt?*

My phone buzzed again, and my shoulders tensed. I made sure Brian wasn't looking before taking a peek, and relaxed when I saw it was Callie again.

> **Callie:** Can you get some stuff for me? Bring it by later? My dad's practically got me on lockdown.

Chewing my lip, I responded: What do you need?

"Who are you texting?"

I glanced up to find Brian staring at my phone, which I tucked back under my leg. "No one."

"Phoebe . . ." He waited until I looked up. His face was kind of pink, and he swallowed nervously. "I just, um . . . if there's anything you want to, you know, talk about . . ."

I frowned. "What? No, there's nothing. Why?"

I could have sworn he glanced over at Scott for a second. The Bishop guy finished the chorale, and everyone applauded. Well, almost everyone. Jorge was leaning back in his seat, trying to get Devon's attention without Scott noticing.

A feeling of foreboding washed over me. *You're being paranoid*, I told myself, turning my phone over and over in my hands. Brian didn't know what happened with me and Scott last night. No one did.

Richard Rogan started correcting the way the Bishop guy rolled his thumbs in when he played, but I was still staring at Jorge. He was gesturing for Devon to hand him something. Scott sat between them, totally oblivious to the exchange going on behind his back. My palms started to sweat under my bandages. When my phone buzzed again, I jumped about a foot. I scanned Callie's text quickly.

> **Callie:** Cool, thx! I need some Nair, a metal nail file, and lotion that has lanolin.

Exhaling shakily, I glanced back up at the guys. Devon was passing Jorge a pair of sticks behind their chairs, both of them clearly trying to be discreet.

I typed my response quickly. No prob. Will get from my roommates.

Right when I hit send, someone let out a loud yelp. Scott leaped out of his chair and pulled Devon's drumstick out of the back of his jeans. Jorge and Devon were doubled over laughing. Nick started cracking up, too, and even Amy was giggling. Nuri pressed her hand over her mouth, then glanced back at me.

Oh god.

Christina shot Jorge a death glare while pretty much the rest of the room started snickering. Mr. Mackey half stood from his seat in the first row and gestured for Scott to sit down. Judging from his purplish-red complexion, the guys were in for a serious lecture after the workshop. I stared down at my shaking hands, hotly aware of Brian watching me.

"You all know, don't you," I whispered. "Scott told you."

Brian cleared his throat. "Well . . ."

I closed my eyes. Scott had actually told everyone. Not only that we'd fooled around—which was enough of a betrayal—but the gory details. It hadn't even occurred to me not to trust him. I'd assumed he wouldn't tell. And that he was embarrassed about what happened, too.

But no. He was just another stupid horny dude who had to let everyone know about the most recent points on his scoreboard. Like last year, when he wouldn't shut up about that Bishop girl. I was a complete moron for thinking the fact that we were actually friends would make a difference in this case.

Suddenly furious, I shoved my phone back in my pocket with trembling hands. "Where are you going?" Brian asked as I started to stand. "Phoebe, hang on—"

"If Mackey asks, tell him I'm sick," I said shortly. Brian grabbed my wrist, and I scowled. "Let go."

He eyed Richard Rogan nervously, but we were sitting too far back for him to hear. Christina, however, was twisted around in her chair and watching us closely.

"Don't just run off," Brian whispered. "We can talk about it after the workshop, okay?"

"Why didn't you tell me everyone knew?" I hissed back. "Oh, wait, I know—you were too busy gossiping with your girlfriend about it."

I wrenched my arm from his grasp and slipped down the aisle and out the exit. But Brian followed, letting the door close softly behind him.

"Phoebe, what the hell."

He sounded more confused than angry, but I was still shaking with rage. "Just leave me alone, okay?"

I headed back to the hotel lobby, walking as fast as I could. Brian kept up at my side, which only infuriated me more. I jabbed at the up button and stood there, fuming, while Brian stood silently next to me. The elevator was on the nineteenth floor and not moving. Perfect.

Finally, Brian cleared his throat. "Look, if you're mad at Scott, you should know that—"

"I'm not mad at him," I snapped. "I know he's a massive jerk. I just didn't realize *you* were, too."

Brian's eyes widened, and I ignored a flash of guilt. "What?"

"When did he tell you guys? Last night, during Halo?" I laughed sourly. "Hope he at least waited for Mackey to clear out. A heads-up would've been nice, you know. But it's fine. I know how hard it is to detach yourself from Christina and do anything on your own."

Brian's face was pale, which meant he was getting pissed. Good. Brian had this infuriatingly calm, even way of arguing that aggravated the hell out of me. My way of dealing with it was to plow over him. And the way I was feeling right now, I really needed to plow over someone. Whether they deserved it or not.

"I've been trying to talk to you all day," he said through gritted teeth. "I texted you this morning, and—"

"Yeah, I got your text. And you want to know why I didn't meet up with you? Because I knew *she'd* be there. Because she's *always* there now. I can't even remember the last time we hung out, just the two of us."

I paused when a bleach-blond woman approached, sexed-up toddler in tow. The woman stepped around me and pressed the up button as if it weren't already lit, then stood right next to us, fussing over her poor daughter's cowboy hat. The elevator was on the fifteenth floor and coming down. Thank god.

"I don't get it," Brian said quietly. "Why is this suddenly about Christina?"

"It's not sudden." I kept my eyes fixed on the elevator doors, willing them to open. "You've been dating for almost a month."

"Well, you didn't seem to have a problem with that until now."

"I don't have a problem with it."

I winced at how pathetic (and untrue) that sounded. Brian cleared his throat again.

"Look, are you . . ." He hesitated. "Are you jealous?"

My head snapped up. "Are you kidding me? No!"

He blinked rapidly behind his glasses. "Then what's your deal?"

"Ow, Mommy, that's too tight!"

We both glanced down at the little girl, who scowled as she loosened the strap of her cowboy hat. Her mother wasn't even pretending not to eavesdrop as she adjusted the hat's angle. The elevator doors slid open at last, and I said a silent prayer of thanks to any and all deities.

"Phoebe . . ." Brian stepped forward, but I waved him off and stepped on the elevator. The pageant mom followed, pulling her kid along and taking out her phone. I stabbed blindly at a random button. Brian just stood there as the doors closed between us.

I had this weird moment where All The Emotions Ever—guilt! regret! hate! anger! shame!—hit me so hard I couldn't breathe. And then the next second, they imploded. Gone. All I felt was a little tugging on my fingers. Numb, I looked down to see the tiny cowgirl holding up a Tootsie Roll with an earnest expression.

"Thanks," I said hoarsely, and took it. She smiled, revealing chocolatey teeth.

"It's my last one," she informed me. Her mother glanced up from her phone and scowled.

"Helvetica Bold Johnson!" she scolded, bending over and patting down her daughter's sparkly denim dress like a TSA agent. "Where *do* you keep hiding these things?"

I unwrapped the candy and popped it into my mouth, then pulled my phone out and started a text to Callie.

Thank you for enlisting me in this noble effort. You have no idea how badly I need the distraction of turkey sabotage. Also you might be my only friend in this entire convention center now, so. Flattered?

I read over it and snorted. Select all, delete. No reason to clue this perfectly normal girl in to the fact that I was completely pathetic. I quickly typed: Grabbing that stuff now, meet up soon?

and hit send. Okay, this was good. I had a plan. Steal some stuff from my roommates, get up to Callie's room as fast as possible, and do everything in my power to avoid every single person from Ridgewood High School for the rest of this convention.

CHAPTER FOURTEEN

VANESSA

Soleil and I did not win the karaoke competition. Unsurprising, since Soleil had spent our whole performance of "Defying Gravity" squinting at her phone screen and tripping over the lyrics, but it didn't really matter, because I'd only ever wanted to sing for the fun of it. It was Soleil who cared about winning.

Her expression got darker and darker as they announced third place (Sherlock and Dr. Watson's rendition of "Bad Romance"), then second place (a guy dressed like a Mountie, belting the crap out of "Livin' on a Prayer"), and by the time they got to first place (a whole bunch of Harry Potter characters singing "Bohemian Rhapsody," with Hermione doing the lead part), Soleil looked like she wanted to murder someone.

"Fine," she muttered to nobody in particular. "Give the awards to the *obvious* song choices."

"I think it was less about the song choice and more about the performance," said Danielle, who was clapping enthusiastically as the first-place winners accepted their trophy on stage. "And those guys were fantastic."

Soleil pointed her murder-face directly at Danielle. "They were totally basic."

Danielle, obviously confused, faltered for a second. "Well, I wouldn't say *basic*. But maybe their harmonies weren't exactly right . . ."

Plus, I thought triumphantly, *at least they knew all the lyrics.*

Up on stage, the DJ thanked us all for being a good audience, and the lights went up, and it was over.

"What a waste," said Soleil as she started following the crowd toward the door.

"I thought it was fun," I replied.

She didn't answer me. Just sort of huffed.

Marziya, jogging a little to catch up with her, said, "But you at least liked our performance, right?"

"Oh, yeah," said Soleil flatly, without even looking at Marziya. "It was great."

Marziya frowned. So did the rest of the Fangirl Trio. I didn't blame them. I mean, come on. Your three biggest fans dedicate a song to you, and you can't bother looking happy about it? I mean, she'd looked plenty happy just a little while ago. When the three of them had come down off the stage and joined us again, Soleil had given each of them a bear hug and then said, "Just you wait till this is over, I am going to *scream* about how awesome you guys are!" But apparently not winning had zapped all her enthusiasm away.

"*I* liked it a lot," I told Marziya. "You guys are all really talented. And the choreography was so great! Have you been practicing a lot?"

"Every weekend for a month." Even though she was talking to me, Danielle was still looking at Soleil.

"Well," I said, "it showed."

"Thanks," said Danielle, kind of sadly.

And, okay, maybe I'd slightly hated her before, when she'd said she was interested in Soleil, but now I felt bad for her. If anyone knew what it was like to be rejected by Soleil, it was me. So I leaned over and added in a low voice, "Soleil thought you were great, too. I could tell. She's just annoyed right now, you know, about the whole not-winning thing. She'll get over it."

Danielle looked skeptical, but she nodded.

Once we were out in the hallway, Soleil stopped walking and rounded on us. She was smiling again, but in this strained way that didn't reach her eyes. "Okay, ladies. Creativity Corner project planning meeting tonight, yes? Want to meet us in our room?"

"We could come over now," said Aimee.

Soleil shook her head. "I need some time to unwind, you get me? Change clothes, have some tea. How about you come over in an hour?"

The three of them nodded, a little row of bobblehead fangirls.

"Come on, Nessie." Soleil started walking away, apparently trusting that I'd follow.

"See you guys in a few," I said with a little wave, and went after Soleil.

She still looked ready to stab someone. Hopefully someone who wasn't me.

"Hey, why don't we go in the hot tub for a bit?" I said. "I bet that'd relax you."

"I don't need to relax," said Soleil, striding down the hall so fast that I practically had to jog to keep up with her. "What I need is to come up with the most kick-ass Creativity Corner routine ever, so I can actually win something."

"You mean so *we* can win something."

"You know what I mean."

I thought about that. Yeah, I did know what she meant. She meant exactly what she'd said.

"Hey," I said, dodging around a girl wearing a unicorn horn, "why didn't you tell them they did a good job?"

"Who?"

"Your Fangirl Trio."

She raised a pointed eyebrow at me. "Yeah, that's because they *didn't* do a good job. I didn't want to lie."

"Oh, come on," I said, even as my churning stomach told me to shut up, shut up, do not risk making her mood even worse. "They were totally fine. Plus that's not even the point. The point is they dedicated a song to you."

"It's not about the song choice, it's about the performance." Her voice went high in a snotty mockery of Danielle's breathy soprano.

"Yeah, unless someone dedicates a song—"

"And they were not totally fine," she continued, talking right over me as we entered the lobby of the hotel. "They were off-key the entire time! Although, heh, how would you know, right?"

"Wait. What?"

Soleil reached the elevator bank, pressed the up button, and gave me a pitying look. "Well, I hate to break it to you, sweetie, but you're a little . . . you know. Tone deaf."

I had no idea what to say. I wasn't tone deaf. I knew I wasn't. I'd been in my school choir every year since the beginning of junior high, and I'd even made Select Choir this year. That didn't happen to tone deaf people.

Before I could regain the power of speech, the elevator arrived. Soleil and I stepped in, and I gathered all the bravery I'd ever had, preparing to defend myself—but then someone else got in, too. The guy in the Mountie uniform. The one who'd won second place for singing "Livin' on a Prayer."

"Good day," he said in this weirdly formal voice, and pressed the button for the eighteenth floor.

Soleil pressed the one for fifteen and didn't reply. The elevator doors slid closed.

"Great job at the karaoke thing," I said, nodding toward the plastic-looking medal that hung around his neck.

The Mountie smiled and touched his wide-brimmed hat. "Thank you kindly. I liked your song, too. You make a lovely Galinda."

"You mean Glinda?" said Soleil, glaring at the guy.

"Actually," he said, "at the beginning of *Wicked*, her name is Galinda. She changes it later to Glinda in honor of her teacher, because he'd been unable to pronounce her name correctly, and when he died, she felt—"

"Hey, look, it's our floor," said Soleil loudly, pushing me toward the opening elevator doors. I gave the Mountie one last wave before I left; he waved back. As soon as the doors closed behind us again, Soleil muttered, "Geez. Mansplaining much?"

"Well," I said, as we headed toward 1502. "He's right. Glinda's name *was* Galinda at first . . ."

Soleil snorted.

I took a deep breath. "Also, I'm not tone deaf."

She chuckled darkly. "Oh, come on. Why do you think we didn't win?"

"Um, I dunno, maybe because you were reading the lyrics off your phone instead of actually performing the song?"

Aaaand cue the return of the murder-face.

"Okay. Sure. And riddle me this, Nessie: Whose brilliant idea was it to look up the lyrics on my phone in the first place?"

"Well, mine," I said. "Because you forgot to memorize them."

"I didn't forget," she said, jamming her key card into the door with such force that it gave her an error message. She tried again. "They didn't tell us we *had* to memorize them. You have to *tell* people that kind of stuff. You have to— Jesus H. Christ, why won't this stupid door unlock?"

I took her card and inserted it like a normal, nonviolent person. It worked fine. We went inside, where she immediately flopped down on her bed, closing her eyes and breathing heavily and, okay, on literally any other day, I'd've taken her silence as my cue to drop the whole karaoke thing altogether. But not today. Not after what she'd said.

"You should apologize to me," I said. It came out kind of shaky, and kind of sounding like a question.

"Ha. Right. For what?"

"For saying I'm tone deaf." My voice was a little firmer now, which, yes, good. "For saying I'm the reason we lost."

She opened her eyes and propped herself up on her elbows. "Oh. Sure. Sorry. I'm *so* sorry I said that, and I *totally* didn't mean it, like, *at all*."

Yeah. Right.

"And for being mean to Danielle and those girls."

"I wasn't mean—"

"Are you StraightFlush?"

Soleil went instantly quiet. She sat up on the bed, really slowly, and fixed me with a look that probably could've melted an entire glacier.

"Excuse me?" Her voice was dangerously soft.

Every cell of my body wanted to turn and flee, but I knew I couldn't do that. Not now. I had to know.

"On your phone," I said. "I pulled up your browser to look up those lyrics, and . . . and, and, see, the page was right there. FicForAll, I mean. It was up, and you were logged in, and it said—"

"You snooped on my phone?"

"No, I didn't. Like I said, I pulled up your browser and—"

"You shouldn't have snooped."

"If you didn't want me to see, you should've looked up the lyrics yourself!"

"Lower your voice, will you?" said Soleil, leaning back on her hands. "You sound like a seven-year-old throwing a tantrum."

She was right; somehow I'd ended up shouting and, okay, fair, I hadn't planned on shouting, but still. I didn't lower my voice.

"Answer my question."

"Don't give me orders."

"Are you StraightFlush?"

Soleil rolled her eyes. "Jeeeesus. Fine. Yes, I'm StraightFlush."

There it was. The truth I hadn't wanted to believe. I let out a long breath.

"You're a sock puppet," I said.

She laughed. "A what?"

"You made up StraightFlush and had him attack your stories so you could make yourself look good and get everyone's attention. Sock puppeting. That's what that's called."

"Oh, grow up, Vanessa. Obviously I wanted to get everyone's attention. I'm a fanfic writer. I wanted readers. That's not sock puppeting. That's *marketing.*"

I shook my head. "It's lying. You lied."

"So?"

"What do you mean, *so?* You created a whole fake identity just to make yourself famous!"

"At least I got famous on my own, instead of riding somebody else's coattails."

"What's that supposed to mean?"

"Let me paint you a picture, Nessie," she said. "FicForAll, circa eight months ago. I post the last chapter of 'I Knew You Were Trouble.' I get thousands of hits in just a couple of hours. Over the next week or so, the entire *Wonderlandia* fandom starts posting fanfic of my fanfic. Missing scenes and sequels and prequels and AU fic and whatever. I read a bunch of them, because who wouldn't? Most of them suck. But one of them's pretty good. So I start reading other stories by this author—an author by the name of Ness—and hey, she's got promise.

"See, I had this idea for a new story. But my fall classes were about to start, which meant I'd have way less time to write—and everyone knows you have to maintain a steady posting schedule in order to keep your fans. So I figure, why not ask her to co-write with me? So I ask. She sends me the cutest email you've ever read, saying it'd be such an *honor* to write with me, blah blah blah. We spend a couple days outlining this new thing together, and we call it 'Carry Me Home,' and we start posting it as we write, chapter by chapter. And you know what happens then?"

My stomach churned. Yeah, I knew what had happened then.

"What happens then," she says, "is that all *my* fans are suddenly interested in this new unknown author's stuff! Her hits start sky-rocketing, and her comments get to the point where she can't even answer them all. And I'll bet you anything she wasn't at all surprised by it. I'll bet you *anything* that she *knew* that was gonna happen. She was *counting* on it happening. I'll bet you anything that was the reason she said yes to co-writing with me in the first place." She grinned at me. "We all wanna be famous, Nessie. I used a sock puppet. You used me. So I'm not sure you're in any position to judge here."

For a second, I had no idea what to say. Not because she was wrong—but because, if you squinted, she was actually . . . well, kind of *not* wrong? Back when she'd first asked me if I wanted to write with her, sure, it had occurred to me that attaching my name to hers would boost my popularity. But it also wasn't the *first* thing that had occurred to me, and it definitely wasn't the main reason I'd said yes.

The main reason was that I'd never written with anybody else before, and I wanted to try it out.

But still. She wasn't totally wrong.

"Well, looks like that's settled!" said Soleil, clapping her hands together. "Wanna talk about our Creativity Corner routine?"

"Soleil—"

"I'm thinking we go with Harry Potter. I know it's so passé, but pandering to the masses might help us win."

"*Soleil,*" I said, and she blinked up at me, looking vaguely annoyed. "No. It's not settled. Just because I got famous from writing with you, that doesn't make it cool that you lied to me about being StraightFlush."

Soleil rolled her eyes. "Fine. I'm sorry I didn't tell you. Happy?"

"No."

". . . No what?"

"No, I am not happy." I took a deep breath and my hands were shaking and I curled them into fists. "You want to know the truth? I haven't been happy since I got here. I've been trying to be, because you're . . . well, you're *you* . . . but you're not . . . you're . . . I mean you're *different*."

"Oh yeah?" she said acidly. "Different from what?"

"Well, first you didn't tell me you had a boyfriend," I began. "And I thought, well, that's weird, but I'll deal. Then you ditched 'Carry Me Home' to read your own story, but I let that slide, too. And then you were so rude to Danielle and her friends just now— Oh! And by the way! Danielle told me earlier that she was interested in asking you out. And do you know *why* she told me?"

"Do tell," said Soleil icily.

"Because she wanted to make sure I was cool with it, because she thought you and I were dating." I paused, just long enough for it to sink in. Soleil narrowed her eyes. "And you know *why* she thought we were dating? The same reasons *I* thought we were dating. You keep posting all this suggestive stuff about us on FicForAll. You keep calling me, like, 'my dear' and 'my love' and whatever. We talked about *sex*, Soleil. Like, not even in a general way. It was *specific*. It was *us*. It was all, like, stuff we'd do if we ever met in real life."

"Oh my god," she said. "I told you, we were just kidding around—"

"No, we weren't," I said quietly. "Maybe *you* started out kidding around and, okay, maybe I was a moron for not seeing it. But I *wasn't* kidding. And if you didn't see *that*, then that makes you just as much of a moron as I was. Unless you *did* see it and you just pretended *not* to see it, in which case you're not a moron. You're just kind of a horrible person."

Soleil wasn't even trying to interrupt me anymore. She sat quietly on her bed, leaning back on her hands, watching me with narrowed eyes.

"I came here thinking I was meeting my girlfriend for the first time. My actual, literal girlfriend. I spent so much time waiting for you to, you know, *do* something. Kiss me, you know, or even just *talk* to me like you do online and on text and stuff. But you didn't—so *I* did—and then you played it off like, oh, no big deal, just a misunderstanding. And maybe it wasn't a big deal for you, and whatever, fine. But me? That was . . ." Deep breath, in and out. "That was my first kiss. You were my first."

For a second, Soleil just sat there, letting my confession sink in, and when she finally spoke, it was in this icy-calm voice: "So either I'm horrible or I'm a moron."

It felt mean when she echoed it back at me, but I stood my ground. "Unless you apologize to me and mean it, then . . . yeah."

"Cool," said Soleil. "Now pack up your stuff and get out of my room."

My jaw went slack because, *what?* Was she really kicking me out? Was she not even going to *try* to fix all the things that were wrong between us?

"You can't just . . ."

"Sure I can," she said smoothly. "Hotel room's in my name. You haven't paid me back for your half yet. So yeah, I can do whatever I want. Have Mommy and Daddy pick you up. Whatever you want. But get out."

I wanted to argue. I *should* have argued, maybe. But I didn't actually want to stay anymore. So I turned around, went into the bathroom, and swept all my stuff off my half of the counter. Not that there was much of it. I took my clothes out of the dresser, and I took my books off my side of the nightstand, and I shoved everything into my suitcase.

"Don't forget your laptop," said Soleil. "Wouldn't want to lose any of those precious unfinished novels that you always abandon after the first chapter."

Clenching my teeth together, I went over to the desk, unplugged my laptop, and slid it into the front compartment of my suitcase.

"Actually, wow," she went on, "this explains a lot. You abandon your novels because you get bored with them, right? You get bored because you never know what the plot is. And you never know what the plot is because original fiction is all about writing what you know, and you don't know anything about anything. You haven't *lived*, unless you count being online all the time. You're so freaking sheltered that you think a little internet flirting means we're *actual girlfriends*."

"At least I don't just change the names of my fanfic characters and try to pass it off as original."

"Get out," she said. "My real friends will be here soon, and we need the rehearsal space."

That was when I remembered something.

"Actually," I said, "remember how I was the one who registered for the Creativity Corner? Under *my* name?"

She rolled her eyes. "So change the registration to my name, duh."

I smiled at her. "Well. No."

"What are you talking about, Nessie? It's not like you're gonna do something without me."

"Who knows?" I said. "Maybe I will."

And I left.

As soon as the door clicked shut behind me, it took everything I had not to collapse onto the floor and start sobbing. But if I did that, odds were good that Soleil would come out and find me, or that Danielle would find me when she and her posse came over, or something even worse, and, just, *no*. I had to get away.

I definitely didn't want to call my parents about this, so that wasn't an option. Maybe I could find Merry and see if they were up for hearing about my drama; I could picture their face already, going all soft and sympathetic when I told them what had happened. But I had no idea where their room was. Actually, I had no idea where *anyone's* room was.

Except . . . no, that wasn't true. That girl from the taxidermy thing. Callie Buchannan. When we'd met and swapped badges yesterday, she'd told me where she was staying, in case I wanted my badge back at the last minute.

A few minutes later, I was knocking on the door of room 1535. And a few seconds after that, Callie was opening it.

"Vanessa, hey!" Her eyes took in the empty hallway, then fell on my suitcase. "Uh, what's going on?"

A lump rose in my throat because, oh god, *so many things* were going on. "I, um. Um." Why, why, why couldn't I get words out? Had I used up all my sentence-forming abilities on Soleil? "I just need, uh . . ."

Callie's eyes widened. "Here, come on in. Let me get you some water, okay?"

I dragged my suitcase inside, and Callie fetched me a cup from the bathroom. I drank the whole thing; she refilled it and handed it to me again.

"Chair," she said, pointing to an armchair identical to the one in my—in *Soleil's* room. "Sit. Talk."

Ugh, no. I'd already done enough talking to fill a lifetime. But I couldn't exactly come into an almost-stranger's hotel room and expect her to let me stay without actually telling her anything, right? So I told her the most basic version possible:

"I had a fight with my roommate."

Callie perched on the edge of the nearest bed. "Your roommate as in your girlfriend? Cirque du Soleil?"

Something loosened in my chest, and I actually found myself kind of smiling. "That's the one. She's not . . . we're not actually . . . See, she kicked me out. You were the only person—I mean, I knew your room number. I'm not asking if I can stay here. I just . . . can I leave my stuff here while I figure out what I'm gonna do?"

"No way," she said.

"Oh." I started to stand up again. "No problem. I'll just—"

"No, no. I mean, you should obviously stay here."

"Wait. Really?"

She spread her arms wide, gesturing at the room. Two huge beds, plenty of space. "I've got this whole place to myself, and . . . honestly, I could use the company right now. So yes, really."

I wasn't going to cry, I wasn't going to cry just because a girl I barely knew was being nice to me, I *wasn't*.

"Do you want to tell me what happened?" she said. "You don't have to if you don't feel like it."

"I really, really don't feel like it." I looked down—and caught sight of something. Something completely awful.

Shooting up out of my seat, I wriggled out of the shirt I was wearing and threw it across the room.

"Uh . . ."

And, yeah, now Callie was staring at me. Well, obviously she was, because I was standing there in jeans and my bra, like a total weirdo.

"Sorry, crap, I'm so sorry," I said, trying to cover myself with my hands. "I'll . . . uh . . . I'm not hitting on you or anything. It's just—it's hers. Soleil's. I've been borrowing her clothes."

Callie's face changed completely. "Ohhhh. Okay. Here, let me get you another one."

She knelt in front of my suitcase, unzipped it, and rifled through until she found a plain black T-shirt. She tossed it over to me, and I pulled it on. "Thanks," I said, sinking down into the chair again.

Callie nodded. "No problem. Make yourself comfortable. Put

on some music if you want; my speakers are over there. I actually have to get back to this, um . . . project."

"That's cool," I said. "I should do some writing, anyway."

I'd said it automatically, partly because Ms. Scherer's critique had been at the back of my mind all day, but mostly because writing was *always* my default escape route when things got stressful. But as soon as the words were out, I realized that actually, for once, I kinda didn't want to write.

"Hey," I said, "what kind of project are you working on?"

Callie's expression turned shifty. "My dad's doing his big Mounting a Strutting Turkey demo tomorrow. And I *might* have a plan to make it go, um, not so smoothly."

For some reason, this perked me right up. "This wouldn't be a vengeancey sort of plan, would it?"

"Decidedly vengeancey," she said. "You have no idea how much he deserves it."

Just like that, I no longer felt like crying at all. "Can I help?"

She looked surprised—not that I blamed her. If you told me an hour ago that I'd actually be offering to help with a taxidermy thing, I'd've said you were nuts, but now? Well, it wasn't like my night could get any weirder, right?

"How are you at mixing stuff with other stuff?" said Callie, grabbing a bottle off the desk. Wait—was that Nair?

"Depends on the stuff," I said. "As long as I don't have to, like, touch anything dead."

"Okay. I'm gonna set you up in the bathroom with some hide

paste and this"—she wiggled the Nair bottle—"which is not mine, by the way."

"Whose is it?" I asked.

"Phoebe stole it from her roommate."

"Ooh, she's in on the vengeancey plan, too?"

"Yup," said Callie. "You just missed her, actually. She should be back any minute—she had to check in with her teacher. Oh, and there's another thing you can help me with! I need to heat up the skin, and it'd be so much easier with two people."

"Wait, *skin?*"

Callie nodded. "Turkey skin. You don't have to touch it. You can be the wielder of the blow-dryer."

This was getting really gross, really fast. "But won't it, like . . . smell?"

She rolled her eyes. "No, it's tanned."

I gave her a pointedly blank look.

"Like a leather jacket. Except made out of a turkey instead of a cow. And not a jacket." She hesitated. "You don't actually have to help me if you don't want. It's really okay. And didn't you just say you have to write?"

I took a deep breath. Yeah, I definitely had writing to do. But on the other hand, Soleil was right: If I really wanted to write original fiction, I had to start living in the real world. Taking risks and having experiences and whatever else people did when they didn't live on the internet all day.

I doubted that she'd meant messing around with dead turkeys, but still.

"No, I want to help. I mean it. Show me what to do."

Ten minutes later, as Beyoncé called for her ladies to get in formation, Callie held up a leathery turkey skin and I carefully pointed the hotel blow-dryer wherever she told me. It occurred to me, then, that I'd been wrong before, thinking that my night couldn't get weirder. It was definitely weirder now.

And I actually really liked it that way.

CHAPTER FIFTEEN

PHOEBE

My plan to spend the evening avoiding everyone from Ridgewood by indulging in poultry vandalism with Callie was thwarted by my way-too-savvy band director.

"IPAC is supposed to be part of your music education," Mackey said, arms crossed. We were standing outside of the main ballroom in B-wing, where the showcase concert was about to start. "You don't get a week away from classes just to come here and hang out in your hotel room."

"But I—"

"Phoebe," he interrupted. "I have a sixth sense for high school drama. You're obviously having some issues with your friends, and I'm pretty sure I don't want to know what those issues are."

I had a sudden, vivid mental image of Scott pulling the triangle beater out of the back of his jeans and cringed. "You definitely don't."

"Right. So you want to avoid them. I get it. Come with me."

He pulled open the door to the ballroom, and I hesitated. "But I was going to . . ."

But I was going to go up to this random girl's room and play with some dead turkeys. Yeah, I couldn't say that. I squeezed my phone in my hand, wishing I hadn't left Callie's room after dropping off the Nair and lotion. But I would've been in big trouble if I hadn't checked in with Mackey after dinner.

He arched an eyebrow. "Yes?"

"Nothing."

I followed him into the ballroom and said a silent prayer of thanks when he turned and walked along the back wall behind the last row. If I had to suffer through this concert, at least I didn't have to sit with anyone else from Ridgewood. Then Mackey stopped outside a black door and spoke to a skinny guy wearing a black IPAC T-shirt. The guy opened the door to reveal a staircase, and Mackey gestured for me to follow him.

"Where're we going?" I asked.

"Sound booth."

My heart lifted a little. And when I stepped into the booth, all thoughts of dead turkeys strutted right out of my head.

A glass window took up most of the far wall, providing a view of the ballroom's stage and most of the audience. The stage was covered in a sampling of pretty much everything you'd find in the exhibit hall: drum sets, marimbas, vibes, timpani, congas, steel drums, and countless other instruments. Below the window was the biggest mixing board I'd ever seen, flanked by two giant Mac monitors. A woman with graying curly hair sat behind the Mac on the right, scrolling down a bunch of audio tracks. She glanced over her shoulder when we entered, then did a double take.

"Jeff!" she exclaimed, getting to her feet. "How's it going?"

"Great, you?" Mackey grinned broadly as he crossed the room and shook her hand.

"Same old," the woman said. "So good to see you again! And this is?"

She glanced over at me, and Mackey waved for me to join them.

"Phoebe Byrd, one of my students." He pointed at my hands. "Of scalpel fame. Phoebe, this is Giovanne Clark."

"Nice to meet you," I said. "And wait—you really heard about the scalpel thing?"

Giovanne chuckled. "Are you kidding? Kid plays a xylophone solo with scalpels in front of a few hundred drummers . . . yeah, people have been talking about it."

For a second, I wasn't sure whether to feel proud or ashamed. But the way Giovanne was grinning at me said *proud*, so I stood a little straighter and smiled back.

"Phoebe's the one I mentioned to you a few months ago," Mackey told Giovanne. "She helped me out with mixing Ridgewood's ensemble recording."

Giovanne's eyes lit up. "Aha, so *this* is the girl with the magic ears?"

My eyes widened. "What?"

"Yup, this is her." Mackey looked amused. "A fact of which she is apparently unaware."

"Magic ears?"

He laughed. "Maybe not magic. But better than average, at least." Turning back to Giovanne, he added: "I'll never forget her first day of band camp. Freshman carrying a drum on the field for the first time. Walks right up to the senior saxophone officer and asks him if he's telling his section to play that sharp on purpose."

"They were, though!" I exclaimed as Giovanne cracked up. "Everyone could hear it, but no one was saying it."

Mackey shook his head. "That's the thing, Phoebe. Most kids are so worried about their own performance, they don't notice how everyone else is playing—especially at first. You've always been more aware of ensemble sound. Why else would I ask if you wanted to help with that mix, anyway?"

I didn't know what to say. Mackey always let me use the band's audio equipment to put together my IPAC summaries, and he'd taught me a lot. But I'd never realized he thought I had an actual talent for this stuff.

"So I was wondering if Phoebe could hang out up here with you during the concert," Mackey said to Giovanne. "She's been missing out on participating in the clinics because of her hands, and I'm thinking she could probably learn a thing or two from watching you work."

"Absolutely!" Giovanne said. "Pull up a chair, Phoebe."

She settled back down in front of the Mac, and I spotted a folding chair leaning against the wall near the door.

"All right, I'm going to sit with the rest of the group." Mackey followed me over to the door. "Phoebe, we're all going to that ice cream place in the hotel lounge after this. If you'd rather head back to your room, that's fine—but check in with Mrs. Hwang. She'll be staying behind, too."

I nodded. "Thank you."

"Anytime. Thanks, Giovanne!" Mackey called before closing the door behind him. I pulled out my phone and sent a quick text to Callie. Sorry, can't make it. Gotta stay at this concert and check in w/chaperone later. I'll come watch tomorrow morning. Going ok so far?

A few seconds later, she replied. No prob. See you tomorrow! I slipped my phone into my pocket and carried my chair over to sit next to Giovanne.

"All right, Miss Magic Ears," she said, adjusting a few knobs on the board. "They'll be starting any minute, so let's do a quick rundown of the channels."

Giovanne launched into an explanation of which instruments were controlled by which of the rows of knobs on the board, and I did my best to memorize each one. That led immediately to a discussion about how to properly mic various percussion instruments, apparently something a lot of sound people kind of failed at.

"Helps to actually be a percussionist," Giovanne told me. "Most sound guys only have experience with drum sets. They—ah, here we go!"

The house lights dimmed, and a few spotlights glowed brighter. The audience cheered and clapped as six performers, all dressed in black, walked out on stage and took their places.

The next fifteen minutes passed in a flash. Watching Giovanne was incredible—it was like the mixing board was an instrument itself, and she was a master. She kept up a running monologue as she worked, explaining how she listened not just for volume and balance, but tone and overall blend. When the ensemble finished and the crowd applauded, she tapped a few keys on the keyboard and the audio tracks on the screen disappeared, replaced with one new track.

"Marimba solo's up next," she told me. "So all the stuff we've been talking about so far, that's critical listening. But analytical listening is just as important, especially when it comes to crafting an album. Any idea what the difference is?"

"Um . . . no."

"Critical listening is the technical stuff," Giovanne said. "Like how you heard that the saxophones were sharp, right? But analytical listening is about intent. As the sound engineer, part of your job is knowing what a musician *means*. What she's trying to say. Take your xylophone solo in that 'Big Top' piece. Tons of people have played that part, but they all say something different with it. What were you saying?"

I thought back on my performance. "Uh . . . please let me get through this without cutting off a finger?"

Giovanne snorted with laughter. "Fair enough. Okay, think about it this way." She nodded at the glass, and I saw a woman walking out on stage and up to the marimba. "She's about to play a solo. She isn't the first person to play these notes and rhythms in this particular combination. But she's going to own it. Make it *her* piece. I want you to listen, and tell me what she *means*."

I nodded and wiped my hands on my jeans. Honestly? I had no freaking clue what Giovanne was talking about. Even without scalpels, the only thing I ever thought about when I played that xylophone solo was not missing any notes. But Giovanne was awesome and I desperately wanted to impress her, so I had to give this a shot.

I focused on the soloist as she raised her mallets over the keys. The applause died out, and she allowed the silence to stretch over several seconds before she began to play.

The solo started with a rapid but soft ostinato on the high end of the marimba, which quickly crescendoed and led into a chromatic, bluesy run down the keys to the low end. After a dramatic rubato, with tempo abandoned as she pulled and stretched the rhythms like putty, the soloist settled into a minor waltz, her left hand keeping time with a chord progression while her right picked out a melody that was both sweet and haunting.

She was an amazing performer, and even though I still wasn't sure how to answer Giovanne's question, I suddenly understood what she'd been talking about. This soloist wasn't thinking about getting the right notes. She was saying something. But what?

Christina would probably know. I pressed my lips together, eyes glued to the soloist but imagining Christina standing there instead. Her solos always had meaning, too. I'd never thought about it before, but they did.

A short chorale swelled into a key change, this one still bluesy but with a little more levity. This led to a more staccato, almost playful section that gradually tapered off into absolute silence. The soloist's eyes were closed, mallets still poised over the keys. I held my breath with her, wondering if the piece was over, and hoping it wasn't.

Then, with a tiny smile, she played the same chromatic run all the way down the keys and settled right into the waltz, but this time faster and in a new key. After a variation on the first melody, she ended with the same ostinato, only this time on the low end of the marimba, softer and softer until it seemed as though her hands were moving but the mallets weren't even touching the keys. There was a suspended moment during which she must have finally come to a stop, but I couldn't pinpoint when it happened.

Her eyes opened, she lowered her arms to her side, and the auditorium burst into whistles and applause.

I let out a slow breath as Giovanne saved that track. "Well?" she asked. "Any ideas come to mind?"

I opened my mouth, fully intending to say, *No, sorry, that was awesome but I have no idea what it meant.* Instead, I said:

"Nostalgia. She was remembering something that made her happy, but she's sad about it, because she misses it."

As soon as the words were out of my mouth, I felt a blush heat up my neck. Because where the actual hell had that come from?

But to my surprise, Giovanne looked impressed. "Now that's a point of view. So what would you do with that?"

I blinked. "What do you mean?"

"You, Miss Magic Ears, future sound engineer. If this was your album you were recording, how would you use that point of view?"

"Er . . ." I felt incredibly stupid. "I don't know what you mean. The piece is over, you've already got the track."

"And what comes after you get all the tracks laid down?"

"Oh . . . mixing?"

"Exactly. That's when we take what they said, consider what they meant, and then shape it so that their point comes across to the listener as vividly and cohesively as possible." I watched as she pulled up another set of tracks and fiddled with a few knobs. "When the musicians finish, the engineers are just getting started. If you want to stick around for a bit after the concert, we can talk more about post-production."

"Sure, I'd love to!"

"Great." Giovanne smiled at me, then glanced on the stage where the next group of performers was taking their places. "So, ready to try again?"

"Yeah," I said, pulling my chair closer. "I'm ready."

CHAPTER SIXTEEN

CALLIE

"Ladies and gentlemen!" boomed a deep, resonant voice from inside Ballroom 2B, far too loudly for this early in the morning. "Here to teach you all the ins and outs of mounting a strutting turkey—pun intended, ha-ha—is two-time winner of the Simon T. Blackshaw Award for the Judges' Choice Best of Show, our very own Mister . . . Hamish . . . Buchannan!"

That was our cue. It was go time.

Dad straightened his glasses, cleared his throat, and gave one curt little nod—his standard psych-up routine when he was about to give a big presentation. It made him seem weirdly vulnerable and human, and for a second, my stomach ached with the thought of what I was about to do. Sabotaging his presentation at a conference this important was kind of a big deal.

But Phoebe was right; he had sabotaged my life, and that mattered way more. He had absolutely no right to go over my head and decide where I wanted to live. I wasn't some dead animal he could bend to his will; I had my own thoughts and feelings. It was time for him to learn that the hard way.

My dad turned and strode into the ballroom, both hands raised to the cheering, whistling crowd like an evangelical preacher. I slipped behind the demo table and made sure all my supplies were in place while he introduced himself. I had assisted him on this demo a bunch of times before, but never for a crowd this big. Every seat was filled, and the back and sides of the room were packed with even more people willing to stand. Jeremy was in the center, three rows back, and Dad's rival Harley was in the front row on the left side, totally unaware of how amazing his day was about to get.

Then I saw Phoebe waving at me through the open door to the hallway. When she had my attention, she gave me a big, cheesy thumbs-up, and I couldn't help smiling. It was super nice of her to come, especially when she wasn't even allowed inside the room, and it made me feel better to know someone had my back.

My dad joined me at the table. "For the purposes of this class," he began, "we'll start with a turkey skin that has been chemically cleaned, tanned in True-Tan Bird Tan solution, drained, and tumble-dried in puffed borax." He held out his hand for the first skin, and it occurred to me that he hadn't even bothered to introduce me as his assistant. Rage bubbled like lava in the pit of my stomach as I passed him the skin and watched him spread the right wing under the overhead camera, which projected its image onto a screen. He didn't thank me.

Considering how little he clearly thought of me, why the hell was he even trying to prevent me from going to Arizona? Was he just using me as a tool to punish my mom?

"We'll begin with the wings," my dad said, his voice infuriatingly calm. "When a turkey is mounted in the closed-wing position, you'll need twelve-gauge wires to help support them. I like to use ten-gauge for my flying turkeys." Without even looking at me, he indicated that I should hand him the wire, and I passed over the one I had dulled with Phoebe's nail file. "I've cut a thirty-six-inch length and sharpened the end, which I'll now insert it through the metacarpal, past the radius, ulna, and humerus, like so . . ."

Dad gritted his teeth as he struggled to push the dull end of the wire through the turkey's wing, then sucked in his breath as it bent and nicked his finger. I held my breath and eyed the audience, wondering if they would judge him for seeming unprepared. But instead they all laughed when he quipped, "This is one tough old bird," then waited patiently while he pulled a sharpener out of his kit and undid my careful wire sabotage. They even chuckled in sympathy at the story he told in the meantime about the hunter who brought him twelve turkeys at once and demanded that they be mounted by the next day.

Callie: zero, Dad: one. That was fine, though. The score would even up soon enough.

Dad sewed the wing incision closed and walked his audience through the process of stuffing tow filler around the wing bones to give the illusion of muscle and cartilage. Then he asked for the WASCO clay to reinforce the skin between the body and the wing joint, and I handed it over. I had to work hard to maintain a straight face as he dug his fingers in, blissfully unaware of the lotion I had mixed with the clay. Now all I had to do was wait for it to work its magic.

Dad's lanolin allergy kicked in about twenty minutes later, when he was beginning to explain the bonded tail-mounting method. As he fanned the turkey's tail feathers over a curved cardboard frame, he had to keep stopping to scratch the tiny red welts that had begun to pop up all over his skin. But he didn't excuse himself to wash his hands. He just wiped them on a towel and carried on applying the filler that would hold the turkey's tail feathers in place. It almost hurt to see how uncomfortable he was, and I wondered if I'd used too much lotion.

He deserves this, I reminded myself. *Think of all the times he's made* you *uncomfortable. How he's ignored you and bossed you around and humiliated you. How he acts like your feelings don't even matter.*

Dad dug his nails into the web of skin between his thumb and forefinger. Callie: one, Dad: one.

As the turkey tail set, I passed Dad the second demonstration skin, which had finished wings and a fully mounted tail, and he started explaining how to fit it around the manikin. "Never stretch a turkey's skin to make it fit over your form," he said as he eased the feathers closed over the rubbery manikin. "Trying to force it will cause it to tear, and pulling the skin too tightly will—aauughh." *Scratch scratch scratch. Scratch.* "Excuse me. Pulling the skin too tightly will make it impossible to properly adjust the feathers. See how easily this skin can be positioned around the form? If your skin doesn't—doesn't close—easily—*gah*." Dad clawed at the red bumps on his wrist so fiercely that I saw a few people in the front row flinch.

"Everything okay?" I asked, all wide-eyed innocence.

"I seem to be having . . . never mind. A fresh towel, please. As I was saying, today I'm using a Sportsman Series standing turkey form . . ."

Between scratches, Dad attached the wing wires to the body, then gestured for me to pass him the container of hide paste. He hesitated and stared into the sticky white goop for a moment too long, and my heart skipped as I worried he might be getting wise to my sabotage. But he seemed to decide that his beloved taxidermy supplies couldn't possibly be at fault, and he scooped out a dollop of paste with his fingers. Callie: two, Dad: one.

"Now I'll apply a layer of stiff Sallie Dahmes Hide Paste to the back and sides of the manikin," said Dad. "This bonds the form to the skin and provides support for the feather roots." He smoothed on the paste, and I crossed my fingers that the Nair and the blow-dryer would do what I'd anticipated.

A few minutes later, Dad scrubbed the extra hide paste off his hands with the fresh towel I'd brought him and handed it back to me. I surreptitiously unfolded it under the table, and when I saw a handful of dark knuckle hairs mixed in with the white paste, I had to bite my lip to keep from smiling. This was going to be epic.

Seemingly unaware that his hands were now totally bald, Dad moved on to showing off his prepared turkey feet and legs. I waited patiently, eyeing the body while he explained the "musculature" he'd created on the legs out of tow and thread. And then the time came to attach a leg to the body, and I held my breath.

"Insert the leg wire through the pre-drilled hole," Dad instructed, "and then reverse it into a U-shape and push it back into the manikin, like so." He grabbed the body firmly . . . and a handful of feathers came off.

My dad broke off in the middle of a sentence and stared down at the turkey like it had betrayed him. He rubbed his thumb across the hide, and a whole new row of loose feathers tumbled onto the prep table. I heard a murmur of surprise ripple through the crowd, and he shot them a scowl. "It's perfectly fine to lose a few feathers," he snapped. "That can be corrected during grooming. We'll just turn that part to the back—"

Dad lifted the turkey, and the skin slid and bunched under his fingers. A few stitches ripped loose as one of the wings drooped precipitously to the left, and when he tried to correct it, another huge handful of feathers pulled loose. Sure, losing a *few* feathers was normal and expected, even for someone experienced. But Dad's turkey now had an enormous bald patch on its side. This kind of thing only happened to amateurs. It was even more perfect than I'd imagined.

Callie: a million, Dad: one.

My dad stared at the ruined bird, his face a mask of shock, and everyone in the audience went dead silent and still. And that's why we could all hear when a woman in the second row leaned over to the man next to her and whispered, "I thought he was supposed to be *the* turkey man?" Someone else laughed, and then murmurs and whispers broke out all over the room. When I glanced over at Jeremy, his eyes were wide, and he had one hand clapped over his mouth.

My mistake was looking at Harley Stuyvesant. He was sitting on the very edge of his chair in his insane, patriotic button-down shirt, gripping both sides of the seat and grinning like he'd been offered a legally obtained dead panda to stuff. With his bushy beard and his little paunch, he looked like a deranged Santa Claus, and I just couldn't keep it together. I let out a snort-laugh.

My dad's head snapped up. For the first time all day, he looked directly at me, and his face flushed a dangerous shade of red. I wasn't sure he understood the reason for what I'd done, but he definitely knew this was my fault. I flinched back a little as his eyes bored into me, sharp as a scalpel.

I forced myself not to look away first. The deed was done, and there was nothing either of us could do to reverse it now. I reached down inside myself, and I found that glowing seed of triumph, and I held on to it tightly. My dad deserved to be exposed for what he was—a smooth, flawless surface with something rotten underneath.

He stared me down, a challenge in his eyes, and I held his gaze. *Still want me at home for the whole summer, Dad?*

He scratched his hairless hands very slowly. He breathed in and out, once, twice, three times. And then he forced a smile onto his face and turned back to the crowd.

"Ladies and gentlemen, we've just learned an important lesson about checking the expiration dates on our chemicals." His voice sounded impressively calm, like this was all a big joke. "Hide paste that's past its prime does not adhere skin to form properly, as you can see from this poor turkey. Fortunately, it was almost time to move on to our finished mount so we can talk about shingling and placing the feather groups." He turned back to me. "You can sit down, Callie. I won't be needing any more assistance."

I could hear the *I'll deal with you later* lurking under his words, but I still wasn't scared. I had way more ammunition on him than he did on me, and I was ready for the fight that was coming.

Dad reached down and removed a finished, ungroomed turkey from the box at his feet, the only one I hadn't messed with. "Now, when a gobbler struts, he bristles his feathers out along his sides and back to make himself look even larger and more impressive. This is called shingling. Let's talk about how to achieve that effect . . ."

I moved off to the side of the room. There weren't any open seats, so I sat down on the floor opposite the door. And when I looked up, there was Phoebe, still watching from the hallway. She pumped both her bandaged fists like she'd scored a touchdown, and I smiled at her and raised both arms above my head, fingers forming Vs for victory. I had won, and I didn't care if everyone in the room knew.

CHAPTER SEVENTEEN

PHOEBE

Maybe it was because I'd only gotten two hours of sleep. Maybe it was the Venti quad-shot iced mocha I'd chugged before the sun was even up. But Callie's super-dignified dad holding a half-bald dead turkey up in front of a roomful of horrified onlookers was the funniest foxing thing I'd ever seen.

After saying goodbye to Giovanne and leaving the sound booth last night, I'd seriously considered not going back to my room at all. But Mackey had already told me that Mrs. Hwang was waiting for me to check in. So I'd gotten in bed by ten, my head still buzzing from my conversation with Giovanne, and pretended to be asleep when Christina and the other girls came in and spent almost two hours talking about The Menstrual Cyclists. I still didn't know if they were kidding about using that name.

Once they'd finally gone to bed, I'd spent most of the night under the covers on my phone, consumed by that particular type of paranoia that only strikes in the middle of the night. Who else had Scott told about our hotel room shenanigans? What if Jorge made a joke about it on Facebook? What if someone found the coffee-soaked underwear I'd wrapped in a Ziploc and buried in a trash can under tons of empty Starbucks cups and crumpled napkins? What if Nuri posted a picture of it on Instagram? What if somehow there was *video*?

To distract myself, I read a bunch of blog posts and articles about sound engineering until I finally drifted off to sleep at around 3:00 a.m. And dreamed that #DrumstickSexToys started trending. So two hours later, after waking up covered in sweat and frantically checking all my social media accounts to make sure there wasn't some sort of new triangle beater meme, I'd snuck out of the room without waking the others.

Now, the high of watching a bunch of adults lose their minds over a Nair-slathered turkey was fading, and I felt a crash coming on. All I wanted was my blissfully empty room and a few hours of real sleep. As I swiped my key card, my eyelids were already starting to droop. But when I opened the door and found myself face-to-face with Christina, I was suddenly wide awake.

"Oh. Hey." I stepped around her and did a quick scan of the room. No Nuri or Amy, thankfully. "I was about to take a nap. Are you heading back out?"

"Actually, I was looking for you."

Great. I walked into the bathroom and half closed the door. "Why, was Mackey asking where I was? Just tell him I'm still not feeling well."

"He wasn't asking. Brian was, though."

My mouth went dry. I grabbed a plastic cup and filled it under the faucet. "Well, tell *him* I'm not feeling well, then."

I heard Christina sigh on the other side of the door. "Are you actually sick?"

"Does it matter?" I asked, irritated. "Look, I'm sure Brian told you we had a fight yesterday. And I really don't want to talk about it. Or about how Scott blabbed to everyone about . . . ugh. I just want to be alone, okay?"

Christina pushed the door open, and I stared down at my cup. "I didn't want to talk to you about Scott," she said coolly. "Or about your fight with Brian. That's your business. I wanted to find out if you had a good reason for bailing on him this morning. And hey, you do. Selfishness."

My head snapped up. "Excuse me?"

"I get that you're embarrassed about what happened with Scott," she went on. "It sucks, and I'm sorry. But it really hurt Brian's feelings when you didn't even show up. You could've at least sat in the back. Or hell, sent him a good-luck text. But no, you—"

"What are you talking about?" I interrupted, setting my cup down a little harder than necessary. "Show up for what?"

Christina's eyes widened. "Are you kidding me?" When I just stood there, she let out a weird little laugh. "Wow. Okay. His solo, Phoebe. This morning, nine thirty."

Oh.

Sharks.

Brian's timpani solo. He'd practiced for months, like I had.

He'd gone on and on about how nervous he was yesterday when Callie was texting me, right before . . . right before I'd called him a massive jerk. And then I hadn't gone this morning. Worse, I hadn't even remembered.

Grimacing, I pushed past Christina and headed for my bed. "How'd he do, anyway?"

Christina grabbed my arm. "That's all you have to say? Seriously?"

I shrugged her off, ignoring the uncomfortable twinge in my stomach. "Is it really that big a deal?" I tried to sound nonchalant. "It's not like I didn't watch him practice it a million times. So I missed one four-minute performance. Not like he's going to run off and cry about it."

Christina shook her head in disbelief. "Aren't you supposed to be his best friend?"

"I was," I said shortly. "But it hasn't really felt that way for the last month."

"Aha." A strange expression flickered across her face, and I silently cursed myself. "So he was right. This is about us dating."

"I didn't—"

"Even though I asked you," she cut in. "I told you I liked him and asked if it was okay, and you said it was. Did you lie?"

"No, I—"

"Are you jealous?"

"No!" I yelled. "God, I'm sick of—I don't—look, people just drift apart sometimes, okay? It happens. It's fine."

"Drift apart?" Christina repeated. "Are you . . ." She paused, looked down, and took a deep breath. To my horror, her voice shook a little. "Is it really that easy for you?"

"Is what easy?"

"Throwing away friendships."

I didn't know what was happening. All I knew was that I was sleep-deprived, and I hated this conversation, and I wanted her to go away. "Are you talking about us?" I managed to croak. "You and me? Because I'm not the one who threw that away."

Christina stared at me, her eyes red and shiny. Several long seconds passed. "You really think that, don't you?" she said at last.

"Well . . . yeah, because it's true. You're the one who started hanging out with those student council girls all the time. You're the one who suddenly wanted to spend every Saturday with them at the mall. You—"

"Unless you asked first," Christina said sharply. "I *always* said yes when you asked me to hang out, Phoebe. Always. Even if it was just to play video games . . . and I've never even *liked* video games."

"Okay, fine, but then you stopped inviting me when you'd all go to the movies or whatever," I retorted. "*You* stopped inviting *me*, so eventually I just gave up trying at all."

"I . . . you can't . . ." Christina sputtered. "Phoebe, you know *why* I stopped inviting you? Because you were obviously miserable! You couldn't stand those girls—you were constantly griping about them to me. *They're such airheads. They're so stupid. Oh my god, why would anyone want to own that many pairs of shoes?* You trashed them every chance you got, even though you knew they were my friends.

So yeah, I stopped inviting you—because if you really thought they were that stupid, you must have thought *I* was pretty stupid for liking them."

"I never said I thought *you* were stupid!" I said, and she let out a bitter laugh.

"You didn't have to *say* it. Just like you don't have to tell Nuri and Amy that you think they're idiots. They know it—it's obvious in the way you look at them. The way you *treat* them. The way you always have to make some sarcastic joke about Nuri being in the shower too long or all our makeup taking up the counter space or just . . ." Christina trailed off, gazing at me. "You know what? You're actually kind of sexist."

My mouth dropped open. *"What?"*

"The way you judge other girls," she said slowly. *"And* guys. Brian couldn't possibly care that his best friend missed his solo, right? *No big deal, not like he's going to run off and cry about it.* Scott must have *blabbed to everyone* about fooling around with you. He didn't, just so you know, but of course you assumed he did. It probably didn't even occur to you that he might be totally into you and also totally mortified that everyone knows what happened. No, girls are all dumb airheads, and guys are all morons who don't have feelings. And you, you're just better than all of us, aren't you?"

I stood there, stunned. Christina had never talked to me like this before. And nothing she was saying made any sense. But the part that disturbed me most was that she didn't seem angry anymore. She looked like . . . well, like she felt sorry for me.

And that—the pity—that was too much. I was done.

"So I'm the jerk here. Got it." I checked my back pocket for my key card and headed to the door. "Thanks for the wake-up call."

My body went on autopilot as soon as the door closed behind me. No tears. No thinking. Just walking to the only room in this hotel I knew belonged to a person who wasn't from Ridgewood. Down the hall, into the elevator, up to the fifteenth floor, turn left, and then I was knocking on number 1535.

When the door opened, I found myself facing not Callie, but Vanessa. Vanessa, wearing pajama pants and a T-shirt with her hair all sleep-messy. I squinted at her, remembering Callie's text last night.

"Did you . . . spend the night here?"

"No! I mean, yes, but not like that." Vanessa adjusted her glasses and smiled nervously at me. "Callie let me stay with her because I had a fight. With my roommate."

She tugged at the hem of her shirt. It was a Weird Sisters shirt, with eyes dotting the *i*'s, like the sticker on my practice pad. A lump hardened in my throat and I swallowed it down.

"That's funny."

"What is?"

"Your shirt. No, I mean, your shirt's awesome," I added hastily when she glanced down at herself. "It's funny that you came here because you had a fight with your roommate, because that's why I'm here, too. I mean, I'm here because I had a fight with *my* roommate, not because you had a fight with . . ." I paused, sighing. "Sorry, I'm delirious from sleep deprivation. So no WTFcon for you today?"

"Eh . . ." Vanessa said. "I wanted to do some writing instead."

"Oh. Callie's not back yet from the turkey thing?"

Vanessa shook her head. "She should be here any minute."

"Ah." I stifled a yawn. "Can I come in?"

"Oh! Of course," Vanessa said, stepping aside. A blanket covered the armchair, and a laptop sat open on the seat. I walked past it and threw myself facedown on the first bed, hoping Vanessa wouldn't ask any questions. I didn't want to talk about what had just happened with Christina. I wasn't even sure I understood half of what she'd said. She'd made new friends and she'd had more in common with them. How was that *my* fault? And Scott—she'd said he hadn't told everyone about us fooling around . . . but that was impossible. Because I sure as hell hadn't told anyone, so how else would they have found out?

And Brian . . .

Well. Christina was right about all of that. I'd forgotten about his solo, and then I'd pretended it wasn't a big deal. And that was *after* I'd called him a massive jerk just for trying to talk to me.

"Am I a giant shark-head?" I mumbled into the bedspread.

"What?"

Rolling onto my back, I watched her walk over to the armchair. "Am I a giant shark-head?"

"No!" she said immediately, picking up her laptop and sitting down. I covered my face with my arm. "Why?"

"My friend Brian's solo was this morning," I said. "And I skipped it to go to the turkey thing. Not on purpose—I actually forgot about it. Although he probably thinks I did it on purpose."

"But he'll understand once you explain, right?"

I shrugged, squeezing my eyes closed. Sure, he'd understand that instead of purposefully bailing on the solo performance he'd been angsting over for months, I'd forgotten about it entirely. Because apparently that was the type of friend I was. Selfish. Just like Christina had said.

And if she was right about that, what else was she right about?

CHAPTER EIGHTEEN

~CALLIE~

I had been looking forward to watching my dad slink off to his room in disgrace after the botched demonstration, shunned by the turkey-stuffing community. But his colleagues and admirers seemed to lose interest in the balding turkey almost immediately, and infuriatingly enough, everyone still flocked to the front of the room when the presentation ended. My dad stuck around to shake every hand and answer every single question, and I stayed in my spot on the floor, marveling at how patient and kind he was to people who weren't related to him. Even Jeremy, who had looked so horrified as he watched that Nair-filled turkey fall apart, came up to shake his hand and clap him on the shoulder.

My dad beckoned me over after everyone was finally gone, and I silently helped him clean up the prep table, which was littered with stray feathers and smears of hide paste and clay. Dad made a big show of dropping all the chemicals into the trash. When everything was packed, I moved to pick up the box holding the finished turkey armature, but Dad snatched it away from me.

"You'll take that one," he said, nodding to the box containing the mangled turkey. "You don't get to touch anything valuable from now on."

I didn't argue. What did I care which turkeys I got to touch? I had only cared about them in the first place because doing taxidermy meant being with Dad, and now that was the absolute last thing I wanted. It would be perfectly fine with me if he lived in the studio, and I lived in the house, and we didn't communicate again until I left for college.

I grabbed the box and trailed behind my dad all the way to the elevator. The convention center was noisy and crowded, but the silence between us felt oppressive, heavy with unspoken words. I wondered if I'd be able to breathe better once we got some of them off our chests and into the air.

The elevator dinged open on fifteen, and my heart sped up as I carried the turkey box down the hall. My dad had never been remotely violent, but a small part of me wondered if he would go berserk and start throwing things the moment we got inside the room. I almost wished he would so I could throw things back.

He didn't. But when the door slammed behind us and he turned on me, all the rage that had been lurking under his eerily calm façade was right there on the surface.

"In the entirety of my career," he started, his voice low and dangerous, "I have never seen anything so wildly unprofessional as what you did today."

I crossed my arms, looked him right in the eye, and shrugged. "Oops. Sorry."

"I know you're being sarcastic, Callie, but you *should* be sorry. Why would you do something so unbelievably stupid after all the conversations we've had about professionalism? Does anything I say make it through to you?"

"You really don't know why I did this?" I snapped. "I bet you can figure it out. You're a smart guy. Go ahead, take a guess."

"Seems to me it's because you're too caught up in your own selfish teenage angst to listen to anything I say. I swear to god, if you weren't my daughter, I'd fire you in a second for—"

"I talked to Mom," I interrupted, and he actually stopped talking. "I know she wants more time with me, and I know you told her I didn't want to go. Did you seriously think I wouldn't find out?"

"It doesn't matter if—"

"Where do you get off thinking you can do that? I'm sixteen, not four. *I* decide where I spend my time, and I'd rather it not be with the parent who destroyed my family!"

Everything went dead silent for five seconds, then five more. It was deafening. When my dad spoke again, his voice was quiet. "Your mother is the one who left, not me."

"It was your fault! You drove her away!"

"She chose *that man* over our marriage. She's a grown woman with free will. I don't know what you expect me to do about it."

"I expect you to *care!*" I shouted.

"Callie, I obviously care. I—"

"You go around telling people she's on a trip like it didn't even happen. I heard you do it with Jeremy."

"It's nobody's business if—"

"Listen, I'm not exactly Paul's biggest fan, either. But at least he cares about what she wants. Why do you think she chose him over you?"

"In case you didn't notice," my dad said, "she chose him over *you*, too."

That felt like a punch to the stomach. I wrapped my arms tight around my waist to hold myself together.

"The court mandated that I give your mother four weeks with you over the summer, and that's what I'm willing to give her," he continued. "She doesn't deserve one second longer. She's an incredibly irresponsible parent, and it's my job to provide you with a stable life."

"You think my life is stable?" I shouted. "I'm alone *all the time* unless I'm in the studio with you! You never eat with me, and none of my friends will set foot in our house because they're too creeped out by all the heads mounted on the walls. You constantly forget to pick me up, and you won't practice driving with me, so I can't get my license. You've skipped Christmas at Grandma's three years in a row because there was some dead animal that couldn't wait one more day to be stuffed. When's the last time you remembered my birthday? Do you even know when it is?"

A tiny flame of panic lit in my dad's eyes. "It's in January. January . . . eighteenth."

"It's the nineteenth. Do you know what you were doing on January nineteenth? You were skinning that cheetah that died at the Bronx Zoo. And do you know what I was doing? Canceling our dinner reservation and eating pizza by myself in front of *16 and Pregnant* reruns. That was some super responsible parenting."

"I'm sorry, but you know what an important project—"

"Do you know what the worst part was? I wasn't even surprised, because you never remember, and you never remembered Mom's birthday, either. When I was thirteen, I started getting her two presents every year because I knew she wouldn't get anything from you. Do you know how many nights I sat there trying to convince her that the fun guy she married still existed, that I still saw him in the studio, and that after this project or that project was done, you'd finally remember there were important things in the real world, too? I stood up for you! But all the projects ended, and there was always something else to skin, and nothing ever got better. And yeah, I *wasn't* enough to make her stay all by myself, and now she's in freaking Tucson, and you're trying to keep me away from her because *she's* irresponsible? Are you seriously surprised that I want to spend time with the parent who cares I exist?"

"She's the one who *left* you," my dad said. "I'm still here."

"You haven't really been here since I was in seventh grade! I mean, yeah, you stock the freezer and put a roof over my head, but you don't actually *notice* me unless I'm holding a scalpel. So I held the stupid scalpel, and I fleshed out your stupid carcasses, because I wanted you to remember that you *had* a daughter. But you know what? I don't care anymore." My nose was suddenly running, and when I wiped it on the back of my hand, I was horrified to find that I was crying. I was furious at myself for showing so much weakness in front of him.

"Callie—" My dad reached for my shoulder, but he was too far away to actually touch me. It was a totally empty gesture, like always.

"No. I'm done. You said you'd fire me in a second, but you obviously don't have the balls to do it, so I'll make it easy for you, okay? I quit."

"Hang on," my dad said. "Let's—"

"I don't want anything to do with you or your taxidermy. I'm asking Mom if I can live with her full-time from now on. If you want to take us to court, fine. Do whatever you want. But the judge is going to be on my side if I tell her you neglect me."

I was all the way to the door before I heard him say, "Callie, wait . . ." He sounded upset, like I had finally gotten through to him, but it was too late. It was *years* too late.

The door slammed behind me, and I fumbled in my pocket for the key card to my room. The door didn't open on my first three tries, and I started to panic; I felt like Harley Stuyvesant's musk ox was sitting on my chest, and if I didn't get inside *this second*, I was going to lose it right here in the hallway. I had a visceral need to be in my bed, where I could curl up in a tiny ball and pull the covers over my head and cry myself out. A scratchy fleur-de-lis duvet had never seemed more appealing.

And then the door opened from the inside, and there was Vanessa, barefoot and rumpled and dressed in a Weird Sisters T-shirt. Behind her, perched on my bed, was Phoebe.

For a second, all I felt was exasperation—seriously, couldn't everyone leave me alone to cry for *one second*? But then I registered the identical expressions on their faces—half embarrassed and half sympathetic—and what was left of my heart dropped directly into my stomach.

I had just spilled my deepest, most embarrassing secrets, and my new friends had heard every single word.

CHAPTER NINETEEN

VANESSA

I used to think there was no worse feeling in the world than being embarrassed. But as I stood there in Callie's doorway, I realized I was wrong, because actually the worst feeling in the world was watching someone *else* be embarrassed.

Callie wiped at her red-rimmed eyes, and I stepped quickly aside as she started to shoulder past me and into the room, except then she stopped right between me and Phoebe and sort of looked around, like she had no idea why she was even here.

Phoebe and I waited for her to say something, and it was . . . awkward. So awkward. Awkward sauce on an awkward sundae, with an awkward cherry on top.

I was about to speak up, like maybe to say I was sorry for over-hearing, or to ask if we should leave, or anything to get rid of the silence—but Phoebe got there first.

"Well, *that* sounded like it sucked!" she said.

Callie blinked a few times, really fast. "Yeah, it really did."

"Sit down." Phoebe gestured toward the armchair. "You look like you're gonna pass out."

So Callie sat, or really she kind of collapsed, just like I'd done last night. That was when I realized this was my chance to pay her back for taking care of me.

I went into the bathroom and filled a cup with water and brought it out to Callie. "Drink up. No passing out, okay?"

She gave me a feeble smile, and then did exactly what I'd said.

"Want to talk about it?" I asked, and took the empty cup back to the sink for a refill.

"No," she replied.

"You sure?"

"No point," she said, and drained the second cup in one gulp. "You guys heard the whole thing, right?"

"Hard not to," said Phoebe. "These walls are seriously thin. We weren't trying to eavesdrop. I swear."

"'S fine," Callie mumbled.

I looked at Phoebe and she shrugged and, thank goodness, maybe she didn't know what to say any more than I did.

"Well," I said slowly, "I can't exactly distract you with turkey blow-drying, like you did for me, but . . . um . . . do you wanna do something else? Do you have a deck of cards or anything?"

"I have an Xbox," offered Phoebe. "Well, it's not *mine*, but I could steal it for a few hours."

"I don't need you to steal more stuff for me," said Callie. "I'm fine. It's fine. I just need to, like . . . sit here for a minute."

Phoebe and I exchanged another look. "You want us to go?" Phoebe asked.

"Yeah, we can leave you alone if you want," I added, even

though I seriously didn't want to leave, not when Soleil could be lurking just about anywhere. "There are some panels I could check out downstairs, I guess, and that fan band The Trash of the Thing is performing later tonight, or—"

"Could I come with you?" Phoebe interrupted. "I won't if it's a huge pain to sneak me in, but I don't want to risk running into anyone at IPAC."

"Wait, why?" Callie asked and, oh, right, she didn't know all the stuff that had happened with Phoebe and her friends.

Wrinkling her nose a little, Phoebe shook her head and dismissed the question with a wave of her hand. "Nothing. Stupid drama. Sorry, I didn't mean to make this all about me."

Callie scrubbed her hands over her blotchy face. "Actually, could you please make it about you for a while? I want to think about literally anything besides my life right now. Misery loves company, right?"

"Yeah . . ." said Phoebe.

"So, I'm miserable. Keep me company." She crossed her arms over her chest and raised her eyebrows and, oh good, we wouldn't have to leave yet. I made myself comfortable on the other bed.

"Okaaaay." Phoebe looked at me, then back at Callie. "I hooked up with this guy the other night. He's in my ensemble."

"Ooh," I said. "Name?"

"Scott. Scott Lloyd."

"Is he cute?" I asked. "Do you have a pic? Can we see?"

Phoebe took out her phone and pressed a couple buttons, then held the screen out, first to Callie, then to me. It was a Facebook profile picture of a guy wearing what looked like busted-up cereal boxes on his arms and head and striking a superhero pose and, okay, if we're being honest here, the costume was pretty awful, but he looked like he was having fun, and that was kind of the whole point of costumes, right?

"Transformer costume," Phoebe explained dryly, and I smiled because under the costume, he did have a nice face, like definitely nice enough that I could see why a person, not a person like *me* obviously, but maybe a more boy-oriented person, might have a crush on him.

"Nice," said Callie. "Okay, so you hooked up with him, and . . ."

"And it was fine for like five seconds until it went nuclear," Phoebe said flatly. "Not *good* nuclear. Mountain Dew coffee on the walls, a bottle's worth of cheap cologne in my hair, triangle beater down Scott's pants kind of nuclear. Are you laughing at me?"

"Sorry!" I said, clamping a hand over my mouth because, wow, I had absolutely no right to laugh. Phoebe's hookup seemed like just as much of a disaster as mine had been, which was saying something, and she was all calm and cool and collected and, yeah, I definitely shouldn't have been laughing. If anything, I should've been taking notes.

So I calmed myself down and tried again: "Okay, though, an actual triangle beater? And like, was it *down* his pants or did it, you know, get stuck up his—"

"No!" said Phoebe. "No, I don't think that's possible from that, er, angle. At least, I hope not."

"I hope not, too," I said. "I've read a couple fanfics where stuff goes up there accidentally, and it's never pretty. Also ones about coffee spilling—although sometimes that's intentional, like there's this one Avengers fic where Tony Stark's got this coffee kink, and there's a threesome with him and Pepper and Steve Rogers, and he pours . . . uh . . ."

Okay, yup, now they were just staring at me.

I cleared my throat. "Anyway. Sorry. Coffee. Mountain Dew. Triangle beater. Go on."

"Uh, right," said Phoebe. "So that happens, and I basically run away. And yesterday morning, I found out that *Scott told everyone*."

"Daaaamn. That sucks," said Callie.

"But I should have seen that coming, right?" said Phoebe. "I mean, he's a guy. That's what guys do. They hook up with whoever, and they brag to their friends about it. He did the same thing with a girl from another school when we were here last year."

"Ugh, I'm sorry," I said.

"Not your fault," said Phoebe. "Anyway, I felt so gross about the whole thing that I went to watch the turkey extravaganza so I wouldn't have to see anyone from my school . . . but I forgot about Brian's solo. That's my best friend, Brian. And then Christina—that's my *former* best friend, she and Brian just started dating—she called me selfish for missing it, and then she said all this stuff about how I judge people and . . ." Phoebe took a long, deep breath. "Girls, right? Everything's always so foxing dramatic. Get a grip."

I looked down at the bedspread. Was I the same way? Dramatic? Was that how Soleil saw me? Was that why she'd kicked me out?

"Guys can be dramatic, too," said Callie, glancing toward her dad's room.

That was when someone's phone buzzed. Phoebe dug hers out of her back pocket and took one look at it and flopped backward onto the bed with a loud groan.

"Speak of the devil," she said.

"Christina?" I asked.

"No. Scott."

"What's it say? I mean, not that you have to tell us or anything, like if it's private or whatever . . ."

Instead of answering out loud, Phoebe tossed her phone onto my bed. I picked it up and read Scott's text: Hey, I'm headin down 2 starbucks. Meet me? 15 mins?

"Omigod!" I grinned at Phoebe, who rolled her eyes. "He wants to meet you downstairs? That's good, right? That's got to be good."

"Oooooooooh," said Callie, as I tossed the phone back to Phoebe.

"There's no 'ooh,'" Phoebe said, thumbing her screen. "He's probably planning on . . . I dunno. He'll stand me up, or he's got a bunch of guys ready to throw Mountain Dew on me, or—"

"Or he just wants to talk to you," I said, because I'd read those fanfics, too, where someone's just screwed up in a humiliating-yet-fixable way, then there's a conversation full of feelings and usually also some apologies, which eventually leads to kissing, then to *meaningful* kissing and then, you know, to other stuff because, hello, obviously, it's *fanfic.*

I didn't say any of that out loud this time, though, and that was probably for the best because Phoebe just said, "Yeah, right." Then she muttered aloud as she typed: "Sorry . . . I . . . feel . . . like . . . sharks . . . see . . . you . . . later. There. Sent." A few seconds later, her phone buzzed again, and Phoebe opened the text and groaned. "He really wants to talk to me, and he'll wait just in case I change my mind. Ugh."

"Maybe you should hear him out," said Callie. "What if he wants to tell you he likes you?"

Phoebe raised an eyebrow. "What if he's got a triangle beater ready to shove down my pants, just to make us even?"

"What if you stopped being paranoid?" said Callie.

"What if boys stopped *completely sucking* so I wouldn't *have* to be paranoid?"

Oh, this wasn't going anywhere good. Someone had to stop this from turning into another fight and, hey, guess who that someone was, just by default?

"Hey," I said, kind of loudly, "what if I told you guys about Soleil being a horrible person?"

Phoebe's expression changed completely. Bouncing a little on Callie's bed, she said, "Ooh, there's new Soleil gossip? Yes, please."

Callie turned toward me, too. "Oh, is this about what happened last night?"

I nodded, and suddenly there were two pairs of eyes laser-focused directly on me, and my stomach twisted a little at being the center of attention, but I took a deep breath and—and, okay, I didn't actually *mean* to tell them the whole story, all the way from the beginning, but I kind of had to, or else last night wouldn't make any sense at all, and once I started talking, I realized it actually felt great to get it all out, and before I knew it, there I was, telling them absolutely everything. Meeting Soleil online for the first time, becoming her co-author instead of just her fan, thinking she was my girlfriend, planning to meet her here at WTFcon.

I told them about all the time I'd spent in our room, waiting for her to kiss me, and I told them about Callie inspiring me to take matters into my own hands, and . . . yeah, and then, I told them about Soleil's reaction.

"So basically," I said to Callie, "you were right."

"I seriously wish I hadn't been," said Callie. "Ugh, I'm really sorry. She is the *worst*."

Phoebe looked at me calmly and said, "Am I allowed to murder her for you?"

"Legally or morally?" I replied, which made them laugh.

Then I told them about accidentally snooping on Soleil's phone and finding out that she'd created her own online arch-nemesis. Then I told them about the fight. In detail.

"And you know the rest," I said, nodding at Callie. "I showed up here, and you put me to work on your turkeys, and then I ditched WTFcon today so I could write instead, but . . . okay, here's the thing. I'm not sure I did the right thing—"

"What are you talking about?" said Phoebe, cutting me off. "You definitely did. You're pretty much my hero for telling that stupid Barbie doll what's what."

My cheeks went hot, and I fought off a grin at the compliment. "No, I . . . see, that Creativity Corner thing? The fanworks competition? I think I should have changed the registration to Soleil's name."

"Are you kidding me?" said Callie. "Why would you do that?"

"Because she was right. She had all these ideas about what to do for the contest, and I don't, and if I'm gonna keep her from entering when I'm not gonna use the registration myself . . . that's just *mean*."

"Serves her right," said Phoebe.

"It really does," said Callie. "Plus, you could still enter on your own, right? Or do something with your other friend, the one with the vulture hat. Merry, right? They seemed cool."

I smiled. Doing a project with Merry sounded like a great idea, except I didn't have their phone number or their room number or anything and, besides, even if they *did* feel like entering the Creativity Corner with me—and, come on, why would they?— odds were they'd already entered on their own.

"Nah," I said. "I don't have any good ideas. I only entered in the first place because Soleil wanted to."

"Just read one of your stories," said Callie. "What about the thing you've been working on today?"

I shook my head. "That's something original, and you're only allowed to enter fanfic. And even then, only if it's under five minutes long when you read it out loud, and only if it hasn't been published online before the convention. All my stuff's online already, so it wouldn't count."

Callie shrugged. "So write something new."

"In the next day?" I said. "No way. I don't even have any ideas! And my co-author's the worst person in the world—"

"In the *galaxy*," muttered Phoebe.

"—plus I'd have to get someone to read it on stage because there's no *way* I'm getting up there by myself, plus I'd need a beta-reader . . ."

"Wait," said Callie. "Wait wait wait."

"You know, someone who edits your stuff before you post it—"

"No, I know what a beta-reader is." She was leaning forward in her chair now, elbows on knees, and I could practically see her coming back to life. "But what you said about editing, and using someone else's voice . . . What if you did something like *A Thousand Words?*"

"The podcast?" said Phoebe, and Callie nodded.

"I don't follow," I said. "Write fanfic of the show?"

"No," said Callie. "Make an *episode* of the show. Like a spec script. You could just walk around and ask a bunch of people the same question, and then edit the clips into a story. That would count, right? Because it's inspired by something else?"

It actually sounded like an amazing idea, only it would be such a lot of work, especially when the contest was just a little over twenty-four hours away and I hadn't even started yet and, gah, did I even know how to *do* something like that by myself?

"I do like how they make stories out of all those different clips," I said carefully. "But I don't know how to actually edit audio stuff or, you know, any of the rest of it, either."

"I do," said Callie. "I could help you. It's not like I have anywhere else to be until Monday."

"And I don't have any recording equipment," I added.

"Sure you do," said Phoebe. "It's called your phone. You do have a smartphone, right?" I nodded. "It's probably got a recorder app already. I'll show you how to use it. And I . . ." She hesitated for a few seconds. "That concert my teacher made me go to last night? He brought me up to the sound booth, and I hung out with the sound engineer for hours. It was pretty badass. I'd love to do some audio for this, if that's okay with you guys. Like a soundtrack or sound effects . . ." Her eyes lit up. "Actually, I've been getting some really amazing sound clips from all the cons already! I bet we could use a lot of them."

I looked back and forth between my two brand-new friends, and they were so eager to help me out even though they barely knew me, and I was not going to cry, I was not, I was *not*.

"What if," I began slowly. "What if we all entered together? It could be our project as a trio instead of mine alone."

"Really?" said Callie. "You'd be okay with that?"

"For sure," said Phoebe. "Can we make it story about how guys are demons but Soleil is actually Satan?"

"We can't plan it in advance," said Callie. "When I went to the workshop with the *Thousand Words* people, they said that was their number one rule. They figure out what the story is *after* they do their interviews. If they do it the other way around, it makes everything seem scripted and trite."

"Mixing," Phoebe said with a little smile. "Figuring out the meaning and drawing it out."

Callie nodded. "Exactly. So the first thing we have to do is figure out what question we're gonna ask everyone."

The room fell silent. Phoebe flopped back down on the bed and stared at the ceiling as she thought, and Callie made soft little *hmm* noises, and I thought about . . . well, okay, mainly I was thinking about the improbability of ending up here in this room, with these two girls. They hadn't been internet friends first. They were both nerdy in their own ways, but neither of them was a fandom person, and yet, somehow, here I was, opening up to them in ways I'd never opened up to real-life people before.

"Hey, guys?" I said. "I think I have the perfect question."

EXCERPTS FROM PODCAST INTERVIEWS

SOLEIL [LAST NAME WITHHELD]
WTFCON

Phoebe: What's your name?

Soleil: Soleil.

Phoebe: And your last name? It won't be in the final project; it's for our records.

Soleil: No last name. Just Soleil.

Phoebe: Like Madonna.

Soleil: Exactly! Or Adele.

Phoebe: Awesome. Wow. Okay, so what convention are you with?

Soleil: WTFcon. That stands for We Treasure Fandom. I'm a fanficcer. I was on a panel the other day and everything!

Phoebe: Aw, I'm *super* sorry I missed that. Well, since you're with WTF, you know about the Creativity Corner contest, right?

Soleil: Yes.

Phoebe: Great. So, a couple friends and I are putting together a podcast, inspired by the format of *A Thousand*

Words. Everything you say will be completely anonymous. Interested in answering a question for us?

Soleil: Ooh, sure.

Phoebe: Okay. Can you tell me a secret you've never even told your best friend?

Soleil: Hmmm. Well, my best friend is my boyfriend, and we tell each other literally everything.

Phoebe: Literally like *literally*, or literally like figuratively?

Soleil: Like both. You get me?

Phoebe: Oh girl, I *so* get you. But, see, we still need something to put in the podcast. So how about a secret you've never told your *second*-best friend?

Soleil: Okay, are you sure this is going to be anonymous? Because this isn't the kind of thing you can just go around telling people.

Phoebe: Totally anonymous. Promise.

Soleil: You know that web series *Wonderlandia*?

Phoebe: Yeah, I've seen a couple episodes.

Soleil: Well, you know the guy who plays the Five of Spades and the Cheshire Cat? Marty Green?

Phoebe: I don't think so— Oh, wait! Is that the cute gay one?

Soleil: Ha! No, he's not gay. He's pansexual, just like me. That means you like *all* genders and—

Phoebe: I know what pansexual means.

Soleil: Ooh, look who knows everything. Marty and me, we met at a convention late last year, and we kinda . . .

you know. *Hit it off*. As in *really* hit it off. As in we *might* be secretly dating.

Phoebe: Marty from *Wonderlandia* is your boyfriend. That's your secret.

Soleil: Marty from *Wonderlandia* is my *other* boyfriend. You can't tell anybody.

Phoebe: Does boyfriend numero uno know about Marty?

Soleil: Oh, completely! We have a polyamorous relationship. That means—

Phoebe: I know what polyamorous means.

BERNICE JACOBSON
WORLD TAXIDERMY CHAMPIONSHIPS

Vanessa: Tell us a secret you've never told your best friend.

Bernice: I'm a taxidermist.

Vanessa: But . . . no, a *secret*. Aren't you here for the taxidermy convention?

Bernice: That's right. I entered two glorious boars for judging!

Vanessa: The ones who . . . um . . . love each other?

Bernice: Yes! Those were mine. Did you see them? This is my very best work.

Vanessa: Yeah, they're . . . they're really nice. But how about a secret?

Bernice: The boars *are* my secret. My best friend . . . she has no idea I'm a taxidermist.

Vanessa: Ohhh. Why can't you tell her about it?

Bernice: I wish I could. But she just wouldn't understand. She's . . . *[lowers her voice]* She's a *vegetarian*.

Vanessa: *[whispers]* Why are you whispering?

Bernice: *[whispers]* You can't say that word here, dear.

WENDI SCHERER
WTFCON

Callie: Can you tell us a secret you've never told your best friend?

Wendi: Oh, that's a really interesting question. Now, how are you planning to—

Guy: Excuse me, aren't you Wendi Sheeran, the literary agent?

Wendi: It's Scherer, but yes.

Guy: Okay, so listen, I know you're not *technically* supposed to do this, but I have this book—

Wendi: Before you go on: Are you signed up for one of my pitch sessions tomorrow?

Guy: Well. No. See, they were charging extra for those, and I'm not exactly flush right now. But if you signed me up, we could both make millions. Billions! That's a guarantee.

Callie: Actually, we were in the middle of an interview . . . ?

Guy: Ooh, are you recording this? Amazing. Keep it. It'll be worth a lot someday. Okay, so here goes. [*voice gets much louder as Guy leans too close*] My name is Guy Stanwyck the Third. That's S-T-A-N-W-Y-C-K. And I am the author of the future bestselling *Blood, Sweat, and Tears* trilogy.

Wendi: The . . . 'scuse me?

Guy: That's right. The first one is called *Daughter of Blood*. The second is—

Callie: Let me guess. *Daughter of Sweat*?

Wendi: [*coughs loudly*]

Guy: I know, it's genius, isn't it? I can't believe nobody's ever done it before, but I guess I'm just a rebel like that. But okay, so here's the thing. It's a trilogy. But! It's the first trilogy . . . in a *trilogy* of *trilogies*! Right? Right? Nine books! Amazing, right?

Callie: Please, please, please go on.

Wendi: No, wait, if you'll just sign up for—

Guy: So it's about this girl named Amethyst Orchid Jones, and she's . . . she's just your average teenage girl, you know? Except *she kicks ass*! And she has no idea how beautiful she is, until—

Wendi: There are still some slots open—

Guy: But listen, this is the best part. Ready? It's *The Hunger Games* meets *Harry Potter* meets *Game of Thrones* meets *Star Wars* meets *Fifty Shades of Grey* . . . but feminist!

Callie: So it's . . . sci-fi and fantasy and also porn?

Guy: It defies genre.

Wendi: Listen, Mr. Stanwyck the Third, I'd love to hear more of your pitch at . . . a later date . . . but I really have to go now. All right? I've agreed to give an interview to this young lady, and I'd appreciate it if you signed up for my pitch session tomorrow.

Guy: But the extra money—

Wendi: Tell them I said you could sign up for free. Password is "Kirkus."

Guy: Omigod, you're amazing. I knew you'd be amazing. Thanks so much! [*retreating footsteps*]

Callie: [*pause*] There's a password for free pitch sessions?

Wendi: Heh. No.

PHOEBE BYRD
IPAC

A secret I've never told my best friend . . . well, I don't think it's a secret anymore, but before this convention my secret was that his new girlfriend really bothered me. I mean, *she* didn't bother me, their *relationship* bothered me. I didn't tell him because I figured he'd think I was jealous—and surprise, surprise, that's exactly what he thought. I'm *not* jealous, for the record. They're both great people, so of course they're a great couple and of course I didn't want to screw that up. They should be happy. But she and I used to be really close, until . . . well, apparently until I dumped her. That's what she thinks, anyway. Even though *she's* the one who made all these new friends. And yeah, okay, she'd still do stuff just with me when I'd ask, and she'd even invite me along when she hung out with them, but those girls were so . . . That's not the point. Yes, it is. They were annoying as hell, and yeah, I told her that, but that doesn't mean I thought *she* was annoying! I mean, yes, I stopped hanging out with them, which meant I stopped hanging out with her, but that doesn't mean I *dumped* her, I just . . . um . . . wait, I think I explained that wrong. Sharks.

TODD FIORI AND NOAH MACIEL
WTFCON

Phoebe: Can you guys tell us a secret you've never told your best friend?

Todd: I have no secrets.

Noah: Yes, you do.

Todd: No, I don't.

Noah: What about Pinky?

Phoebe: Pinky?

Noah: His stuffed penguin. He sleeps with it.

Todd: Everyone knows that.

Noah: What about that time you went skinny-dipping in our neighbor's pool?

Todd: That photo was on Facebook.

Phoebe: Um, were you tagged?

Todd: Yes.

Phoebe: I'm going to need to see that. For . . . evidence. Podcast. Science. [*clears throat*]

Noah: Here's a secret. *He refuses to read Harry Potter.*

Phoebe: EXCUSE ME?

Todd: That is not a secret. That is simply something of which we do not speak.

Phoebe: That which shall not be named?

Todd: What?

Phoebe: Sweet jackals.

Noah: *See?*

Phoebe: Why won't you read it?

Todd: It's so mainstream. It's unoriginal.

Noah: Nope. That's not why. Tell her the real reason.

Todd: [*sigh*] Well, the entire *concept* of boy wizards—

Noah: Nope.

Todd: It's actually the fact that Dumbledore is—

Noah: *Nope.*

Phoebe: Um.

Noah: Do you want me to say it, hon? I'm gonna say it. *He has an ex named Harry Potter.*

Phoebe: What. *What.*

Noah: Dude totally sucked.

Todd: He . . . scarred me.

Phoebe: Heh, I see what you did there.

Todd: What?

JILLIAN BRZOZOWSKI
AND BEIGE BRZOZOWSKI
LITTLE MISS CITRUS

Jillian: Excuse me, are you with the press? I saw you interviewing that woman over there.

Vanessa: Well, I am doing interviews . . .

Jillian: Perfect. Come here, Beige! We're going to talk to this young lady.

Vanessa: Your daughter's name is . . . Beige? Is that a family name, or . . .

Jillian: Oh no. Color names are very in right now. Beyoncé named her daughter Blue, did you know that? We considered Magenta, but I think Beige is classier. Neutrals go with everything.

Vanessa: Um.

Jillian: Beige! Say hello to this nice lady.

Beige: [*tearful*] I WANT A DOUGHNUT.

Jillian: Beige was first runner-up in the talent competition yesterday. I'm so proud of her. Can you sing into the recorder, honey?

Beige: YOU SAID I COULD HAVE A DOUGHNUT. YOU PROMISED. MOMMY, I WANT—

Vanessa: *Okay.* So. Can you tell us a secret you've never told your best friend?

Jillian: Who, me? I don't see why you want to talk about that. Have you ever met a five-year-old who sings

Wagner? I bet you haven't. You should've seen her little Valkyrie breastplate, it was so—

Beige: I HAVE A SECRET.

Vanessa: You can tell me a secret if you want.

Beige: Mommy can't know. I want to whisper it.

Vanessa: Okay.

[rustling]

Beige: *[whispering]* Mommy says I have to hate Delancey because she's my arch-ne-me-sis, but I want to be her friend because she gave me a lollipop, and it turned my mouth purple, and Mommy was MAD, but purple is my favorite color, and it's Delancey's favorite color, too.

Jillian: Beige! What are you telling her? Why don't you show her your tap routine for tomorrow?

Vanessa: *[whispers]* I think it's okay to be friends with whoever you want.

Beige: *[whispers]* Even though I'm supposed to crush her?

Vanessa: Even then.

Jillian: Beige? Wouldn't you like to dance?

Beige: NO. I WANT A DOUGHNUT. YOU SAID.

Jillian: She's so contrary these days. She never listens to me. I don't know what to do with her. Good thing her sister Ochre is almost old enough for the toddler category. She's so much more . . . obedient. Where did—Beige! Beige, honey, where are you going?

VANESSA MONTOYA-O'CALLAGHAN

Okay, this is kind of dumb, because I agreed to answer this question. The question was *my idea*, even. But . . . wait, let me start over. My name's Vanessa, and I'm here with WTFcon. And I'm supposed to say a secret that I've never even told my best friend. But the problem is . . . um. Problem is, I don't think I have a best friend. My school's really big and cliquey, and there are some nice people there, but nobody who I really click with, you know? So, I had this online friend named Sol—uh, named Sarah, and I thought we were best friends. Actually, I thought we were way more than best friends, but it turns out she never thought that at all, and we had a fight and— Ugh, I'm sorry. This isn't even useful. Let me start over. My answer to the question is that I can't answer the question because I don't have a best friend.

SCOTT LLOYD
RIDGEWOOD HIGH SCHOOL

IPAC

Callie: Hey, can you answer a question for a podcast I'm putting together?

Scott: Um, I'm waiting for someone . . . but sure. I can talk until she gets here.

Callie: Tell me a secret you've never told your best friend.

Scott: Oh. Uh. I don't really have any secrets. It's impossible to . . . just, everyone knows everyone's business. At least, with my friends.

Callie: There has to be *some*thing you've never told them!

Scott: Well, there is . . . there *was*. There's stuff I *wish* I hadn't told them. Does that count?

Callie: What kind of stuff?

Scott: Just . . . I don't know.

Callie: Like *relationship* stuff?

Scott: [*laughs uncomfortably*] I, um . . . have you had any luck getting anyone to let a total stranger record that kind of secret?

Callie: You'd be surprised! Besides, it's all anonymous.

Scott: Well . . .

Callie: Come on, spill.

Scott: [*laughs again*] Okay, so my school's percussion ensemble comes to this convention every year, right? And last year I hooked up with this girl from another school. Everyone knew because, well, I told them.

Callie: You mean you bragged about it?

Scott: Well . . . yeah. Anyway. This year, I hooked up with another girl . . . from my school.

Callie: And you told everyone again?

Scott: No! I really didn't this time. Not at first . . . but they all found out anyway. And then, yeah, I talked about it when they asked. But I kind of wish they didn't know at all. Because . . .

Callie: Because you're embarrassed about it?

Scott: No, no! Because I *like* her. Like, a lot.

Callie: Really? Does she know that?

Scott: I don't know. I don't think so. It's already weird because we've been friends for a long time, you know? She got kind of freaked out and took off. I bet she thinks this is just like what happened with that girl last year, that I don't care. But . . . I do. I really didn't want her to go.

Callie: So are you going to tell her?

Scott: Well, I was. But . . . well, it looks like she's not gonna show up, so. I guess she's not interested either way.

HARLEY STUYVESANT
WORLD TAXIDERMY CHAMPIONSHIPS

Phoebe: Tell us a secret you've never told your best friend.

Harley: And why would I do that, young lady?

Phoebe: I mean, you don't have to. We're putting together a podcast, and we're trying to get diverse—

Harley: *Okay*, I'll tell you. I saw the Spice Girls in Dallas, when they were on their reunion tour. It was the best night of my life.

Phoebe: So tell me what you want? What you really really want?

Harley: I'LL TELL YOU WHAT I WANT, WHAT I REALLY REALLY WANT.

Phoebe: Yup. Yup, okay. I think . . . yup, that's all we need. Thank you. *Thank* you.

Harley: Zig-a-zig-AHH.

CALLIE BUCHANNAN
WORLD TAXIDERMY CHAMPIONSHIPS

So, my mom left my dad and me a little more than a year ago because she wanted to "start over." It's not like it was a total surprise or anything—things hadn't been good between my parents since I was in middle school. But obviously, I was still seriously angry and upset. I mean, my dad had pretty much stopped paying attention to my mom, but he'd stopped paying attention to *me*, too, and I had always imagined that if he and my mom split up, I'd live with her. We'd have, like, this adventure, start a new life, just the two of us. But then one day she was just gone, and I was still in the same place I'd always been.

But here's the thing: even though I was furious, there was this tiny little part of me that actually felt kind of *hopeful*. Because I figured that if Dad was my only parent, if he saw that I didn't have anyone else, he'd finally remember that he had a daughter. Like, that fun guy who used to hang out with me when we weren't in the studio had to be in there somewhere, right? And now that I'd basically lost my mom, it just seemed fair that I'd finally get my dad back.

I can't believe I was so stupid. Life isn't fair, and things change, and even with my mom gone, my dad didn't give a crap what was going on with me when I wasn't assisting him. I should've seen right away that he didn't have any capacity for real human feelings anymore. Maybe he never did, and I was just too young to understand that. I'm not really mad at my mom anymore. I totally get why she left now. And I can't wait to do the same thing.

MERRY NOVAK
WTFCON

Vanessa: So can you give me your name for my records? I mean, I know it's Merry. But is that short for anything?
Merry: Not anymore. My birth certificate says Meredith. And there were a couple years in high school when I told people it was short for Meriadoc—

Vanessa: Aw, *Lord of the Rings*!

Merry: That's the one. But yeah, I like just plain Merry.

Vanessa: Cool. Okay, so here's the question. Tell me a secret you've never even told your best friend.

Merry: Ohhh. Interesting. Hm. Well, how about a secret that's so brand-new that I haven't had a *chance* to tell my best friend yet?

Vanessa: That works, sure.

Merry: I met someone that I like.

Vanessa: Ooh, really?

Merry: Really. It's just a crush thing at this point. I don't even know her that well yet. But I'm hoping that'll change.

Vanessa: Yeah? Are you seeing her again soon?

Merry: Well. Yes.

Vanessa: What's she like?

Merry: Um, she's really pretty, in this offbeat-nerd kind of way. Really nice hair. Really great smile. Really friendly, you know? Just a nice, cool person. And she has these awesome glasses. They're these green tortoiseshell frames, and they look so great on her.

Vanessa: Oh! You mean like mine?

Merry: Yyyyyes. Like yours. And she writes fanfiction with . . . okay, her co-author's not my favorite person, but . . .

Vanessa: Wait.

Merry: [*laughs quietly*]

Vanessa: But you mean . . .

Merry: Yeah.

Vanessa: But!

Merry: Yeah.

Vanessa: That's, um. I. You're! Um! Hey, look, I'm late to meet my—um, but I'll catch you later, okay? Bye!

JEFF BELL (BISHOP HIGH SCHOOL)

IPAC

Callie: Can you tell us a secret you've never told your best friend?

Jeff: Sure. Last summer, I stole my teacher's car.

Callie: [*pause*] Wait, what?

Jeff: This is anonymous, right?

CHAPTER TWENTY

PHOEBE

As soon as we reconvened in Callie's room, I texted Nuri. Callie got to work uploading first her audio clips, then Vanessa's, onto her laptop. I flopped down on the bed and shook my phone, like that would make Nuri respond to my text faster. She checked her phone compulsively; this was clearly a power play, making me wait. I could imagine her and Amy right now. *"Can you believe her, asking us to cover for her after that fight she had with Christina?" "Ugh, who cares. Tell her you'll do it just so we don't have to share a room with her for another night."*

Okay, maybe that wasn't *exactly* what they were saying. For all I knew, Christina hadn't even told them about our fight. In fact, she'd probably gone straight to Brian so they could commiserate over what a rotten best friend I—

My phone buzzed. Sure, I'll just tell my mom you're in the shower when she checks in. But where are you staying? Are you okay?

I blinked, surprised at Nuri's concern. I typed my response and tried to ignore the inner voice, which sounded a lot like Christina, nagging me about judging other girls. I'm fine. Crashing in a friend's room. As soon as I hit send, I winced and added: A girl. No need to fuel any more gossip about Phoebe's Adventures in Sexland.

Callie's phone buzzed, too. She checked it, then scowled and rolled her eyes so hard she could probably see her own brain. "Are you *kidding* me with this?" she muttered.

"Everything okay?" I asked.

"Look." She held up the phone for us to see. "After everything that happened earlier . . . *this* is all he has to say to me?"

Vanessa and I leaned in to read the screen, which was displaying a text from her dad.

Dad: Do you know where the small pliers are?

Vanessa blinked. "Um. Wow."

"Dude," I said. "I'm sorry. That guy is a serious shark-head."

"Whatever. He's totally incapable of talking about actual human feelings. It's not like I didn't know that already." Callie tossed her phone on the floor and held out her hand for mine instead. "Can I get those audio clips of random sounds?"

"Sure. They're labeled in the recorder app."

"Thanks."

I kicked off my shoes. Time for a subject change to happier things. "So, who'd you guys talk to? Get any good interviews?"

Callie opened her mouth like she wanted to say something, but then changed her mind, closed it, and started typing furiously. I looked over at Vanessa, but she was acting super weird, too—she was curled up in the armchair, hugging a pillow to her chest and staring into space, her eyes super wide and unfocused behind her glasses.

"Um," I said. "Am I missing something here?"

"What? No! Nothing!" Callie glanced at me with an expression so guilty I almost laughed. "I mean . . . okay. There is something. Just . . . please don't be mad."

"Why would I be mad?"

Callie tapped a few more keys, then swiveled around to face me. "I went down to Starbucks and interviewed Scott."

My mouth dropped open. So did Vanessa's. "You—what?" I sputtered. *"Why?"*

"Because you said you weren't going to go and I knew he'd be there, and it's not like he knows you have anything to do with this project, so I figured it was a good opportunity for you to hear his side of the story without actually having to confront him. The guy clearly wanted to explain himself to you and he deserves a chance, and . . . well, and I thought if he really *does* like you, you'd want to know." Callie paused, giving me a smile that was part teasing, part uncertain. "Even if you're pretending you don't care because you're incredibly stubborn."

I tried for maybe half a second to look pissed, then shrugged and smiled back. "Well. Maybe just a little."

Visibly relaxing, Callie turned back to her laptop. "Sooo . . . wanna hear what he said?"

Well, obviously.

But also, no.

Because I could tell from her slightly smug expression that Scott had said something . . . well, *something*. And I'd almost gone down this road with him before. Like last year at IPAC, when a tiny part of me had thought our mutual competitiveness over the snare solo competition was kind of flirtatious, and then he'd gone and hooked up with that Bishop girl. Obviously, Scott and I were better off as buddies. I had accepted this. I *still* accepted this.

Then, completely without my permission, my brain started replaying the way he'd very gently massaged my palms with his thumbs. The way he'd kissed me, those first few seconds that were really soft and tentative, and—

"She's *blushing*!" Callie exclaimed, and I jumped. Vanessa laughed.

I sighed. "Just shut up and play the stupid interview."

Snickering, Callie turned back to her laptop. A second later, her voice came through the speakers.

"Hey, can you answer a question for a podcast I'm putting together?"

"Um, I'm waiting for someone . . . but sure. I can talk until she gets here."

Oh cats. I squeezed my eyes closed and fought the urge to tell Callie to turn it off. He'd actually sat down there and waited for me. I was such a jerk.

His interview was short, but by the time it ended my stupid emotions were all over the place again. *I like her. Like, a lot.* He'd told a complete stranger that, and he sounded like he meant it, and already I couldn't help imagining what would've happened if I'd gone down there to talk to him.

I'd assumed Scott wasn't capable of getting feelingsy, but he was. I'd assumed he didn't like me that way, but he did. I'd assumed he'd immediately bragged to all of our friends about hooking up with me, but he hadn't.

Christina had been right. About *everything*.

I exhaled slowly and stared at my knees.

"Wow, you really had no idea he liked you," Callie said. "So . . . think you'll go for it?"

"He sounds really nice," Vanessa added.

"Cute, too," Callie told her. "Even more in person than in that photo. And it's sweet that you've been friends for so long. I mean, I'm sure that makes it kind of weird, like he said, but the good kind of weird, don't you . . ." She trailed off, then scooted her chair closer to me. "Hel-*lo*? You okay?"

Swallowing, I nodded. Then I shook my head. "It's not that. Scott. I mean. I don't. Christina . . . She . . ." My voice got all cracked and weird, so I stopped talking.

An awkward silence descended. But I couldn't say anything, not until I was positive I wasn't going to cry. After several long seconds, Callie stood up and grabbed her purse.

"All right," she said. "I'm going to raid the vending machines, and then once we have the appropriate supplies, we can talk about it."

"Doritos," said Vanessa immediately.

Callie gave her a withering look. "Obviously."

A few seconds later, the door clicked closed behind her. I sat there, thankful Vanessa wasn't pressing me to talk. Actually, she wasn't even looking at me. She was picking at a loose thread on her pillow, her eyes all unfocused again.

"What's up with you?" I asked.

She stiffened. "What do you mean?"

"I mean you've been acting kind of weird ever since we got back."

"Oh." Her cheeks blazed pink. "Um. Well, it's just . . . something that happened when I was interviewing . . . someone."

I raised my eyebrows. "Oh yeah? A good something, or a bad something?"

Her mouth opened and closed a few times. Then she smiled down at her pillow.

"A very good something."

The way she said it was so funny, so sweetly innocent in a way that would've sounded fake coming from anyone else, that I couldn't help laughing. Vanessa buried her face in her pillow, but her shoulders were shaking with laughter, too. I was trying to decide whether or not to ask more when Callie returned with an armload of snacks and drinks.

"Rations for the night," she announced, dropping a bunch of bags of Doritos on the bed, along with . . .

Moaning, I nudged one of the bottles of Mountain Dew with my toe. "Seriously?"

"That's the only kind that was left . . . oh." Callie snickered. "Sorry, I forgot about your sordid past with Mountain Dew."

Vanessa was already ripping into a bag of chips. I wasn't hungry, but the smell of artificial cheese made me realize I desperately needed therapy in the form of MSG-laden corn products. "Was there anything spicy?" I asked, rummaging through the bags until I spotted a Salsa Verde. "*Yes*. Mine."

I leaned back against the headboard. Vanessa propped her feet up on the bed.

"I haven't been to a sleepover party since elementary school," she said. "This is fun. As long as neither of you draw on my face when I'm sleeping."

Callie's eyes widened. "Did that happen to you?"

"No, to another girl. I didn't draw on her," Vanessa added quickly. "The other girls did. And they didn't use permanent marker or anything."

"Still sounds more like fun than my sleepover experiences," I told her. "I think the last one I went to was winter break freshman year, at this girl Jen's house. I only went because Christina invited me. They spent the whole time painting each other's nails, so I went downstairs and played Jen's brother's Xbox by myself."

I wanted to find out if you had a good reason for bailing . . . and hey, you do. Selfishness.

My stomach churned again, and I crammed five chips in my mouth and crunched furiously in an attempt to get Christina's voice out of my head. Callie reached for a bottle of Mountain Dew.

"I tried having a sleepover once, in middle school." Her tone was a little too light. "They all called their parents and asked to go home before we could even order pizza."

"What? Why?" Vanessa asked.

Callie smiled tightly. "Turns out most twelve-year-old girls don't react super well when they unexpectedly encounter dead warthogs in dark rooms."

Vanessa's face blanched. "Oh."

"I'd be down for a dead warthog sleepover," I told Callie, and her eyes lit up.

"Yeah?"

"Yeah. But only if you let me paint their nails. Or, um, hooves, I guess?" She and Vanessa laughed, and I added, "Apparently I'm such a rotten person that I'd be better off hanging out with stuffed warthogs than other girls, anyway."

Dinosaurs. I'd meant for it to come off as a joke, but instead it sounded self-deprecating and whiny. Callie and Vanessa stopped laughing immediately.

"What are you talking about?" Callie asked gently. I swallowed and wished there was any soda besides Mountain freaking Dew.

"I'm talking about me being a jerk," I said. "Christina was right. I dumped her. I didn't think that's what I was doing, but it was. She always did stuff she wasn't interested in just to hang out with me, but I wasn't willing to do the same for her. And I should've been because . . . because she's awesome. She's an awesome friend, and I messed up." My throat felt scratchy, and the spicy cheese powder wasn't helping. "And now I've pulled the same garbage with Brian, too. I suck."

"I'm sure you can fix it, though," Vanessa said immediately. "Right?"

"I don't know. Would you forgive your best friend for treating you like that?"

Vanessa wrinkled her nose. "Well, if that was *all* my so-called best friend had done, then probably I'd forgive her. But . . . I mean, you guys have met Soleil, so . . ."

"Oh god." I closed my eyes and fought down the sudden urge to laugh. "Yeah, I should probably warn you. I kinda sorta interviewed her."

"*What?*"

I opened my eyes, fully expecting Vanessa to be furious. Instead she looked mildly terrified.

Callie, though, bounced up and down in her seat a little. Apparently our podcast project was helping distract her from the fight with her dad, because she looked fifty times peppier. "Oh my god, what'd she say?"

"You can hear it for yourself," I said. "Apparently she's dating one of the actors from *Wonderlandia*. Marty Green?"

Vanessa sat up straight, eyes narrowed behind her glasses. "Uh, no. She is definitely not dating Marty Green."

"Secretly," I added. "She said he's her *other* boyfriend. They met at a convention last year, and—"

"Yes, they did," said Vanessa. "For like fourteen seconds. In an autograph line. She wrote this huge fangirly blog post about how his eyes were *so big* and his hands were *so soft*."

I grinned. "And I'm guessing they didn't keep in touch after?"

"Unless you count the time when she tweeted something about the show and he retweeted it?" said Vanessa. "Definitely not. I mean, she didn't shut up about *that* for like two whole weeks. Believe me, if Soleil were hooking up with the *Five of freaking Spades*, I'd know about it. The entire internet would know about it."

"So she's a pathetic liar," Callie said.

"A pathetic, *delusional* liar," I added.

Vanessa kind of shrugged, and Callie added, "You're better off without her. You know that, right?"

Blushing, Vanessa ducked her head and grabbed another bag of chips. "I guess. It's just . . . Yeah, she's not who I thought she was. Not at all. But even without the oops-we're-not-really-dating part, it still sucks losing a friend, you know? It's not like I have all that many."

She sounded like Callie had earlier: a little too nonchalant. Callie must have sensed it, too, because she nudged Vanessa's foot with her own.

"You might have lost one this week," Callie said. "But you gained two."

I smiled. "Cheesy. But true."

"Hey, it's after eleven," Callie said, scooting back over to her laptop. "Should we listen to the rest of these clips and see what we've got to work with?"

"Start with Vanessa. Apparently she got *a very good something*," I added, waggling my eyebrows suggestively.

Callie's face lit up. "Oh, really? From who?"

Vanessa squeaked something unintelligible and went back to hugging her pillow like it was a life raft. Callie turned back to her laptop. "Well, these clips are all labeled. Let's look at who you interviewed." After a second, she cleared her throat. "Bernice? Who's that?"

"From your convention." Vanessa told her. "That woman with the two boars, you know . . ."

"The Humping Boars Queen?" I exclaimed. "Aw, does she want to mount you, too?"

Vanessa responded by throwing her pillow at me. I caught it and tossed it on the floor. "I don't think that's the right one," I told Callie.

"Next one is Jillian Brow . . . Broz . . . zos . . . yeah."

"Pageant mom," Vanessa said, looking slightly more composed. "I feel sorry for her daughter."

"I feel sorry for *all* of those girls," Callie murmured. "Let's see, then you interviewed . . . oh, hey, Merry!"

"Oh, good call interviewing them," I told Vanessa. "I don't know why I didn't think to . . ." I stopped, because Vanessa's face was quickly going from red to nuclear. "Um. Callie."

Callie spun around in her chair, and her eyes widened. "Oh. *Oh.*"

"What'd they say?" I leaned forward eagerly, but Vanessa shook her head, mute.

"Did you get a secret out of them?" Callie asked. Vanessa nodded.

"And that secret was the *very good something*?" I pressed. Another nod.

Callie arched an eyebrow. "And would that *very good something* by any chance have to do with *you*?" Pause.

Nod.

"*Ha!*" I yelled, thumping my fist on the bedspread in triumph and smashing my chips in the process. "Merry likes you!"

"So can we still use the clip?" Callie asked teasingly. "Or is it not suitable for younger audiences?"

"Oh my god, nothing like that—no!" Vanessa said, curling up into a little ball. "I didn't even tell them that I . . ."

"Like them, too?" I supplied, and she nodded again. "Well, what *did* you say?"

"I don't even remember. Something gibberish. Then I freaked out and ran away."

"Aw," Callie said. "I'm sure it wasn't as bad as you think. Let's listen."

"Oh god. Fine." As Callie opened the clip, I returned to attempting to drown my guilt in spicy powdered cheese.

But for the first time all day, I felt hopeful. So far, this IPAC had sucked in about a zillion different ways. I'd royally screwed up with Brian and Christina, and very possibly with Scott, too. I'd met Callie and Vanessa, though, so the convention wasn't a total bust. Sure, we barely knew each other. But I'd confessed all my friendship screwups, and they still seemed to think I was worth keeping around.

A strange thought occurred to me. Back in my room, Christina was probably having a similar evening with Nuri and Amy, eating junk food and laughing and griping and just . . . hanging out. Thinking about Christina made my chest ache worse than ever, but it also made me smile. If I could bond with these girls I'd only just met, maybe there was a chance I could fix things with the one I'd known since sixth grade.

CHAPTER TWENTY-ONE

CALLIE

Vanessa, Phoebe, and I all fell asleep on one of the double beds in a tangle of laptop cables and empty Doritos bags. When I woke up hours later, light was streaming through the curtains, someone's knee was wedged into the back of my shoulder, and there was a Mountain Dew bottle resting against my forehead. I batted it away and scrambled into a sitting position, certain I was late to shop for coyote throats or something. But then yesterday came back to me in a horrible rush—the sabotage, the yelling, the accusations—and I remembered that my coyote-throat-shopping days were over forever. That rock-on-my-chest feeling started up again, and I fought for a deep breath.

This is what you wanted, I told myself. *He can't order you around anymore. You're free.*

The thing was, I didn't really feel free. I just felt lonely.

I forced myself to retrieve my phone from where it had been lying on the carpet all night. There was one text from my dad, and despite everything that had happened yesterday, a tiny part of me still hoped it would contain an apology or at least a request to talk later. But all it said was, Please confirm you're alive in there.

The tiny spark of hope flickered and died. Alive, I wrote, and then I turned the phone off and dropped it back on the floor. I extracted my laptop from under Vanessa's foot, moved onto the other bed with my headphones, and started listening to yesterday's interviews again. If I had learned one thing from my dad, it was that burying yourself in your work was a pretty effective coping strategy.

The other girls woke up half an hour later, when Vanessa rolled over and accidentally elbowed Phoebe in the stomach. Phoebe made us all coffee—Mountain Dew–free—and we dove right back into podcast-land without bothering to change out of our pajamas. We made pretty good progress for a couple of hours, piecing together clips and crafting our narrative, but soon all three of us were too hungry to think.

"Room service?" I suggested. "I don't feel like moving."

The moment I said it, I thought of my whole family curled up on a big hotel bed, eating our room service burgers, and suddenly I wasn't very hungry anymore. I was relieved when Phoebe wrinkled her nose and said, "I'm not paying twenty bucks for a mediocre sandwich."

"There's a crepe kiosk in A-wing that's not bad," Vanessa said. "I can head down there and grab us some stuff, if you want. I have to turn in our Creativity Corner form anyway."

Phoebe grabbed her jeans off the floor. "I'll walk out with you.

I need to take care of a couple of things, too. What do you feel like eating, Callie?"

"Eh, whatever," I said. "I don't really care. Get me something with cheese."

Phoebe rolled her eyes on her way out of the room. "Well, obviously. We're not monsters."

They'd only been gone a few minutes before there was a knock on the door, and I left the interview tracks playing as I got up to answer it. "Sorry, I forgot to give you money," I said as I pulled it open. "Let me get—"

But it wasn't Phoebe or Vanessa. It was Jeremy.

"Oh!" My hands flew up to fix my messy ponytail, and then I realized I wasn't wearing a bra, so I left my snarled hair alone and crossed my arms over my chest instead. "I, um— What are you—"

"Hey, I brought you these." He held up a box of saltines and a bottle of ginger ale. "Are you feeling any better?"

"Am I . . . what?"

"Your dad told me you were sick. When we had dinner last night? I wanted to make sure you had everything you needed."

He was such a freaking *good person* that it made me want to hit him and hug him at the same time. "I'm— Thank you," I managed. "That's so nice of you. But I'm actually not sick."

"That's weird. I could've sworn he said you couldn't eat with us because you had a stomach bug. Maybe I misunderstood."

"He didn't even tell me you guys were having dinner. We aren't really speaking right now."

"Wait, *what?*"

"We had a huge fight." I almost told Jeremy more, but then I remembered how he'd shut me down the other day. He had made it very clear that he wasn't interested in our family drama. I waved my hand like I could erase the few words I'd already said. "Don't worry about it. Do you want to come in for a second?"

Jeremy looked a bit bewildered, but he said, "Yeah, okay."

He followed me inside and set the crackers and ginger ale on the desk, and I grabbed Vanessa's hoodie from the back of the chair and wrapped it around myself. I was suddenly very aware of all the empty chip bags and soda bottles scattered around, and I gathered some of them up and crammed them into the tiny trash can. Soleil's shirt was still crumpled in the corner, so I stuffed that in, too.

"I don't know. I don't think so," said Scott's voice from my laptop speakers. *"It's already weird because we've been friends for a long time, you know?"*

"Sorry for the mess," I said. "I didn't eat all of these chips myself."

"I wouldn't judge you if you had. Doritos are the best. What are you listening to?"

"Well, I was," said Scott. *"But . . . well, it looks like she's not gonna show up, so. I guess she's not interested either way."*

"I'm working on a project with some friends," I said.

"Cool. A radio thing?"

"Sort of. It's for—"

And then my computer skipped to the next track, and *my* voice came out of the speakers. *"So, my mom left my dad and me a little*

*more than a year ago because she wanted to 'start over'. It's not like it
was a total surprise or anything—"*

I lunged for the laptop and slammed it shut, but it was too late.
A crease appeared between Jeremy's eyebrows. "Was that . . . you?"

"Um. Yeah." And then, for no reason I could fathom, I said,
"Sorry."

"Why are you apologizing? Cal . . . did your parents split up?"

I looked at the floor. "Yeah."

"Oh my god," Jeremy said. "I'm so sorry. Why didn't you
tell me?"

I shrugged. "You said you didn't want to hear about my family
stuff."

"I didn't mean— Man, I had no idea you were going through
that. Your dad didn't mention anything about it." Jeremy sat down
on the edge of the bed. "So . . . where did she go, exactly?"

"Arizona. She moved in with her boyfriend. Paul. I guess they
had already been together for, like, a while. Not that she told me.
My family's not super big on telling me things, as it turns out."

"Do you still see her?"

"I didn't want to for a while, but we're back on pretty good
terms now, so I see her during school breaks and four weeks during the summer. I wish it was more. I actually just found out the
other day that she asked if she could take me for the whole summer, but my darling father said no without even asking me. He
told her I refused to go and that she'd have to take us to court if
she wanted more time with me." I swallowed hard. "That's what
we fought about, actually. I mean, that and the fact that I totally

ruined his demo yesterday. On purpose. And I told him I was going to go live with Mom full-time. So . . . yeah."

Jeremy's eyes widened, and I wondered for a second if he was going to reprimand me for being an awful person. But he just said, "*Man*, Callie. This all sucks so much."

I nodded. When I'd told Phoebe what was going on with my family the other day, the words had come out just fine, riding a wave of anger and adrenaline. But now it felt like they were piling up in my throat, stopping my breath. "Just twenty more months until I turn eighteen, and then I don't have to live with anyone. I can make it that long, right?"

"Hey," Jeremy said, his voice so gentle it hurt. "Come here."

I went over and sat next to him on the bed. He put a hand on my back, and it felt safe, like someone was anchoring me. My eyes filled up with tears, which I tried my best to blink away.

"They love you so much," Jeremy said. "Both of them."

"You don't know that."

"Sure I do. I basically lived at your house when you were little. I saw how you guys were together."

"It's not like that anymore."

"Your dad couldn't stop talking about you last night, about what an advanced taxidermist you are. He showed me like twelve pictures of the raccoon you mounted. It's really good. He loves having you in the studio with him."

I shook my head. "He only wants me there because I'm useful. I could send a raccoon-mounting robot in my place and he wouldn't even notice the difference." I sniffled hard. "It's just . . . if he doesn't even care about me, why is he trying to keep me from spending time with Mom? I don't understand why he won't let me *go*, you know? It's like he's just holding on to me out of spite."

"He's holding on to you because he wants to keep you close," Jeremy said. "Remember how you said the other day that he was crazy controlling? He wouldn't try so hard to keep you near him all the time if he didn't want you around. He's probably afraid he's going to lose you like he lost your mom. It must've been a huge blow for him when she left so suddenly."

"It wasn't at all. It's not like he paid any attention to her when she was there, so why should he care that she's gone? He doesn't even miss her."

"I'm sure he does," Jeremy said. "I bet he's hurting a lot. Sometimes people don't realize they have a good thing until it's too late."

I knew Dad was angry at Mom for abandoning us, but he'd never acted *hurt*. After she left, he stopped talking about her completely, like she had never existed at all. I had always assumed it meant he didn't care, and the possibility that it might mean something else made my stomach turn over in an uncomfortable way.

"Well, that's stupid," I said. "He should've paid attention when it actually mattered, and then maybe she wouldn't have left." I reached for a tissue from the bedside table. "If I leave, too, maybe he'll actually decide *I'm* worth something."

"Or maybe he doesn't want to let you leave because he knows exactly how much you're worth already."

I didn't know how to respond to that, so I shrugged.

"Listen, I don't want to tell you what to do or anything, so take my opinion with a grain of salt," Jeremy said. "But maybe you shouldn't write him off completely? Try to understand his side of things a little bit? I know he's not the most open person in the world, and he's not very good at talking about his feelings. He obviously hasn't made you feel very loved, and your anger at him sounds pretty justified. But I think it's possible you two are kind of going through the same thing. So, just . . . think about that?"

I didn't want to think about it. My fury was safe and uncomplicated, a lofty tower where I could lock myself away and judge him. I didn't want to consider the possibility that all those times Dad and I stood next to each other at the prep table, passing tools back and forth, he was suffering in silence, like me.

But at the same time, I couldn't completely dismiss what Jeremy was saying. The reason I'd kept assisting my dad all this time was because it was the one way I could bridge the vast distance between us. As long as there were raccoons to stuff and birds to flesh, there was a reason for us to communicate, and I *needed* that—I had already lost one parent, and I couldn't lose the other, too. Maybe Dad was doing the same thing. After all, Mom had offered to pay for him to hire another assistant for the summer, and he'd turned her down. It was possible he really did want *me*, specifically.

And now I had snipped the few remaining threads holding us together.

"This *sucks*," I said.

Jeremy gave my back a little rub. "I wish I could help."

I reached for another tissue to wipe my blotchy face, and my eyes fell on the blue registration folder sitting on the night table. I hadn't opened it since our first day here, but I knew there was a ticket to tonight's awards banquet tucked into the right-hand pocket. And as nervous as it made me, I suddenly knew what I had to do.

"It's okay," I said. "You've helped a lot already. But I think I can handle the rest on my own."

CHAPTER TWENTY-TWO

⫸VANESSA⫷

As soon as Phoebe and I left Callie's room, Phoebe started texting. From the look of extreme stress on her face, I guessed it was one of her band people—maybe even that guy Scott.

"Hey," she asked, as I pressed the down button on the elevator. "Can I meet you at the crepe place after you drop off the forms? Brian said he'd meet me for a few minutes."

Oh, so not Scott. Brian, her best friend.

"Sure," I said.

The elevator arrived, and the doors opened to reveal two guys— a Gandalf and a skinny guy holding a mounted jackalope—eyeing each other distrustfully.

We rode in silence until the third floor, where Jackalope Guy stepped off. As soon as he was out of earshot, Phoebe whispered, "Fly, you fool!"

Gandalf, of course, cracked up.

When we reached the convention center, I wished her luck with her friend, then headed off to the A-wing, Creativity Corner form in hand. There was no line at registration, so I stepped right up to the desk, where a bored-looking, pink-haired woman was doing something on her phone.

"Um, 'scuse me," I said.

She jumped, startled, but then gave me a huge smile once she'd recovered. "Hey, look! A real live human to talk to! You looking for an agent pitch session slot? We've only got one left."

I smiled to myself, remembering Callie's interview with Ms. Scherer, and how that awful-sounding guy had interrupted them. "No, actually. Sorry. I've got my entry form for the Creativity Corner. Do I give that to you?"

"Indeed you do," she said, holding out her hand. I handed the paper over, and she skimmed it, muttering to herself. "Names of participants, good . . . format, oh, interesting . . . name of— Oh, hey, sweetie. Your entry needs a name."

I pushed my glasses up my nose, looking down at the empty space on our form. "Um. Well, we don't have one yet. And it says you have until four o'clock to email audio-format entries . . . ? Right?"

She nodded. "Four o'clock for the actual material, yeah, but they do need a title now. It doesn't have to be perfect. They're judging you on the content, not the title."

"Oh. Okay, hold on." I pulled out my phone, intending to send an emergency group text . . . but then I had an idea. It was kind of dumb, but it worked pretty well for the way our story was shaping up so far, and the other girls wouldn't be mad if I didn't ask them first, right? No, they weren't like that. I took the form back from the pink-haired woman, grabbed a pen off the desk, and wrote our title in all caps.

"*A Thousand Feels*," she read with a smile. "Very nice. You're all set! And you have the email address to send your final file, right?"

I nodded. "Thanks!"

And I started to walk away, toward crepes and my friends and another several hours of surprisingly fun editing work. But then I stopped.

The night before last, after Callie had fallen asleep, I'd had an idea for a new story. I'd taken my laptop into her bathroom so my typing wouldn't wake her up, and I'd kept Ms. Scherer's advice in mind, and I'd started writing. And I'd continued writing all yesterday morning, instead of going to any of the panels at WTFcon. Now I had five brand-new pages of something I actually really liked, something I actually wanted to *continue*, and I'd just been told that there was one agent pitch session left, and if that wasn't the universe trying to tell me something, then I'd eat a taxidermy jackalope.

Heart absolutely pounding, I went right back to the registration desk.

"Sorry, hey, hi," I said. "Um, how much for that agent thing?"

Twenty minutes later, I was waiting for my turn in the hallway outside room A-21—the very same room where Soleil, on that first panel of hers, had ditched "Carry Me Home" and read one of her solo stories instead.

In my left hand, I clutched the first five pages of my own solo story, which I'd printed from the A-wing's business center.

My right hand held my phone, which I'd just used to send a text to Callie and Phoebe. I'd apologized for how I was gonna be late, explained why, and said I'd grab our crepes as soon as I was done. Phoebe replied almost immediately with, Don't worry about the food! I got it! Callie, a few seconds later, added, Good luck!

There were six or seven people waiting in the hallway, and every single one of us perked up when the door to room A-21 opened, and sure enough, out stepped the WTFcon volunteer in charge of keeping the pitch sessions organized.

She squinted at her tablet, then looked up at us. "Karen?" A dark-skinned, spiky-haired girl raised her hand. "Holly Bowen-Davies is ready for you. And . . . Vanessa?" I raised my hand. My sweaty, shaking hand. "Wendi Scherer's ready for you."

Karen and I exchanged tight smiles, and we followed the volunteer into A-21. The room was totally different from the last time I'd been here. All the audience chairs had disappeared, leaving a space that was empty except for four desks, one in each corner. Behind each desk was a professional-looking person. Two of them were talking to people already, and the other two were just sitting there, waiting.

"Karen, Holly's over there," said the volunteer. "And Vanessa, there's Wendi."

Yup, there was Wendi. Sitting behind a desk, perfectly coiffed and super professional and so intimidating that I came pretty close to turning and running out the door and out of the convention center and out of Florida altogether. But I took a deep breath. I tucked my phone into my pocket, clutched my five pages, and started walking toward her.

"Hi there," said Ms. Scherer, as soon as I got close enough. She gestured toward the folding chair that faced her. "Have a seat. Hey, weren't you in my workshop the other day?"

I nodded as I sat. "I'm, ah, Vanessa."

"And I'm Wendi," she said in the same friendly teacher voice she'd used at the workshop. "Nice to see you again."

I nodded and nodded. Then stopped nodding, because I should probably actually *say* something, because that was the whole point of this, right? Me saying things?

I put my pages on the desk and rubbed my hands on my denim-covered thighs to get some of the sweat off and took a deep breath and tried to get my thoughts in order.

Ms. Scherer—or *Wendi*, apparently—glanced down at my pages. Her eyes moved, like she was reading. "Is this the same story we talked about in the workshop, Vanessa?"

I nodded—then made myself stop. "No."

"All right," she said. "I ask because I remember you saying that you hadn't written anything beyond the first chapter. And it's not usually a good idea to try to find an agent for a book before it's finished."

"I know," I said truthfully. She'd said the same thing in the workshop. "And I'm not actually, uh. I don't want an agent. I mean not *yet*. Not right now. Um."

She raised her eyebrows. "In that case, I should probably ask why you signed up for one of my pitch sessions. Since the whole point of pitching your book is, well, trying to find an agent."

For some reason, the fact that she was kind of sarcastic made me like her more. I started talking.

"Okay, so yeah, I know that's the point of this—pitching and stuff—but I actually wanted to talk about what you said in the workshop." She frowned politely, tilting her head a little to the side. "You gave me notes. You said my dialogue was good but it needed to point toward something. And you said the seeds of my book needed to be in the first chapter. And I said I didn't know how to do that because I didn't know what the rest of the book was about yet, so you had the whole class talk about stuff I could pull from the dialogue and make into a story."

Wendi nodded. "Did any of the class's ideas resonate with you?"

"Some," I said. "But I'll be honest: Most of what, um, resonated with me was how I had this huge fight with my roommate later that day, and it made me think about . . . about . . . I dunno, people's personalities? And character motivations, and getting inside other people's heads, and . . . and I'm not sure how to describe it. But I wrote it down." I put my fingertips on my five pages and pushed them a few inches toward her. "I know this probably sucks, because it's just a first draft and I haven't even looked it over or anything, but that's because I wasn't even planning on coming here today. I literally just signed up twenty minutes ago. But, see . . . um, I took your notes. I made the dialogue point toward something. And I . . . um, I wanted to see if you think I'm doing it right."

Wendi glanced at her watch, and then, apparently satisfied, picked up my pages. "Well, let's take a look, shall we?"

I tried not to be nervous—which was really hard, since she was reading my pages right in front of me. This was so different from posting a chapter online and waiting for the comments to start rolling in. Different and mildly terrifying. But also sort of awesome? Maybe?

I looked at the other agents, who were deep in conversation with the people who'd signed up for their pitch sessions, and I looked at the volunteer, fiddling with her tablet over by the door, and then I looked at the empty stage, where Soleil had read "I Knew You Were Trouble" to a packed room.

She'd been nervous, too.

I'd remembered that, the night after she'd kicked me out. How nervous she'd been, how well she'd hidden it. It had made me wonder, in retrospect, what else she'd been nervous about. That was the main reason why I'd picked her as the viewpoint character in my new story, instead of myself. Well, a fictionalized version of her. But still.

After approximately twelve lifetimes had passed, Wendi put my pages down. She was smiling.

"This," she said, "is a huge improvement."

I let out a long, long breath, and then I let myself smile, too. "Really?"

"Really," she said. "Your workshop chapter was lovely. I told you that, and I meant it. But that felt like a slice of life, and nothing else. Two friends talking about a boy they both like. So what? Why should I care what happens next, right?"

I nodded. She'd said the same thing in the actual workshop.

"But this?" she said, pressing her index finger right into the middle of my new first paragraph. "This feels like the beginning of something. You've created tension in the difference between what your narrator is thinking and what she's saying out loud to her friend. She's got an agenda. She wants to present herself a certain way—a way that matches the online image she's created—and she's terrified of being found out, right?"

I nodded. Yeah, that was right—in the story, at least. In real life, I'd probably never know for sure what Soleil had been thinking when she'd first met me. But here, on paper, where I had the freedom to take what I knew, change it as I saw fit, fill in the blanks with whatever I wanted . . .

"And at the end of the chapter," Wendi went on, "when her friend catches her in a lie, she completely freezes up. Her reaction seems disproportionately large, given how small her lie was—but it seems to me that you might have done that on purpose. Did you?"

"Yeah," I said. "Because it's the tip of the iceberg, you know? First it's that one little lie, then it's a bigger one, then an even bigger one, and on and on and on."

"So what's your narrator hiding?" asked Wendi. "What's the big secret that she doesn't want her friend finding out?"

"I'm . . . um, see, I don't think she has one."

Wendi did that politely confused head-tilt thing again.

"Okay, no, I swear this makes sense," I said. "See, she wants to be interesting and mysterious. She wants people to *think* she's got some big secret. But she doesn't. She's just totally normal. She goes to school, she's got a boyfriend, she likes shopping and clothes and books. She's just this really average person. And she *hates* being average."

Wendi pursed her lips. "Interesting. And what about her friend? Does she stay in the story long enough to figure out what's going on?" I nodded. "What will she do?"

"I'm not sure yet," I said. "But I think I'll figure it out as I go along."

"I think that's a good idea." Wendi reached into the pocket of her blazer and pulled out a business card. "And when you have a complete manuscript, I'd love to read it."

My cheeks blazed. I took the business card. My palms were sweating again. "Um. Sure, yeah. Okay. Thanks."

"I think our time's up," Wendi said, nodding to someone behind me. The volunteer, probably. "But one more question. You never told us your narrator's name. Was that also intentional?"

"Oh," I said. "No, it wasn't. But I think she lies about that, too. She doesn't like people knowing her real name, so she uses her online name."

"And what's that?" asked Wendi.

I smiled. "Luna."

The volunteer came over to get me, and I left A-21 with my heart racing and Wendi's business card clutched in my hand.

Outside, more people had joined the small crowd waiting for their pitch sessions—and right there among them, in jeans and a T-shirt that said *Burdened With Glorious Purpose* in neon-green letters, was Merry.

I hadn't seen them since the interview yesterday afternoon, when they'd confessed to having a crush on me. As in, an actual crush. On *me*. And now there they were, sitting on the floor with one of the girls I'd met at Soleil's panel, looking all . . . all *cute*.

"What if I suck?" said Merry's friend. Trish? No. Tiff. That was it. "What if I totally freeze up and forget what my book's even about?"

Merry laughed. Even their laugh was cute. "Come on, you've worked on that thing for two years. You won't forget. You'll be great."

Cute *and* supportive of their friends. Arg, arg, arg.

"Can I run my pitch by you one more time?" said Tiff.

"Go for it," said Merry.

So Tiff started talking. Part of me wanted to wait around until Tiff went inside, so I could have a few minutes alone with Merry and ask them if they'd really meant it, about crushing on me, but the very thought of it put a knot of nervousness in my stomach that, combined with the nervousness that still lingered from talking to Wendi, was way, *way* too much to handle. I could talk to Merry later, when I'd had a chance to calm down.

And besides, I had to get back to Callie's room so we could finish our podcast.

CHAPTER TWENTY-THREE

PHOEBE

After a not-so-quick stop in the IPAC exhibit hall, which seemed twice as crowded as it had the other day, I was running late to meet Brian. But it was a necessary stop. This apology was going to take more than words.

I hurried to the Starbucks, passed the long line that thankfully included no one I knew, and found Brian sitting at a small table in the back. There were two cups in front of him. Instinctively, I glanced around for Christina before taking the empty seat.

"Hi," I said nervously.

"Hi."

"Where's Christina?"

Brian frowned slightly. "She didn't come. Why?"

"Then whose . . ." I stared at the cup closest to me. Venti iced mocha. *Dinosaurs.* "Did you get this for me?"

"Of course."

He said it like he was genuinely surprised I'd even asked. And suddenly I was crying. I was crying in a Starbucks because a boy bought me a drink, and I was trying really hard not to hate myself for it.

Brian looked truly alarmed now. He handed me a bunch of napkins and stayed silent while I blew my nose.

"Okay," I said at last. "Here's the thing. I'm sorry I missed your solo. I'm sorry I . . . I forgot about it entirely, because I was too wrapped up in my own stupid problems. I'm sorry for all that stuff I said about you and Christina, and I'm really, *really* sorry I called you a massive jerk, because you're pretty much the nicest human in existence. This week has sucked because . . . well, for a lot of reasons, but it wasn't right for me to take it out on you. And I hope you can forgive me. And thank you for the drink. And . . . and that's all." I grabbed the iced mocha and started draining it.

"It's okay," he said. "Phoebe? Hey, you're gonna give yourself brain freeze."

I set the empty cup down, slightly out of breath. "Sorry. I haven't eaten yet today. It's . . . *okay*? All that stuff I did was *not* okay. I suck."

Brian smiled. "No, you don't. Between the scalpel thing, and then your solo, and what happened with . . . I mean, I get why you've been upset."

I felt dangerously close to tears again. "So, um . . . how'd your solo go, anyway?"

He ran his hand over his head and shrugged. "Pretty good."

"Pretty good?" I attempted to smile. "Can't you just brag for once?"

"Brag about what?" he asked innocently. "About winning for the second year in a row? Or about getting offered a spot for an early audition at Oberlin next fall?"

"What?" I yelped. "Are you serious?" When he nodded, I threw my arms around him, knocking my cup over and sending ice skittering across the table. He laughed and hugged me back before setting the cup upright. "Oh, hey!" I reached into my pocket and handed Brian a velvet pouch. "I got this as an apology present, but I guess it's a good congratulations present, too. And also a, um, necessary replacement."

Brian opened the pouch, and suddenly—probably due to the overdose of caffeine and relief—I felt so giddy, so on the verge of hysterical laughter, that I had to clamp both hands over my mouth.

Brian's lips twitched when he pulled out the gold triangle beater. I'd even had the vendor tie a little bow on it. He studied it for a moment, eyes twinkling behind his glasses.

"Thank you." Brian smiled at me, his expression one of polite confusion. "But are you sure this is for me? Seems like a better present for S—"

"Do not *even*," I interrupted, but he'd started cracking up before he could finish the sentence. I threw my napkin wads at him. "I have to ask, even though I'm not sure I want to hear this. If I didn't tell anyone, and Scott didn't tell anyone . . . how did you all find out what happened, anyway?"

I peeked up at him, and he blinked a few times. "Seriously, you don't know?"

"No freaking clue."

"Ah." Brian's face reddened a little. "Er. Well. We were all in the room next door playing Halo, so . . ."

I frowned, confused. But suddenly I remembered listening to every single word of Callie's fight with her dad through the wall. The very *thin* wall.

"Oh god." I sat up straight and stared at Brian in horror. "You *heard* us?"

"Um . . ."

"Noooooooo." I thunked my head on the table. Then I did it a few more times for good measure. "No. No. No."

"I'm really sorry," Brian said, and I could tell he was trying not to laugh again. "If it makes you feel any better, Christina spent the whole time trying to get Jorge and Devon away from the wall."

"Oh yeah, that makes me feel a ton better," I said to the table. "So what, after that, Scott came in to play Halo, and everyone started giving him grief?"

"Not exactly." Brian cleared his throat. "We heard you leave, and then Jorge and Devon and Nick went in, and Christina followed, I think just to tell them off, so I went in, too, and, you know . . . the whole room smelled like cologne and there was coffee all over the wall and floor, and my . . . er . . ." He coughed again. "The bed was all messed up, with sticks and mallets all—"

"Stop." I held up my hand, palm flat, my forehead still glued to my other arm. "I already know what it looked like. It looked like . . ." I waved my hand, like I could pull the perfect, most humiliating word out of the air.

"Fun?" Brian said teasingly, then snickered when I flipped him off. "Well, was it?"

"Was it what?"

"Fun."

"Are you seriously asking me this right now?" I said into my elbow.

"I seriously am."

"Why?"

"Because you've had a thing for Scott for a while."

"What?" My head shot up so fast, I felt slightly dizzy. "How did—I mean, no I haven't."

Brian raised an eyebrow. "Okay, if you say so."

"Why'd you think I did?"

"I don't know." He shrugged. "The way you act around him sometimes. And not just around him, but . . . okay, remember when you found out he'd asked Amber to Homecoming first and she turned him down? And suddenly you *hated* her."

"What?" I wrinkled my nose. "No, I didn't. Why'd you think that?"

Brian's eyes widened. "You seriously don't remember? Amber was my lab partner in chemistry last semester. You started calling her Science Barbie."

"Oh, come on," I said. "I only called her that a few times."

"Phoebe." Brian gave me a stern look. "Every. Single. Day. I'd leave chemistry, get to lunch, sit down, and you'd ask, *How'd it go with Science Barbie today? Did Science Barbie blow anything up? Was there a chemical accident, or is Science Barbie's lipstick* supposed *to be purple?*"

I winced. Those were definitely things I'd said. Only I'd never realized how often I said them. And I guess I'd never heard how mean and petty they'd sounded. I thought I was just being funny.

"And that only started after Homecoming," Brian added. "So yeah, I figured you were jealous."

"Ugh." I slumped back in my chair.

Brian gave me a gentle kick under the table. "You were right about one thing you said yesterday. I should've warned you that everyone heard you and Scott. I kept trying to get you to tell me what happened instead, because . . . I don't know. It's frustrating sometimes, how hard it is to get you to admit when something's bothering you. I guess I wanted you to go first for once. But that was dumb, because this time I already knew about it."

Brian's phone buzzed, and his brow furrowed as he read the text.

"Is that Christina?" I asked, and he hesitated before nodding. "Tell her to come over here. Or, I mean, see if she wants to."

"Really?"

"Please. But just her," I added hastily.

"Don't worry, everyone went to that Mexican restaurant after the clinic." Brian kept typing, and I made a mental note to take a different route to the crepe place. Then I glanced at the time on my phone and cringed. Callie was probably wondering what was taking us so long.

Now I felt anxious all over again. With Brian, I'd only had to apologize for being a jerk the last few days. With Christina, I'd been a jerk the last few *years*. What the hell could I possibly say to her in the next five minutes that would make up for everything I'd done?

"How are your hands?" Brian asked, setting his phone down.

"What? Oh." I looked down at my palms. "Better. I took off the Band-Aids last night."

"Good. There's a drum set clinic in half an hour, if you want to come?"

I toyed with my straw. "I would, but I've got a . . . thing."

"A thing?"

"Yeah, it's . . ." I wrinkled my nose. "You remember the taxidermy girl from the lobby?"

"Sure."

"We're making a podcast. For a contest."

Brian squinted at me. "A taxidermy podcast?"

"Ha, no. It's sort of a storytelling podcast. We're making it with another girl who's here for that fan convention. Although," I added, sitting up straighter, "I did learn some stuff about taxidermy. For example, did you know Nair can take the feathers off a turkey?"

"Um . . . no?" Brian rubbed his hand over his head again. "What exactly have you been doing all week?"

"Actually, so during the showcase concert the other night? Mackey brought me up to the booth and introduced me to the sound engineer—Giovanne Clark, remember?—and we ended up talking for hours, and—" I glanced up and saw Christina making her way toward us through the crowded café. "And it was really cool. I'll tell you about it later." I swallowed as Christina pulled a chair up to our table. "Hi."

"Hi."

We smiled tentatively at each other, and she glanced at Brian. "So . . ."

"Want me to go?" He half stood, but I grabbed his arm.

"No, I only have a minute anyway." I took a deep breath and turned to Christina. "All that stuff you said was true."

Her eyes narrowed for a second, like she thought I was being sarcastic. "What?"

"You were right," I told her. "About how I . . . you know, why we stopped hanging out. And everything else you said, too. About me being selfish."

Christina winced. "I shouldn't have said that. I was mad, and—"

"It's true, though." I tried to smile. "And I'm sorry. And . . ."

What was I supposed to do now? *I gotta go do a cool thing with some girls I just met, but maybe we can hang out later and pretend I haven't been a jerk for the last few years?* But I had to go—this was the last day I'd get to spend with Callie and Vanessa before heading back to Austin early tomorrow morning on the bus.

The bus. Hey.

"Maybe we could . . . oh, wait. Never mind."

"What?" she asked.

"Nothing, just . . . you guys probably want to sit together tomorrow, right? On the bus, I mean."

Christina's expression cleared. "Oh, you want to sit with Brian? Sure!"

"No, I was going to ask if, uh . . ." I made a face, annoyed with myself for being so flustered. Christina's eyebrows shot up when she realized what I was getting at, and she crossed her arms and smiled expectantly at me.

"Yes?"

"Ughhh, this is *so* middle school," I moaned, and they both laughed. "Fine. Want to sit with me on the bus?"

Christina tapped her chin and pretended to consider it. "Well . . . I guess that would be okay."

"Okay. Hey, maybe we can talk about audio stuff for The Menstrual Cyclists," I added. "I saw the mics y'all were checking out in the exhibit hall and those are all wrong for what you're trying to do. I can help you out with that . . . if you want, I mean."

"Oh yeah?" Christina tilted her head. "Nuri and Amy are coming over to my place this Friday to talk about the recording. Maybe you can come, too?"

"Sure, yeah. That'd be fun."

We grinned at each other. Then I stood up, mostly because I had to get back to Callie and Vanessa, but a little bit because I suspected my tear ducts were about to betray me again. "I'll see you guys later tonight, all right? Have fun at the clinic."

"Have fun with the turkey podcast," Brian said, and Christina's face screwed up in confusion.

"The *what?*"

Laughing, I waved and started weaving around the tightly packed tables. I was so relieved, I almost felt like I could've floated right over them. It might take a while to fix things with Christina, but a twenty-hour bus ride seemed like a good place to start.

CHAPTER TWENTY-FOUR

VANESSA

We figured editing our mini-podcast wouldn't take more than a few hours, but Phoebe stocked up on enough crepes to get us through a whole day, just in case. And it was a good thing, too; we ended up working right up until our deadline.

Well, *working* was maybe not the most accurate description of what we were doing. There was definitely work involved: figuring out how to make an actual story out of the dialogue we'd recorded (mostly Callie and me), and figuring out which audio clips to add, and when, to create the effect we wanted (mostly Phoebe).

But along the way, we kept getting distracted by, say, turning on actual episodes of *A Thousand Words* for inspiration (Callie), or sharing cool facts about the percussion instruments we were hearing in our clips (Phoebe), or imagining what it might be like to kiss Merry and totally zoning out on what was actually happening in the room (me). Luckily, though, we always got each other focused again. We were a good team.

At quarter to four, we stopped working and played back our whole finished podcast, just once, to make sure we hadn't done anything horribly stupid in the editing process. Five minutes later, the recording ended—and for a second, the three of us just kind of sat there, smiling stupidly at each other.

Then Phoebe said, "Well *done*, ladies!"

And that was it. That was our project, finished.

I emailed the file to the moderators. We each ate one last crepe. We went through our suitcases and picked outfits for the Creativity Corner: a dress printed with hot air balloons for Callie, jeans and a red shirt for Phoebe, and jeans and the puffy-paint *I <3 Harry Potter* shirt for me. Yes, I'd already worn it once, and yes, there was apparently some unspoken set of convention rules that made my shirt uncool, but screw that, right? I loved that shirt, and the pits didn't smell or anything, so I was going to wear it.

And then? Off we went, down to the A-wing ballroom.

I had a flimsy plan in mind for if we needed to sneak Phoebe and Callie in, but it turned out not to be necessary; for whatever reason, the security people waved us through without even a glance at our badges. So we snagged a trio of seats and waited for the show to begin.

At five o'clock on the nose, the house lights went down. Cheers rose up from the audience. And a short black girl in Hogwarts robes walked out on stage: Beth, the same person who'd moderated Soleil's panel on that first day. My stomach twisted at the reminder of my ex–best friend—but I told it to shut up, because this wasn't about Soleil, not anymore. This was about me and my two new friends.

Beth explained that she would be the emcee for the event,

and explained how it worked. There were five categories: Visual Arts, Prose, Audio/Video (anything that starred fans themselves instead of featuring clips from the source material; this was where our podcast would be), Fanvids (clips of movies and TV shows and things, set to a song, like a music video), and Performances. And there were five judges: one who specialized in each category.

We got to see all the Visual Arts stuff first, projected in a slideshow on a screen that rolled down from the ceiling above the stage. And then there were fanfic readings, and, okay, I'll be honest, I didn't really hear or see *any* of them. Because as soon as they started showing stuff, my stomach erupted into butterflies, and all I could do was sit there between Phoebe and Callie, wait for our podcast, and hope there wouldn't be a mass exodus from the ballroom as it played because we sucked so much.

The Audio/Video category was up next. There were some filks—people rewriting lyrics to popular songs so they were about fandom stuff instead of whatever they'd originally been about—and some original songs. And some seriously cool videos, some of which looked professionally edited—including this one called "Look, Ma, We Fixed It," where two girls cross-dressed to re-create a scene from *Sherlock* that, in their version, ended with Sherlock and John making out.

And then Beth said, "Our final piece in Audio/Video is called '*A Thousand Feels*: A Mini-Podcast in the Style of *A Thousand Words*,' created by Callie Buchannan, Phoebe Byrd, aaaand Vanessa Montoya-O'Callaghan."

I reached out and took my new friends' hands. Callie laced her fingers through mine. Phoebe squeezed so hard it almost hurt.

Here we go, I thought.

A THOUSAND FEELS:
A TRANSCRIPT

[fade in, sound of thirty people drumming on rubber practice pads—a comforting sound, like heavy rain on a rubber roof]

SOLEIL: Okay, are you sure this is going to be anonymous? Because this isn't the kind of thing you can just go around telling people.

JEFF: This is anonymous, right?

PHOEBE: Totally anonymous, promise.

GUY: Okay. So, here goes.

[crowd noises; sound of a toddler crying]

GIRL FROM COSTUME COMPETITION: Who are you supposed to be?

PHOEBE: What's your name?

CALLIE: Which convention are you here for?

SOLEIL: WTFcon. That stands for We Treasure Fandom.

HARLEY: The World Taxidermy Championships.

JEFF: IPAC. Indoor Percussion Association Convention.

[Sound of a marimba being played. Player messes up, laughs, plays phrase again correctly.]

WENDI: These conventions are so fascinating to me. People come to them for the panels and workshops, obviously. But it seems like most of them are really here because they're desperate to be seen.

GIRL 2 FROM COSTUME COMPETITION: Cauldron cakes! Two for a sickle!

GUY: It's genius, isn't it? We could both make millions. Billions! That's a guarantee.

HARLEY: [*singing*] I'll *tell* you what I want, what I really really want!

PHOEBE: It's like an awesome geek parade.

WENDI: For some people, this is probably the only place they feel like they can be themselves. They just want to find their people and connect.

GIRL 3 FROM COSTUME COMPETITION: I think you should dress like that *all* the time.

GIRL 4 FROM COSTUME COMPETITION: Oh, totally.

LITTLE GIRL: Mommy, my wig is itchy!

WENDI: People seem to find cosplay really freeing. I once showed up in a Stormtrooper costume and walked around the trade show floor all morning just to see what it was like.

BERNICE: This is my very best work.

VANESSA: Why can't you tell her about it?

BERNICE: I wish I could, but she just wouldn't understand.

TODD: That is simply something of which we do not speak.

[*sound of haunting melody played on a thumb piano*]

VANESSA: Problem is—

WENDI: At home—

VANESSA: I don't think I have a best friend. There are some really nice people there, but nobody who I really click with, you know?

PHOEBE: She and I used to be really close, until . . . well, apparently until I dumped her. That's what she thinks, anyway. Even though *she's* the one who made all these new friends.

VANESSA: I thought we were best friends.

CALLIE: We'd have, like, this adventure, start a new life, just the two of us. But—

SCOTT: I guess she's not interested either way.

JILLIAN: She never listens to me.

TODD: He . . . scarred me.

PHOEBE: I'm not jealous, for the record.

CALLIE: I can't believe I was so stupid.

WENDI: It's interesting how sometimes you can be surrounded by thousands of people and still feel like you're completely alone.

[sound of steel drums]

BEIGE: I HAVE A SECRET.

TODD: I have no secrets.

SCOTT: I don't really have any secrets. It's impossible to . . . just, everyone knows everyone's business.

TODD: Everyone knows that.

BEIGE: Mommy can't know. I want to whisper it.

CALLIE: Come on, spill.

BEIGE: [*whispers*] Mommy says I have to hate Delancey because she's my arch-ne-me-sis, but I want to be her friend because she gave me a lollipop and it turned my mouth purple and Mommy was MAD but purple is my favorite color and it's Delancey's favorite color, too.

MERRY: I met someone that I like.

VANESSA: [*whispers*] I think it's okay to be friends with whoever you want.

BEIGE: [*whispers*] Even though I'm supposed to crush her?

MERRY: It's just a crush thing at this point. I don't even know her that well yet. But I'm hoping that'll change.

SCOTT: I hooked up with another girl . . . from my school.

PHOEBE: His new girlfriend really bothered me. I mean, *she* didn't bother me, their *relationship* bothered me. I didn't tell him because I figured he'd think I was jealous.

SCOTT: I bet she thinks this is just like what happened with that girl last year, that I don't care. But . . . I do.

HARLEY: [*singing*] If you want my future, forget my past—

SCOTT: I *like* her. Like, a lot.

GUY: She's just your average teenage girl, you know? Except *she kicks ass*!

MERRY: She's really pretty, in this offbeat-nerd kind of way. Really nice hair. Really great smile.

GUY: And she has no idea how beautiful she is—

MERRY: [*laughs quietly*]

HARLEY: It was the best night of my life.

CALLIE: There was this tiny little part of me that actually felt kind of *hopeful*.

PHOEBE: They're both great people, so of course they're a great couple.

SCOTT: It's already weird because we've been friends for a long time, you know? She got kind of freaked out and took off.

CALLIE: One day she was just gone, and I was still in the same place I'd always been.

SCOTT: I really didn't want her to go.

JILLIAN: Honey, where are you going?

WENDI: I really have to go now, all right?

[sound of a gong being hit]

CALLIE: The weird thing is . . . I know this doesn't even make any sense, really. But I kind of feel like these two girls I just met while I've been here . . .

VANESSA: . . . they already know me better than anybody at home.

PHOEBE: They just . . . we really clicked, you know? Which is weird, because I barely even know them.

SOLEIL: We tell each other literally everything.

CALLIE: I wish I'd met them sooner. I feel like this last year would've been a lot easier if they'd been around.

VANESSA: I hope they still want to stay friends after we leave.

HARLEY: *[singing]* FRIENDSHIP NEVER ENNNNNDS . . .

PHOEBE: Aww, you guys said that, too?

VANESSA: We all said the same thing!

CALLIE: You guys are the best.

PHOEBE: Okay, bring it in. Group hug. This is happening.

CALLIE: Oof—

VANESSA: Awwwww.

[laughter]

[fade out]

There wasn't a mass exodus. People actually clapped. Sure, that didn't necessarily mean anything, since people were clapping for literally everything—but there was something super cool about applause for a thing that I'd helped create.

Still, I couldn't help looking back and forth between my friends and asking, "It's actually good, right? I'm not just imagining that it's good?"

"Oh yeah, it's good," said Callie.

"It's *great*," said Phoebe. "We're amazing."

The Fanvids category was next, but while there was some stuff in there that I liked (a couple Harry Potter vids, plus a seriously amazing Disney Princesses one, and even a really short *Wonderlandia* one), most of them weren't fandoms that I knew very well. So I clapped politely along with everyone else, and waited for the Performances category to start. That was going to be fun.

Or so I thought, until Beth announced the first piece in the category: "Our first entry is called 'The Many Loves of Draco Malfoy,' created by Aimee Hughes, Danielle Kozlov, Marziya Malik, aaaand Soleil."

No. No no no. No *way*. She wasn't here. Our entry had been under my name, not hers. I'd misheard.

Except then Phoebe said, "Are you *kidding* me?" so loudly that a couple people turned around to glare at her—so, no, I hadn't misheard.

"Gross," said Callie.

My legs tensed with the desire to stand up and get the hell out of there as fast as I could. But I stayed in my seat. I had to. This was my convention as much as hers.

"She's friends with the emcee," I told them. "Bet you anything that's how she got herself an entry."

Callie gave me a sympathetic smile. Phoebe rolled her eyes and snorted.

A Beyoncé song started playing. No, wait, not solo Beyoncé. Destiny's Child. "Say My Name." A chorus of laughter rippled through the audience, because of course she'd pick something like that. It was classic and funny and ironic, all at the same time, and hey, you had to give Soleil this much: she knew how to please a crowd.

"Oh my god," murmured Phoebe, as Soleil and her posse took the stage, one by one.

Soleil was dressed as Draco, in Slytherin robes and a spiky blond wig, because obviously she had to be the title character. Danielle was dressed as Harry. Marziya was Professor Snape, and Aimee was . . . Luna Lovegood, maybe? Or Fleur Delacour? I couldn't actually tell which.

The dance was exactly what Soleil had described, back when she'd first told me the idea. A totally overwrought dance of epic, unrequited longing—made even funnier when Soleil's three new besties changed costumes offstage and came out again dressed as Hermione, Ron, and Sirius Black. And then as Neville, Tonks, and Lucius.

Basically, it was a tribute to every fanficcer who'd ever shipped Draco Malfoy with *anyone*, and the audience clearly loved it, and the thing was, I probably would've loved it, too, except that Soleil's performance kind of ruined the whole thing. Not only because it was Soleil, either, although that definitely didn't help. The way she stretched and writhed and grimaced was so over the top, so incredibly look-at-me-look-at-me, that it probably would've made me want to puke even if we *were* still friends.

"Not as good as our podcast," whispered Callie when it was over, as everyone clapped. Phoebe grinned. I tried to grin back, but mainly I just tried to believe her.

The other performances were a blur after that.

But I pulled it together when Beth came back out on stage and announced that the judges were deliberating—because that was when she asked all the contestants to gather beside the stage so we could line up and take a bow.

Phoebe shouldered her way through the crowd, Callie and me trailing in her wake. And when Beth called the Audio/Video contestants up on the stage, and we all lined up and waved at the crowd as they applauded us, I wasn't thinking about Soleil at all.

Then the Performances contestants took their bows, too, and Soleil and her Fangirl Trio stepped off the stage—and came right over to me. She crossed her arms over her chest, smiling smugly as she approached, and the urge to flee crept over me again. But, again, I didn't. Because I could feel Callie and Phoebe hovering right behind me, like Soleil's three minions were hovering behind her—except, no, not like that at all. Callie and Phoebe weren't minions. They were actual friends.

"Good performance," I told Soleil, because someone had to take the high road, right?

"Thanks," she said, eyeing my puffy-paint shirt with a smirk. "Same to you—although, wow, what was that I heard in your little podcast? Can't stop using my voice for your own benefit, can you?"

"Literally nobody benefits from your voice," said Phoebe. "And that's literally as in *literally*."

"Oh yeah. I remember you now." Soleil spared a second to level a death glare at Phoebe, then looked back at me. "Well, whatever. It's not like you even used the good parts of my interview, anyway."

I snorted. I couldn't help it. "Your *alternative facts* about Marty Green. Right."

"Aw, Marty. I'll tell him you said hi, okay?" She smirked. "By the way, how are all those novels of yours coming along?"

Behind her, Danielle and Marziya exchanged a look. I wondered what she'd told them about me and my writing—but it didn't actually matter, did it? Especially not after my pitch session this afternoon.

"Actually, pretty great," I said. "I showed something new to that literary agent again today. She said it was a huge improvement. Then she gave me her business card so I can send her my manuscript when it's done."

Behind me, someone murmured, "Aw *yeah*, she did." Phoebe, probably.

In front of me, Soleil's eyes were practically bugging out; this was clearly not the answer she'd expected. If she were a cartoon character, steam would be coming out of her ears.

So obviously, I kept going: "And actually, it's all because of you. You said that thing about living my life and writing about what I know. So that's what I've been trying to do. And it turns out you were right. So hey. Thanks."

"I was— What's that supposed to mean, I was right?" She sounded so confused. I didn't blame her. Here she was, trying to insult me, and I totally wasn't taking the bait.

"It means," I said slowly, "that you and Wendi gave me constructive criticism, and I took it. You should try it sometime."

Now she looked confused *and* pissed off. My work here was done.

So I turned to my actual friends and said, "Come on, guys. They're about to announce the awards."

We found a spot to stand in, far enough away from Soleil that I wouldn't be tempted to look at her. And as Beth came back out on stage accompanied by the judges, Phoebe leaned over and whispered, "You? Are my hero."

There were eight awards in total. First, each of the five judges gave a Best in Category award to a piece in their own specialty category. (In the Audio/Visual category, our podcast lost to some song about a character from *Supernatural*. Weird choice, but whatever.) Then, all five judges voted on first, second, and third place for the overall competition.

Third place went to a *Doctor Who* fanfic. I didn't really have an opinion about it, since everything before the Audio/Visual category had been kind of a blur—but when the author went up on stage to accept her yellow ribbon, she looked like she was actually crying from happiness. So that was nice.

Second place went to the Disney Princesses fanvid. I cheered pretty loudly for that; it had been one of my favorites. The vidder, who was named BrandyBuckBeak and dressed as Captain America, complete with the mask and the shield, gave the crowd a patriotic salute as Beth pinned a red ribbon to his chest.

First place went to a video called "Missing Scenes From *Harry Potter and the Order of the Phoenix*," which consisted almost exclusively of footage of Remus Lupin and Sirius Black sneaking away from Order meetings so they could make out. The actors who played Remus and Sirius—who I was pretty sure were also the Sherlock and John who'd placed third at the Karaoke Extravaganza—were pretty awesome, and the whole thing looked like a blooper reel from an actual movie. I wasn't at all surprised that it had won.

So yeah, Soleil's stupid dance thing didn't win anything, which, yay. And our podcast didn't win anything, either—but I didn't even care that much, actually. All the stuff I did care about had already happened.

After the ceremony was over, Phoebe said she had to catch up with a couple of her percussion people, and Callie said she had to find her dad. Which was fine, since they both promised to meet me back here for the Farewell Ball—but as soon as they left, I started feeling a little glum. I'd spent the whole day with them, and it was weird not to be around them now, even if it was only for a little while.

Someone tapped my shoulder. *Soleil*, I thought, and tensed. But when I turned around, it wasn't Soleil at all. It was Captain America, wearing the second-place ribbon. The mask had come off—which meant now I could see who it was underneath. Dirty-blond hair and dimples and cuteness and *oh god*.

"Hey," said Merry, grinning their face off.

"Oh, hey!" I said. "Oh. *Oh*, that was you? That Disney Princess fanvid?"

"That was me," said Merry proudly.

"It was, um. It was really good." Ugh, my tongue felt sluggish and horrible and completely incapable of making words.

"So was yours," said Merry. "That was some of the coolest editing work I've ever heard. I'm really surprised you guys didn't win anything."

My face went hot, and I had to change the subject, because if they gave me one more compliment, I would explode right there.

Fortunately, that was when someone in a convention center T-shirt came over and told us we had to clear the room.

"So, hey, what was that song?" I asked, as we moved with the crowd toward the door. "The one in your princess vid? I don't think I know it."

"You don't know Meredith Brooks?" said Merry, their eyebrows shooting up. "Come on, that's only the greatest song of all time! How have you been alive this long without knowing that one?"

"I haven't been alive *that* long," I said, which was probably number one on the list of the absolute dumbest things I could have said and where, where, where had my brain gone?

"It's been my personal anthem since I was about eight." Merry waggled their eyebrows. "And I *know* you're older than eight."

"Seventeen," I said.

"Only two years younger than me," they said. "Sweet. Plenty of time for you to learn about important music before you go to college."

"Are . . . uh, are *you* in college?"

They nodded. "I'm a freshman at Valencia. Right here in the great city of Orlando."

"Valencia?" I said. "Seriously? I'm totally applying there next year! I mean, a bunch of other places, too, but—that's so cool."

"What about now?" Merry asked. "Where are you from?"

"Right here in the great city of Orlando," I replied. "Well, technically Winter Park, but nobody who isn't from here knows where that is, so I usually say Orlando."

There was a pause. My stomach fluttered, and Merry's smile widened. "We're neighbors."

I nodded. We were out in the hall now, surrounded by a rapidly thinning crowd, and Merry didn't seem like they had any intention of moving any farther.

Pause.

Pause.

Awkward, awkward pause.

I wasn't allowed to just, like, grab them and kiss them right here in the hallway, right? That wasn't a thing people could do?

"Hey," said Merry. "So . . . I overheard you and Soleil talking before the awards got announced. It sounded like— Okay, stop me if this is none of my business, but . . . did you guys have a fight?"

"Oh. Yeah." I sighed. "It turns out she's a slightly horrible person."

Merry didn't look remotely surprised. "Wanna talk about it?"

I'd done more than enough talking last night. So I just shook my head and said, "It's a long story."

"Well, are you okay, at least?"

"Yeah," I said with a smile. "I think so."

"Good," said Merry. "Because I'm about to be really awkward at you, and it'll go way better if you're in a good mood."

". . . Oh yeah?"

"So, um. That thing I said before."

"What thing?" I said.

"When you were interviewing me."

Oh god. *That* thing. I pushed my glasses up my nose and tried very hard not to die.

"I was just sort of wondering," they went on, "if you maybe—"

"Yes!" The word exploded out of me before I even knew it was there. "Ilikeyoutoo. Yesyesyes."

So apparently I was a lunatic. Cool.

Merry burst out laughing. "I was actually going to ask you something else. But that's very good to know."

My face was on fire. Probably literally. "Uh. Sorry, what were you gonna ask?"

"If you'd go to the Farewell Ball with me. As my date. I mean, I figure we're both going anyway, but we could maybe walk in together, at least? Maybe dance together . . . ?"

"I'd . . . yes. That'd be awesome."

Merry nodded thoughtfully. "And maybe . . . maybe I could get your number? Text you after the con is over so I can ask you out for coffee?"

Was this seriously happening?

"Probably a good idea," I said. "And just in case you were worried, I'm gonna say yes."

Merry put their hand dramatically to their chest. "Oh, thank heavens."

"Especially to the ball part," I added. "*Especially* if you're up for, say, dancing together where we can be sure Soleil will see us."

"Make her jealous?" said Merry. "I like it. And I can be like 'Here's my super-hot girlfriend Vanessa!' really loudly where she can overhear."

I laughed. "And here's *my* super-hot . . . uh . . ."

Yikes. Was there a gender-neutral version of the girlfriend/boyfriend thing?

Merry raised their eyebrows. Not like a challenge. More like they were waiting to see what I'd come up with.

"My super-hot personfriend," I said at last.

Merry laughed again. "Aw, I love that! Yeah, I'll totally be your fake personfriend for the evening."

"Fake for *now*." Great. Yet another dumb thing that I probably shouldn't have said.

But Merry nodded. "For now. Let's go out for coffee next week, and then see what happens."

I pushed my glasses up again. "Yeah. Yeah, that sounds good."

"Meantime," they said, "wanna get something to eat before the dance?"

"You're not, um, eating with Tiff and . . . what was her name again?"

"Jaya," said Merry. "And nah, they're waiting in line for autographs. Not really my scene. We're all gonna meet up later. So . . . dinner?"

I checked my phone. It was a little past eight, which meant I had plenty of time before I was supposed to meet back up with Callie and Phoebe. "Yeah. That sounds good."

"And maybe some ice cream after?" they said.

"That sounds good, too."

"And also maybe you'll let me kiss you?"

"That—" I cut myself off, realizing what Merry'd just said. I swallowed hard. "Yeah. That . . . yes, that also sounds . . . very good. Very."

Merry reached up and touched a finger to my cheek, right above my jaw. It was a single, simple point of contact, but it sent little zings of *yes yes yes* all through me, and suddenly my whole body was awake, alert, and ready.

I'd written the words over and over again, in tons of different fanfics. Bodies being drawn together like magnets. Leaning closer without meaning to. All that stuff. I'd written it, but I'd never actually understood what it felt like until right this second. Because Merry was moving closer, and I was, too, and then *lips on mine* and then *arms around me* and then *tongue* and it was *awesome* and—

"Yeah, you get some, Cap!" shouted a voice from somewhere nearby.

Merry and I pulled apart, giggling like loons as we looked for the source of the voice. Turns out, it was some girl dressed as the Black Widow, which was pretty appropriate. She waved. I waved back. Merry gave her a Captain America salute.

"So how about crepes?" said Merry, holding out their arm like an old-timey gentleman.

"Or," I said, putting my hand on their elbow, "we could forget dinner and just go right to the ice cream."

"Skipping to the best part, huh?" said Merry, and leaned over to kiss my cheek. "I knew I liked you."

CHAPTER TWENTY-FIVE

PHOEBE

Ranking so low in both the ensemble and solo competitions at IPAC had really sucked. But not placing in the Creativity Corner thing didn't bother me at all.

Because even now, standing in the lobby waiting for Scott, I kept hearing snippets of conversations and creating a soundtrack in my mind, editing and rearranging to alter the mood and even the meaning of certain lines. *I really didn't want her to go*, accompanied by a mournful violin, indicating sadness and regret and extreme melodrama. *I really didn't want her to go*, followed by a trombone *wah wah wah*, indicating the line is a joke and you'd be an idiot to take it seriously. *I really didn't want her to go*, spoken over low, disjointed chords gradually growing louder, indicating that something terrifying was about to happen.

I really needed to practice that whole "hearing intention" thing.

I glanced nervously at the elevators and tugged at the hem of my new Weird Sisters T-shirt. I'd bought it after we'd left the Creativity Corner, both because I liked Vanessa's and because it seemed appropriate enough dance attire without going full costume.

"Hey, Phoebe."

I whirled around and found myself facing Scott. "Oh! Hi."

He smiled tentatively, stretching his arms out a little and flexing his fingers. So he was nervous, too, which somehow made me feel both better and worse. When he opened his mouth to start talking, I stopped him.

"Sorry, but there's something I need to tell you before you say anything." I took a deep breath. "First, I'm really sorry I didn't meet up with you yesterday. I should have. But that girl who interviewed you for her podcast? That's my friend Callie. I swear on my life I didn't know she was going to talk to you. But she did, and . . . I heard it. Everything you said."

Scott blinked. "You did?"

"Yeah."

His shoulders relaxed. "Thank god."

"What?" This was not the reaction I'd expected. "You aren't mad or anything?"

He shrugged. "Nope. Saying that stuff to some random girl was easier than saying it to you. And look," he added, his smile vanishing. "I know you probably didn't believe it when I said I didn't tell everyone, but—"

"No, I do," I assured him. "I talked to Brian. I know they, um . . . heard us."

Scott didn't even answer. He just slumped back against the wall and mouthed *thank god* to the ceiling. I started snickering, and he grinned at me. "What? I figured you were going to hate me forever."

"I don't hate you." As soon as I said that, I realized this was the part where I was supposed to tell him how I *did* feel about him. But I couldn't. I'd been trying to psych myself up for this for the last two hours, but the fact was, I wasn't ready yet.

But neither was he. After all, he'd just told me it had been easier for him to tell "some random girl" how he felt about me. And he was clearly relieved he didn't have to say it to my face. We were both bad at this, but maybe that was okay for now. No reason to rush anything.

So instead of saying *I like you* or whatever a more romantically inclined person would say, I went with: "Got any plans next Saturday?"

Scott's eyes lit up, and he stepped forward. "No . . ."

"Halo?"

"Sure!" His smile turned slightly wicked. "Wait, actual Halo, or . . ."

I rolled my eyes, trying not to laugh. "Yes, actual Halo."

"That works, too."

The silence that followed managed to be both awkward and electric, and I stared down at my shoes. "Although, I mean, that *was* fun, before. Well, until . . . you know."

"I thought it was *all* fun."

I looked up. Now he was grinning in that very specific way he did when he was challenging me. I crossed my arms and smiled back, hoping I looked like someone whose pulse wasn't racing out of control. "Yeah? Well, coffee-soaked underwear isn't really my thing, just FYI."

He nodded. "I'll keep that in mind for next time."

"Next time? That's a pretty big assumption," I said lightly.

"I know."

Cats. We were both grinning like idiots by now, and my face and neck were probably beet red, and my stupid body was basically betraying me in every possible way. I needed to end this conversation before it turned into Phoebe's Adventures in Sexland: The Sequel.

"I need to get going," I told him, taking a step back. (And how had we ended up standing this close, anyway?)

"You're not going to the showcase concert?"

I shook my head. "No, I've got the Farewell Ball."

"The what?"

"It's a, um, dance. At the fan convention. I made some friends this week who'll be there, so . . . What?" I added, because Scott was looking at me funny.

"Nothing! It's just . . . a *ball*? Seems kind of girly for you," he teased. "Gonna get a fancy dress, get your hair and makeup done?"

I flinched and instinctively opened my mouth to fire off a defensive retort. Then I paused and thought about what he'd said.

"Yeah, so what if I am? Anything wrong with that?"

Scott's brow furrowed. "Well . . . no?"

"Okay then." I smiled. "See you later?"

He smiled back. "Yeah."

I waved and headed across the lobby, my pulse gradually

slowing to a normal rate. As I passed the registration desk, I heard a vaguely familiar woman ranting at the poor receptionist. "I demand this hotel compensate me for at least one night's stay. Really, the entire thing should be free. This was the most important week of my Beige's life, and neither of us could sleep a wink thanks to that horrible man next door with all those dead animals. The *smell*!"

I half wanted to call her out on that—I'd spent enough time in the taxidermy trade show to know the animals didn't smell at all. I glanced at her tiny daughter, who stood several feet away from her mother, gazing openmouthed at a huge group of WTFconners in costumes, clearly on their way to the dance. Beige's face was scrubbed clean now; no wig, no black leather. She took a few steps toward A-wing and, for a second, I thought she was going to make a run for it. Then her mother glanced over her shoulder.

"Beige! You stay right here next to me!" The little girl stopped in her tracks, crossed her arms, and pouted.

Shaking my head, I headed toward the bridge to the convention center. A second later, someone nudged my arm.

"Poor kid, right?" Merry said.

I grinned. "Seriously. Hey, Vanessa!"

On Merry's other side, Vanessa smiled at me, her cheeks pink. "So, it looked like things went well with that Scott guy?"

My eyebrows shot up. "Were you guys spying on me?"

"Not on purpose!" Vanessa exclaimed at the same time Merry said: "Obviously."

As soon as we entered the convention center, I could hear the *thump thump thump* of some pop song coming from the A-wing ballroom.

"Yeah, it was . . ." I trailed off, because that was when I noticed they were holding hands. "Hey. *Heyyyy.*"

Vanessa turned bright red, but she was smiling so hard it looked like her cheeks might split. Merry swung their clasped hands back and forth, beaming at her, and Vanessa somehow blushed even more.

"Okay, stop," I told them. "This is, like, an illegal level of adorable. You might get arrested."

Merry sighed loudly. "Oh well. Lock us up, if you must."

Vanessa tried to look scandalized and, when she failed miserably, pointed at my Weird Sisters shirt instead. "Hey, that looks familiar! Is it—"

"Not yours! I bought one after the Creativity Corner," I told her as we reached the ballroom. Merry let go of her hand to pull the doors open for us, and I leaned closer to Vanessa. "And don't tell Callie, but I bought her one, too—I'm gonna try to hide it in her suitcase before she leaves. Seemed like we should all three have one, you know?"

Vanessa didn't say anything. Just beamed at me, her eyes all shiny. I grinned back. And maybe my eyes were a little shiny, too. And maybe I didn't care. I linked my arm through hers, and Merry took her other hand, and we walked into the dance together.

CHAPTER TWENTY-SIX

CALLIE

The Creativity Corner awards hadn't made me nervous at all, but as I left the safe embrace of the pop culture junkies and made my way toward the taxidermy awards banquet, my stomach started tying itself in knots. I clutched my ticket in my sweaty hand and forced my feet to keep moving, even though it would've been so much easier to forget the whole thing and head straight to the Farewell Ball with my friends.

Vanessa had stood up to Soleil even though she'd been terrified. Phoebe had swallowed her pride and shouldered the blame for ruining her friendship with Christina. If they could be strong, so could I. I *had* to do this, or nothing would change, and I'd be miserable forever.

The C-wing ballroom door was open, and I could hear applause coming from inside. The crowd sounded pretty lively, considering the banquet had been going on for two and a half hours already. I wasn't sorry to have missed most of it; four years ago, my parents had made me sit through the entire thing in case Dad won one of the big awards at the end. Most of it was a blur, but I remembered the giant, intricate napkin sculptures on the tables, the girls in prom dresses who'd sung the national anthem, and the way the emcee had led everyone in the Lord's Prayer, which I hadn't known. I also remembered the way my mom had asked a waiter for "the vegetarian option" just to see the shocked and appalled expressions on everyone's faces. Dad had rolled his eyes and acted exasperated, but I could tell he thought it was funny.

I held up my ticket, and the bored girl at the door waved me through. The inside of the room looked like a charity ball crossed with a rodeo; about two-thirds of the people were dressed in suits and floor-length gowns, and the remaining third wore denim and camo, bolo ties and cowboy boots. People murmured quietly among themselves as the emcee announced award after award. The tables were littered with the remains of dinner, plates scattered with gnawed bones and pools of gravy, and my stomach lurched again. I forced myself to look away and scan the room for my dad.

I spotted Jeremy right away, sitting at the head table in an impeccable black suit and a red bow tie. There was Bernice, the lady with the boars, in a flowered dress; she had a blue ribbon on the table in front of her, and I was sad to know she wouldn't be able to show it off to her best friend. Harley Stuyvesant's shock of white hair made him super conspicuous, even across the room, and I almost laughed out loud when I thought of him belting out Spice Girls lyrics. I'd never be able to look at him the same way again.

And then I spotted my dad, sitting toward the right side of the room at a table full of strangers. I took a deep breath and went over.

"Hey," I whispered.

He looked up, and for a second it was like he didn't even recognize me. "Callie? What are you doing here?"

"I'm—I thought I'd—" My eyes fell on the ribbons sitting in front of him: first place for turkeys, third for large mammals. "Oh wow, the turkeys won? Congratulations." In the lower divisions, everyone who scored more than ninety points got a first place ribbon, but in the master division, there were only three awards total. Getting one was kind of a big deal.

"Thank you," he said, but he sounded wary, like he couldn't trust that I actually meant it.

Someone touched my shoulder, and I turned to find a tall stranger behind me. "Here, honey, take my chair," he said in a Southern drawl. "I've gotta go catch my flight."

"Oh, okay. Thanks." I scooted the chair up to my dad's table, and the guy next to him moved over to make space for me. Being so close to my dad made me feel trapped, but I kept my eyes on the emcee and took deep breaths. Soon the banquet would be over, and I could say what I needed to say, and then I could go find my friends and have one last night of fun before I went home.

The emcee moved on to the big awards of the night, and the room went quiet. The Best in World Collective Arts Award went to a group of Japanese guys for their herd of running gazelles, and Judges' Choice Best in Show went to Harley for his musk ox, which made my dad let out a frustrated huffing sound. As the emcee started listing the winners of the Competitors Awards, which came with cash prizes, I realized my dad was twisting his napkin under the table. He wasn't just annoyed about his rival's success; he was actually *nervous*.

But he didn't need to worry. Even though the judges had chosen to award only eight of the twelve possible Best in World titles this year, my dad still got one of them for his beloved strutting turkeys. The winners got a standing ovation as they posed together for a picture at the front of the room, and I stood up, too. If he was going to be all-consumed by his work, at least it was nice to know it was some of the best work in the world.

The emcee finished up by reminding everyone about the wind-down party, and I shuddered. My whole family had gone the first time I came to this convention, and even though I had only been in third grade, I had a clear memory of a burly taxidermist singing a karaoke ballad about cowboys. I also remembered dancing with my mom, who spun me in circles until I fell over laughing.

My dad's progress back to the table was slow; everyone wanted to shake his hand. My knees felt a little wobbly, but I stayed standing as I waited for him. Being on my feet made me feel a little more in control.

He finally arrived, picked up his ribbons from the table, and tucked them gently inside his jacket. And then he turned to me and said, "So."

"So. Um. We should talk."

"All right," he said. "Let's go outside."

We made our way out of the ballroom and took the escalator down to the ground floor, and as we walked through the sliding glass doors, I realized I hadn't left the hotel at all in nearly five days. The Florida air was so humid it felt like soup in my lungs, but it was still a relief to breathe it in. There were palm trees lining the driveway, each with its own individual spotlight, and I listened to them rustle as I gathered my thoughts and my courage.

"So," my dad said again.

There wasn't really a good way to say any of the things I wanted to tell him, so I just launched in. "I know you're probably still pissed at me about the demo. You said some pretty awful stuff to me yesterday, and I probably deserved it. But I still can't believe you went behind my back and lied to Mom about me, and I think you deserved the stuff I said to you, too."

"Callie, I—"

"I want to spend the summer with her," I said. "She did a really crappy thing last year, and she shouldn't have left us like she did. But she's making a big effort to have a normal relationship with me now, and we're finally in a pretty good place, and we need time together. I'm not going to let you stop me from having that. If you really want to go to court over it, we can, but if I say I want to go out there, I'm pretty sure the judge is going to let me."

"I really don't think—" my dad started, but I held up my hand.

"No, listen. You need to let me say everything I want to say, okay?"

He nodded, and I took a deep breath.

"I'm not going to ask Mom if I can live in Arizona full-time," I said. "I thought about it, and I want to come home and finish high school in D.C. But you and I have to start trying harder with each other, even though we're really different people, because we're a family, and families don't get to just . . . *quit* like that. They get mad, and they fight, and that's fine, but in the end, they try to be there for each other. And maybe we'll never be super close, but you're what I have, and I'm what you have, and we've got to do better."

My dad stood there in silence for a minute. I wondered if he was gearing up to say something about how disrespectful I was being on his big important night. But instead, he nodded slowly. Maybe it was the way the light from the lobby was hitting his face, but he suddenly looked older to me, more tired than I had ever seen him.

"You're right," he answered. I couldn't even remember the last time he'd said that to me.

"I miss the way things used to be, with all of us together, and I think maybe you do, too." The words made the lump in my throat spring back up, and I struggled to swallow it down. "But I'm still here, even though she's gone, and I still need you to be my dad."

"I know," he said quietly. "I'm sorry. I know I've made some mistakes. And I want you to come back home. I really do."

"I will, but only if we try harder. We have to actually talk to each other, and not just so you can tell me how much I suck at everything."

My dad scrubbed a hand over his face. "That's not . . . I was just trying to help you, Cal. I know I can be a little harsh, but you have so much potential, and . . . I just don't want to see you waste any of it."

"That's not what I need from you, though. I need you to listen to me and support me and ask me questions about stuff I care about. Real-life stuff, not just work stuff. When I said I was quitting as your assistant, I was serious. I want to be your kid, not your employee."

He nodded again, and when he looked at me, I felt like he was actually seeing me for the first time in two years. Not like yesterday, when he saw straight through me to the bad things I had done. This time it was like he was just looking at his daughter.

"I'll start," I said. "Congratulations on the turkeys and the Best in World. That's really great. I know you worked incredibly hard, and the animals came out beautiful."

Dad smiled a little. "Thank you, Callie."

"And I think your mounts are way better than Harley's."

His smile got a little bigger. "They are, aren't they?"

"Yeah, they really are. Now you go. You say something real to me."

He was quiet for so long that I started to wonder if he even remembered how to talk about things other than taxidermy. But then he said, "You mentioned something about going to a class the other day?"

"Yeah," I said, because even though it was vague, it was something. "It was a workshop with the hosts of this podcast I love. It's called *A Thousand Words*. They were here for the fan convention that's happening in A-wing."

"And . . . how was that?"

"It was amazing. I learned so much. And then these girls I met and I made our own podcast in the same style for this competition. That's what I was doing last night and today. I can play it for you in the car on the way home, if, um, if you're interested."

His eyebrows furrowed. "On the radio?"

"No, I have it on my phone."

"Your phone? But how . . ."

"We can play it on the car stereo." He still looked baffled, and I rolled my eyes. "There's a cable, Dad. The phone connects to the car. I'll set it up."

And then I was laughing. It just felt so *normal*, a sixteen-year-old girl getting frustrated that her dad didn't know how to use technology. It had been so long since anything in my family had felt remotely normal.

"Hey," I said. "Do you want to meet my friends? They're over at this dance in A-wing. I could introduce you."

"I should really—" he started, but then he broke off. "Yes. Okay."

And there it was. He was trying.

I led the way, and when we reached the hall full of people dressed as My Little Ponies and Princess Leias and anime characters, Dad moved a little closer to my side. The dance was already in full swing in the ballroom; disco balls flung colored specks of light everywhere, and the beat of a Katy Perry song throbbed loudly enough that I could feel it deep in my chest.

"Callie, over here!" someone called, and I turned to see Vanessa waving at me from the food table. As I got closer, I noticed that her other hand was entwined with Merry's, and I gave her a huge, cheesy *OMG, you did it* smile. She beamed and looked at the floor.

Phoebe joined us, a cup of punch in each hand. "Hey, you made it! You want one of these? I can get more." She looked back and forth between my dad and me, then raised her eyebrows like, *How did it go?*

I smiled at her. "I'll get some later. Guys, this is my dad. He just won this huge taxidermy award. Dad, this is Phoebe and Vanessa, the girls who made the podcast with me. And this is—"

"—Merry, my personfriend for the evening," Vanessa jumped in. Even in the swirling, rainbow-colored lights, I could tell she was blushing. "It's nice to meet you, Callie's dad."

My dad blinked. "Person . . . friend . . . ?"

"Excuse me," said a voice behind me. "Are you the girls who made the podcast?"

"Yeah, we—" I started, but when I turned around, the words died on my lips. Standing right in front of me were the hosts of *A Thousand Words*.

"I thought I recognized your hair," said Anica. She was wearing an orange dress, and she glowed under the colored lights. When she held out her hand, the stack of wooden bangles on her wrist clinked together. "Hi, I'm—"

"I *know*," I said. "Oh my god. I— You—" I turned to Vanessa and Phoebe. "These are—Anica—Rafael—*A Thousand Words*. Hosts. Like, right here. I—holy sh— Um. Sharks. Holy sharks."

My cheeks were flaming now, and I had apparently forgotten how to form sentences. I realized I had been holding on to Anica's hand for way too long, and I let go.

"Callie's a big fan," Vanessa said. "Hi, I'm Vanessa, and that's Phoebe."

"Hey," Phoebe said. I could tell it was taking everything she had not to laugh at me.

"We loved your entry for the Creativity Corner," Rafael said as he gave my hand a firm shake. His voice was even better up close, despite the noise of the dance. All I wanted in life was for Katy Perry to shut up so I could hear him better.

"Thank you," I breathed. "Thank you so much."

"You guys are really talented storytellers," Anica said. "Do you have your own podcast?"

Phoebe shook her head. "This was our first time."

"Seriously? Wow. What a spectacular first attempt."

Vanessa smiled at me. "Thanks! It was really fun."

"You should keep going for sure," Rafael said. "We'd love to hear more from you guys."

"If you have any questions or you need someone to listen to your stuff, feel free to reach out to us," Anica said. "We love helping people who are just starting out. Here's my card. My email is right here at the bottom."

I reached out and snatched the card before anyone else could get it. It was just normal card stock, but it felt electric, like it was buzzing in my hand. I was pretty sure my head was about to explode.

"I'm— You guys are so inspiring," I blurted. "I've listened to every single episode of *A Thousand Words* like ten times. The one with the fourth graders! And the one with the *veterans*, and— The way you put stories together, it's— I *love* you guys."

Anica laughed. "Thank you. We're really honored."

"Keep up the good work, okay?" Rafael said.

Anica squeezed my arm, and then she and Rafael turned to go. I watched her until her orange skirt disappeared into the crowd.

Vanessa squealed and slung her arm around my shoulders. "They liked it!"

"They want to hear *more* from us," I said. "I think I'm going to faint."

Phoebe laughed and pressed a cup of punch into my hand. "Steady, friend. You better drink this." I drained it in two gulps and handed it back.

"We could do more episodes, you know," Vanessa said. "Longer ones. It's not like we'd have to be in the same place to keep working together."

Phoebe nodded hard. "We totally could."

"Those people," my dad said. "They . . . ran the class you went to?"

"Yes!" I said. "They're *so* amazing. I'll play you their podcast on the way home, too. It's way better than ours."

"They certainly seemed impressed by you girls," he said. "Well done."

The Katy Perry song finally ended, and Lady Gaga started blasting through the speakers. "I love this song!" Merry yelled, grabbing Vanessa's hand and tugging her toward the floor. "We have to dance!"

Vanessa stumbled along behind them. "You guys, too!" she shouted over her shoulder. "Come on!"

Phoebe followed right away, arms snaking up over her head and hair flying out behind her as she twirled around and around. Vanessa laughed as Merry grabbed her by the hips and pulled her closer. None of them were good dancers, but all three of them looked so happy as the swirling lights played over their upturned faces, and it made them beautiful.

I turned to my dad. "Do you . . . maybe want to dance with me?"

Spinning around a crowded ballroom floor to "Born This Way" with his adrenaline-drunk teenage daughter was probably the last thing in the world my dad wanted to do. But he only hesitated for a minute before he offered his arm to me.

"All right," he said. "Let's dance."

And we did.

EPILOGUE

BEIGE

Mommy said I had to stay right next to her while she talked to the lady at the tall desk because it wasn't safe to walk around the hotel alone because of stranger danger. But I wasn't alone because I was with Delancey.

There was a room with swirly lights that were lots of different colors, and they were really pretty when they spun around. There was a banner over the door and I could read the word *BALL* on it. Delancey said the word before that was *FAREWELL*. I was good at sounding out words but Delancey was faster because she was already six.

There were lots of people dancing inside the room and I wanted to dance too. I wondered if we would get in trouble if we went inside but Delancey went right in because she is very brave. Nothing bad happened, so I followed her. There were lots of people wearing costumes like it was Halloween and I saw a boy dressed like Rainbow Dash from *My Little Pony: Friendship Is Magic*. I liked Rainbow Dash but she was not my favorite pony because Twilight Sparkle was purple and purple was my favorite color. It was Delancey's favorite color too.

A girl with green glasses and curly hair came up to me and at first I wasn't going to talk to her because of stranger danger, but she wasn't a stranger because she was the girl I told a secret to yesterday and if you tell someone a secret, they are not a stranger.

"Hi," she said. "You're Beige, right?"

I nodded yes even though I did not want my name to be Beige. I wanted to be named Violet because that was another word for purple.

The girl smiled at me. She was with another girl and they were holding hands and I wanted to hold Delancey's hand, so I did. Her hand was sticky but I didn't care because she was my friend.

"Did your mommy get you a doughnut yesterday?" she asked.

I was happy to be in the room with the swirly lights but when she said that I remembered about yesterday and I got mad again. Mommy *said* she would get me a doughnut if I placed in the pageant, and I got second runner-up, but then she said the hotel didn't sell doughnuts and it wasn't her fault and *Beige, you're trying my patience.*

I shook my head no.

"See that table?" The girl pointed across the room at a table with a pretty tablecloth that was purple. "There are doughnuts over there, if you still want one."

The girl she was with laughed and said, "You know this kid?" And the girl in the green glasses said, "Yeah, I interviewed her yesterday." Then they kissed, but I did not want to kiss Delancey so I didn't.

I ran through the dancing people with Delancey until we got to the table, and there were no doughnuts, but there were doughnut holes, which are not the same. But they still taste good so I took the whole box. Delancey took a bunch of cookies with pink frosting and then we crawled underneath the table so the tablecloth hid us like my cousin Casey and I do on Thanksgiving.

"Beige?" somebody yelled, and when I peeked under the tablecloth I saw Mommy's shiny black shoes, but I didn't want her to find me so I did not come out.

"Have you seen my daughter?" I heard her say, but I still did not come out. I ate a doughnut hole with white sugar all over it and the sugar went on my dress and I laughed and Delancey laughed too. Mommy would be mad about the sugar but right now she couldn't see me so I didn't care. She would also be mad that I was with Delancey because she was first runner-up and I was second runner-up so she was the enemy and also *you're not here to make friends, Beige.*

But I stayed under the table and held Delancey's hand and ate more doughnuts and didn't answer Mommy yet, because the girl with the green glasses said I could be friends with whoever I wanted.

A BRIEF NOTE ON TAXIDERMY:

As Callie tells Vanessa during their first conversation, the idea that taxidermists enjoy killing animals for sport is a common misconception. Though commercial taxidermists do prepare trophies for hunters, many scientific taxidermists are naturalists, have degrees in zoology, and are employed by natural history museums to create dioramas that educate the public. In order to properly mount an animal, it's important to understand exactly how it looks, behaves, and moves while it's alive, so these taxidermists spend long periods of time studying living animals of the appropriate species before taking on a project. All the animals that end up in dioramas these days are acquired in an ethical way; for example, a museum might essentially "call dibs" on a snow leopard in a zoo while it's still alive, then hand it over to a taxidermist once it dies of natural causes to be incorporated into a display about snow leopard conservation.

The mouse on our cover, lovingly dubbed Maggie Wormtail MouseRat, was taxidermied for us by Brooklyn-based illustrator Grace Robinson. No mice were harmed for the express purpose of this cover; Grace ordered her frozen from a pet shop, where she was intended to become snake food. Instead, her image has been immortalized by Scholastic, and she is now living a long and happy afterlife on my bookshelf.

—Alison Cherry

ACKNOWLEDGMENTS

Like the conventions that inspired it, this book would not have been possible without a huge team of people helping it along, every step of the way. A huge thank-you to our families and friends, who've been listening to us talk about taxidermy, percussion, and fanfiction for longer than has probably been comfortable. And thank you in particular . . .

To our fellow writers in the woods—Claire Legrand, Jenna Scherer, Lissa Harris, Mackenzi Van Engelenhoven, Melissa Sarno, and Jen Malone—for listening to our early drafts, acting out scenes with us, and giving us the feedback we needed to keep going.

To our lovely posse of beta readers—Sarah Enni, Meghan Deans, Nina Lourie, and Kayla Olson—for your gentle, kind, and incredibly helpful notes; and to Kathy Dawson, for your fantastic feedback along the way.

To Sam Escobar, for lending us a necessary perspective on some of the language choices.

To taxidermist extraordinaire Allis Markham, for sharing your insider knowledge with us and for being generally awesome.

To Grace Robinson, the creator of Maggie Wormtail MouseRat, who graces the cover of this book. We are in awe.

To our book fairy godmother, Amanda Maciel, for giving us the collective "oh, *this* is how it should go" moment that inspired us to finish our half-drafted and long-abandoned manuscript, and for being our spy on the inside. (Say it with us now: Hercules MULLIGAN!)

To our amazing agents—Brenda Bowen, Holly Root, and Sarah Davies—for your boundless enthusiasm for this book, for always being there for us when we need you, and for being three of the most badass ladies we know.

To our publisher, David Levithan; our designer, Maeve Norton; our production editor, Melissa Schirmer; our copyeditor, Beka Wallin; and the whole Scholastic team, for making this an incredible experience for us. We are sorry you had to deal with having a taxidermy mouse in your office. But not that sorry.

To our amazing editor, Matt Ringler, for your passion and warmth, for your fabulous ideas, and for generally being an excellent human. You are the big brother we've always wanted.

And, last but not least, to our readers. Thank you for reading, you wonderful weirdos.

ABOUT THE AUTHORS

Alison Cherry (Callie) is the author of the young adult novels *Red*, *For Real*, and *Look Both Ways* and the middle grade novels *The Classy Crooks Club* and *Willows vs. Wolverines*. Aside from a long-standing morbid fascination, she has no personal experience with taxidermy. She lives in Brooklyn with her two (live) cats.

Lindsay Ribar (Vanessa) is the author of *The Art of Wishing*, *The Fourth Wish*, and the Andre Norton Award–nominated *Rocks Fall, Everyone Dies*. She lives in Manhattan, works in the publishing industry, and spends far too much time reading fanfiction on her phone. Ask her about her Harry Potter tattoo.

Michelle Schusterman (Phoebe) is the author of the middle grade fantasy novel *Olive and the Backstage Ghost* and the upcoming *Spell & Spindle*, as well as the I Heart Band! and The Kat Sinclair Files series. She's also the co-author of the Secrets of Topsea series, writing as M. Shelley Coats. Michelle lives in Queens with her husband and bandmate, their chocolate lab (who is more of a vocalist), and an exhibition hall's worth of percussion instruments.